SNOWBLIND

The figure with the high-powered rifle aimed for the lift.

Eric jumped. Pain shot through his left knee when he hit the ground. Wind-driven snow stung his face as he lay gasping for breath. Grimacing, he managed to stand up in the increasing wind.

Waves of blowing powder streamed across the rugged terrain. Eric found both skis, but only one pole. When he tried to step into his bindings, the pain doubled. Finally, using the pole to crutch his left leg, he pushed off.

The bright orange trail markers disappeared in the blinding blizzard, and Eric found himself in deep powder. Leaning back on his skis, he made slow, painful turns. Nothing looked familiar. Viciously jolted by an unseen mogul, he managed to maintain his balance, but he lost direction. Each turn brought more pain. Visibility was limited to the terrain immediately ahead.

And then suddenly the mountain dropped away, and Eric was falling . . .

ICEBOUND

by
Rick Spencer

A SIGNET BOOK
NEW AMERICAN LIBRARY
TIMES MIRROR

PUBLISHER'S NOTE

This novel is a work of fiction. Names, characters, places, and incidents either are the product of the author's imagination or are used fictitiously, and any resemblance to actual persons, living or dead, events, or locales is entirely coincidental.

NAL BOOKS ARE AVAILABLE AT QUANTITY DISCOUNTS WHEN USED TO PROMOTE PRODUCTS OR SERVICES. FOR INFORMATION PLEASE WRITE TO PREMIUM MARKETING DIVISION, THE NEW AMERICAN LIBRARY, INC., 1633 BROADWAY, NEW YORK, NEW YORK 10019.

SIGNET TRADEMARK REG. U.S. PAT. OFF. AND FOREIGN COUNTRIES
REGISTERED TRADEMARK—MARCA REGISTRADA
HECHO EN CHICAGO, U.S.A.

SIGNET, SIGNET CLASSIC, MENTOR, PLUME, MERIDIAN AND NAL BOOKS are published by The New American Library, Inc., 1633 Broadway, New York, New York 10019

First Printing, November, 1983

1 2 3 4 5 6 7 8 9

PRINTED IN THE UNITED STATES OF AMERICA

CHAPTER 1

The small Strelabahn gondola swung down into the summit station on the Strelagrat. Lift attendant Franz Stenner opened its door and pulled two pairs of skis from the side rack carrier. As the two occupants stepped from the swinging car, Stenner pointed at the Grundig digital clock on the wall near the exit door. The time was 4:04 and the notice below stated that the lift closed at 4:30.

"Guten Tag," he said. *"Die Gondel wird in dreissig minuten geschlossen."*

The skier wearing a canvas knapsack nodded at the young Swiss attendant and grinned. "Right, mate."

The other man took the skis, stepped behind Stenner, and slid a ten-inch blade into the young man's back. Bubbling through the clean puncture, Stenner's left lung deflated and collapsed. He tried to cry out but wasn't able to make a sound.

As Franz Stenner lay dying on the concrete floor, his murderer peeled open the knapsack's Velcro tabs and extracted two Cordura nylon assault rifle cases.

The afternoon sky over Davos darkened as slate clouds slowly swallowed the jagged white horizon. Across the valley, the alp Jakobshorn disappeared in a snow squall. Within minutes, gray flakes began to fall from the ominous leaden overcast and the frigid air on the Strela began to move.

Eric Ivorsen's legs were tired, and it showed. His skiing was off. Ticking the surface with his right pole, he leaned into a stop, spraying snow onto a boulder at the side of the slope below the lift. He closed his eyes, leaned his head back, and sucked in several deep breaths of the thin alpine air. Above him, the lift's gondolas glided silently toward the Strelagrat summit. As his breathing returned to normal, Eric looked up and sighed. Of the dozen gondolas within his view, only one had skis in the carrier. The Plexiglas window opened and the passenger beamed down at him. His grin was wide, his face tan, and his hair white. He looked like a distinguished businessman on holiday—healthy, happy, and full of life.

"One more run!" he yelled. "I'll wait for you at the top!"

Still trying to catch his breath from the last run, Eric shook his head, amazed at the older man's stamina.

"We won't be back for at least a year!" the man yelled, grinning.

Eric nodded and smiled back.

Watching the lift's car disappear in a swirling gust of wind-driven snow, Eric took a deep breath and pushed off. Drifting powder, just beginning to coat the existing crust, quickened the surface. He leaned forward and dropped over a steep pitch, taking on speed. As he swept down and over a ledge below Schönboden, a wave of white wind momentarily obliterated the trail. He slowed, relaxing his knees, allowing the terrain to dictate his speed. After several boneshaking jolts, he slowed even more and did not let go again until he reached the tree line and the trail to the base station.

Hidden within the concrete walls of the summit station, the assassins waited, watching empty gondolas climb from behind a snowcapped rise to the last lift stanchion and then descend to the unloading platform before them. Unattended, the cars automatically swung around the huge cable wheel and out again into the snow to begin the journey back down to the base station.

Recognizing the Rossignol skis on the carrier rack of a rising car, the two men raised their guns. The car bumped along the rollers on the stanchion and began to descend. Snow that had piled up on the forward window of the car shook loose and blew away. The passenger, preparing to unload, looked up and saw the two armed men. He frowned for a moment, confused. He recognized neither and thought for a second they might be police. Then he looked carefully at their unorthodox weapons. Covering his face with his arm, he threw himself down into the small space between the seats.

As the car swung down into the station, the deafening roar of a sawed-off Perazzi Mirage 12-gauge shotgun exploded in the concrete vault. The snow on the gondola, the Plexiglas window, and five inches of sheet metal disappeared.

The second gunman opened fire with an Ingram Mac 10 machine gun. A spraying blast of fire and lead cut a swath of destruction from one side of the gondola to the other, chopping the victim's skis in half. When the car swung around, the shotgunner fired again and the rear window splintered into oblivion.

With freezing wind whistling through its shattered shell, the gondola rose slowly out of the lift station for its return trip down the mountain. When the car once again reached the apex of the stanchion, the damaged door, slapping back and forth in the buffeting wind, broke and fell away. The car glided down and out of sight.

The man with the shotgun reloaded. His partner smiled, revealing a mouthful of bad teeth.

The attendant in the base station advised Eric that the lift would shut down at 4:30. Eric nodded, removed his gloves, and stepped into the tiny car. Exhausted and hungry, he was thankful that it would be the last run. The deteriorating weather had emptied the slopes—there were no other skiers on the lift ahead of him and none behind.

As the car ascended, snow fell faster and the wind began to sing across the cable above. Eric decided that the journey back down to Davos would be more work than fun.

He tried to make himself comfortable in the cramped car, but his size made it impossible. Muttering to himself about gondolas designed for midgets, he pulled his gloves back on and looked up the mountain at the empty cars descending.

Just beyond the halfway point, Eric spotted the damaged car, its door and windows gone. As the gondola glided closer, he could see the gaping bullet holes, the splintered Rossignol skis, and a crimson trail dribbling onto the snow below. He ripped open his window as the ravaged hulk floated by, carrying his bloodsoaked ski companion. The older man stared back at him through half-closed glassy eyes.

When he recognized Eric, the older man's eyes widened and he strained forward, desperately trying to speak.

"Jump!" he managed to gasp, a look of pleading in his eyes. "Get away!"

Numb, Eric watched the car sink toward the base station. With fear and anger fisted in his gut, he fought to think logically. Breathing short gasps, he told himself that the older man would be okay.

Trapped in the slow gondola, he squinted up toward the summit but could not see. Frustration quickly became anger. Exploding with rage, Eric rammed his fist against the car's window, and it burst. Snow slashed through the jagged hole as the car continued its steady climb.

Raising his legs, he set his boots against the latch and pushed. The sheet metal was no match for his powerful legs. The door ripped open and slammed against the car. He sat down on the gondola's slippery floor, his legs swaying in the blistering wind. Ice and snow whipped into the car.

The car glided up to the rise before the summit.

Reaching out with one hand and gripping the door edge with his other, he pulled his skis and poles from the side rack. As he dropped them to the swirling snow below, he lost his grip, and fell.

When the car lifted into the view of the Strelagrat summit station, the assassins saw only an empty car with its door flapping in the wind.

They shouldered their weapons, stepped into their skis, and took off for the hunt.

Pain shot through his left knee when Eric hit the ground. Wind-driven snow stung into his face as he lay gasping for breath. Grimacing in pain, he swallowed hard and managed to stand up in the increasing wind. Balancing his weight precariously on his right leg, he looked around and saw one of his poles protruding from a snowbank. He hobbled toward it, limping badly.

Waves of blowing powder streamed across the rugged terrain, but Eric found both skis. The desperate search located only the one pole. When he tried to step into his bindings, the pain seemed to double. On the second try, he locked his right boot into the Salomon 727 bindings but found he could not apply any pressure with his left leg. Holding his knee straight with his hands, he pushed again, crying out. Finally his boot clicked into the binding. Using the pole to crutch his left leg, he pushed off. Snow poured down from the sky and surrounding peaks as the entire Strela became engulfed in a wicked storm.

The bright-orange trail markers disappeared in the blinding blizzard, and Eric found himself in deep powder. Leaning back on his skis, he made slow painful turns. Nothing looked familiar. Viciously jolted by an unseen mogul, he managed to maintain his balance, but he lost direction. Each turn brought more pain. Without goggles, visibility was limited to the terrain immediately in front, and then suddenly the mountain dropped away and Eric was falling.

Windmilling, he managed to stay upright until his skis grabbed surface, but he was completely out of control. His right tip caught, and a split second later his skis were torn from the bindings. Eric snapped over and hit the frozen ground with a sickening thud that drove the wind out of his lungs.

Bouncing down the icy incline, Eric began tumbling. When at last he slid to a stop, he had only his ski pole. Snow and ice were caked white in his dark hair.

Stunned and nearly unconscious, he lay motionless. Slowly, he revived, then methodically began surveying body damage. He could curl his toes. His legs moved but his left knee was swelling. Both hands worked, but his right elbow had been badly twisted. As he sat up in the deafening wind, snow spilling down his neck, a shuddering chill shook him.

Above the howl of the storm, he heard a distant guttural shout.

"*Nach rechts!*" the voice commanded.

"Don't see 'im, mate," another voice yelled back.

A few seconds passed, then Eric heard the voices again, farther away, farther down the slope. Now at least he knew which way was down.

Snow filled his gloves as he crawled, dragging his pole. An entire section of bank gave way, sucking him away from the trail, but he crawled on, stabbing into the crust to pull himself up. When he reached hard surface, he struggled to his feet and tried to walk, but the combination of the high Raichle boots and damaged left knee forced him to descend sideways, crablike, using his ski pole as a crutch. Each uncertain step was painful. The bone-chilling wind anesthetized some of the pain but weakened his muscles. An hour of unrelenting torture passed before he stumbled into the protection of the tree line.

Frostbitten and exhausted, he trudged through the deepening snow and finally staggered out of the dark forest into the hilly streets of Davos. Carefully avoiding the area near his hotel, he limped down the winding streets toward the railroad station. Out of breath and ghostly white from the ordeal, he stumbled across the Talstrasse to a phone booth. With his arm slung over the phone box for support, he placed a call to the Paresenn-Rettungsdienst, the rescue service, and was told that a man injured on the ski lift had been taken to Zurich.

Still clutching a bent and broken ski pole in his fist, Eric Ivorsen collapsed in the first-class section of the 17:47 train to Landquart and Zurich just as it was pulling out of the station.

Four blocks away in the restaurant Pot au Feu, Gunter Toombs motioned to have have his wheelchair moved closer to the table. With the fork in his left hand, he impaled a small potato, raised it to his mouth, and began chewing slowly. His right hand, gloved in gray velvet, lay lifeless in his lap. His dead right eye remained fixed in his head, staring forward, while his left eye stared down at the food. He ate without speaking to either the buxom young woman at his side or the two men sitting across the table.

"You have completed your assignment?" he asked finally,

his good eye moving back and forth between the two skiers.

There was a moment of silence before the English-speaking gunman replied, "We shot only the old man."

Gunter Toombs's steely eye narrowed and the muscles on the left side of his face tensed into a cruel half-smile. His right side remained still—dead and unseeing.

CHAPTER 2

Maggie McCabe squinted up at Hohensalzburg Fortress from an outdoor table in Salzburg's Mozartplatz café. The castle's gray stone turrets glistened as the night frost melted in warm morning sunlight. Three hundred feet below, the first cablecar of tourists began an ascent to the castle's base. Twisting a telephoto lens onto her Pentax LX, Maggie aimed the camera up at the nine-hundred-year-old castle and clicked off several shots. When the cablecar crept into frame, Maggie put down her camera and quickly snatched a tissue from her bag. She sneezed twice, and then winced when she tried delicately to wipe her nose, sore and reddened from two weeks of an unremitting cold.

"Oh Lord," she sighed, closing her eyes.

"*Gesundheit,*" the waiter said as he placed a glass cup of steaming tea in front of her.

"Thank you," she sniffed in a thick voice.

Sipping her tea, she watched a group of tourists gathered under the Glockenspiel Tower across the square. She reached into her bag, extracted a Yashica FX-3 with a wide-angle lens, and took four shots of the scene. The morning haze, just beginning to burn off, gave the narrow streets of Old Salzburg a natural softness.

Maggie returned to the Pentax to scan for interesting scenes and subjects. As she panned across to the Waagplatz, a blurred figure filled her lens, and she pulled back to focus. The image of a man sharpened into view—young, sitting alone at a café table. Although his hair was dark, he looked Nordic—tall and broad-shouldered, with a healthy tan. Dressed in gray slacks, a lightweight Harris-tweed jacket, and white cotton shirt open at the collar, he sat with his long legs crossed and appeared to be relaxed, simply enjoying the warmth of a spring day in Austria. Maggie clicked off a shot. She zoomed in for a close-up and captured him once full-face and, as he turned to call the waiter, twice in profile. Then her nose began to twitch and she had to lower her camera to sneeze. When she looked up again, his table was empty. Realizing that he had seen her, Maggie hoped she hadn't embarrassed him by taking the pictures.

A sip of hot tea made her throat feel better, but did nothing to lift her spirits. She decided to tackle her budget. Opening her wallet, she separated the different currencies into small piles on the table, trying to calculate their values. She stared down at the notes, coins, and a conversion table, looking perplexed. A long shadow fell over the table.

"An audit?" The voice was deep, friendly, American.

Maggie looked up into the face of the man she'd just photographed.

"I'm afraid I'm not doing too well," she said, pocketing her tissue. "I've been in five countries in two weeks and I've given up trying to keep it all straight," Maggie admitted.

"Maybe I can help," he said, pointing at each pile. "This is worth three dollars and forty-two cents. Your Swiss francs are worth twelve dollars and seven cents, the deutsche marks are worth eighteen dollars and fifty-five cents, you have thirty-nine dollars and four cents in schillings, and sixty-two dollars in guilders. If you take the whole pile to the bank, they will give you back two thousand one hundred eighty-nine schillings."

"That's amazing," Maggie observed.

"I'm good at numbers," he replied.

"You're American?" she asked.

"Princeton, New Jersey. My name's Eric Ivorsen."

"Maggie McCabe, Tampa, Florida," she said and then sneezed.

"May I join you?"

"If you don't mind catching a cold," she sniffed.

Eric set his ebony walking stick against the edge of the café table and eased into a chair, carefully keeping his left leg straight. He looked directly into her green eyes and said, "You're entirely too pretty to be giving people colds."

Smiling at the compliment, she bowed her head slightly, and her chestnut hair glinted in the sunlight.

"What brings you to Salzburg?" he asked.

"Vacation," she replied.

"A long stay?" he asked.

"I leave for home tomorrow."

"Too bad," Eric replied and glanced up the mountain.

"Why?"

"You'll miss springtime in Austria."

"Well," she sighed, "be that as it may, I have to get back to work."

Eric motioned the waiter and in fluent German ordered coffee, croissants, and assorted jams. He looked again into Maggie's eyes.

"Did you enjoy your visit?" he asked.

"The airline lost my luggage, which contained my money, I came down with this incredible headcold, and I've reached the credit limit on my MasterCard, leaving me with what you see spread out before us. As a result, I've been forced to stay in expensive hotels rather than guest houses, because only the hotels take credit cards. After two weeks of carrying all my possessions around in my camera bag, I've met only one tall dark stranger, and if I ask you to be honest, you will no doubt admit that Mrs. Ivorsen and all the little Ivorsens are patiently waiting for you back in Princeton."

"Sorry to ruin your streak of bad luck," he answered, "but I'm not married."

Maggie laughed, embarrassed at her display of self-pity. The waiter brought a tray with coffee and two croissants. Eric broke open the warm roll, spread it with boisenberry jam, and offered it to Maggie.

"What are you doing in Europe in the middle of the spring semester?" she asked, accepting the treat.

"I'm not on the university's faculty," he replied, "My association is with the Plasma Physics Lab."

"Plasma physics? As in blood?" she asked.

"No," he explained, "plasma as in the the fourth state of matter. Solid, liquid, gas, plasma."

Maggie's expression did not change, but her interest in Eric Ivorsen disappeared. His slightly condescending tone reminded her of Carl, and the last thing she needed was to be reminded of Carl. She decided to terminate the conversation as soon as possible and get on with her assignment.

After ten minutes of small talk, she finished her tea, thanked him for the croissant, and stood to leave. When Eric stood up, she saw him grimace in pain. He gripped the handsome walking stick tightly in his left hand, leaning heavily upon it. As he unfolded, she realized that he was even taller than she had guessed.

"Well," she said, looking up and extending her hand, "thanks again. It was nice to meet you."

"I'd like to take you to dinner," he said, shaking her hand.

"I'm sorry, but as I mentioned, my luggage took a vacation of its own. I wouldn't have anything to wear, and I'm really not feeling that well. Thanks anyway."

Eric released her hand, smiled, and nodded goodbye. Maggie joined a group of tourists headed for the Hohensalzburg cablecar station. When she looked back across the Residenzplatz, he was still staring at her from the café.

She spent the morning sight-seeing and taking photographs for the travel section of the *St. Petersburg Times*. When she returned on the cablecar, she strolled back to the small café, but Eric Ivorsen was nowhere in sight. Just as well, she told herself. At 5:30, she returned to her hotel, tired, depressed, and sure she was about to spend the last night of her trip like all the others—alone, sneezing, and wondering what had happened to her fantasy of romance and adventure. But when she opened the door to her room, she was surprised to find a large box plopped in the middle of the bed. Intrigued, she untied the ribbon, pushed aside the tissue, and discovered an emerald-green wraparound silk evening dress and three pairs of dress shoes identical in style but different in size. A note from Eric explained that he would be at a table for two in the Weinrestaurant Alt Salzburg at 7:00 and he hoped not to dine alone.

* * *

At 7:30, Eric, still sitting by himself, ordered a bottle of Gumpoldskirchner and stared out the window at the lights of Salzburg. The waiter uncorked the crystal-cool wine, poured a glass, and departed.

"It's not healthy to drink alone." The voice was soft, feminine.

Eric turned slowly. Maggie smiled, candlelight sparkling in her eyes.

"You are," he said slowly, "simply stunning."

Maggie beamed. The waiter brought another wineglass.

"The dress fits beautifully," she said.

"I noticed."

Eric, in fact, could not take his eyes off of her. He shook his head in admiration as she sat next to him.

"It's therapeutic as well," she said with a smile.

"How so?"

"My cold seemed to clear as soon as I put it on."

Eric leaned close and said, "I'm glad you changed your mind."

"A little hard to resist," Maggie admitted. "This is the nicest thing that's happened to me in the last six months."

The waiter presented menus and poured a glass of wine for Maggie.

She frowned slightly, turned to Eric, and asked, "How did you know where I'm staying?"

"This afternoon—your hotel key was lying on the table next to your Swiss francs and deutsche marks."

Maggie nodded, opened her menu, and stared at the incomprehensible writing. Eric watched her, taken by a beauty that he had somehow underestimated earlier in the day.

"Are you familiar with Austrian food?" he asked finally.

Maggie blushed a little before answering, "I've been eating most of my meals alone. I haven't been too daring."

"May I order for both of us?"

"Sure," she answered, handing him her menu.

Eric signaled the waiter and said, "*Herr Ober, ich mochte gerne Komenymag Leves Nokedival, cevapcici, und schaschlik, bitte.*"

"What exactly is all that?" Maggie asked.

"Burger, fries, and a Coke," Eric answered seriously.

She stared at him until he laughed and admitted, "Caraway-seed soup, peppered barbecued meatballs, brochettes of lamb with onion and peppers."

Taking a sip of the wine, she asked, "How does a New Jersey boy come to speak German so well?"

"I live in Princeton now, but I was raised by my uncle, all over the world actually."

Maggie sighed. "This is my first trip out of the United States."

"And you leave tomorrow to get back to your job?" When she nodded, Eric asked casually, he hoped, "What business are you in?"

She didn't detect the cold directness of the question.

"Photographer," she replied. More interested in learning Eric's background than revealing her own, she asked, "How is a person raised all over the world?"

"My parents were killed in a climbing accident when I was fourteen, and I went to live with my bachelor uncle. He decided that conventional education was inappropriate. More accurately, he thought it was boring. Uncle Charles is something of a rogue. He has an extraordinary ability in mathematics—but whereas my father had a fellowship at the Institute for Advanced Study in Princeton, Uncle Charles counts cards in Monte Carlo."

Eric refilled their wineglasses.

"At first, I traveled with Uncle Charles and his lady friend on a sailing yacht that he had acquired in a game of backgammon. One morning when we were moored off Cannes, Uncle's lady friend appeared on deck *au naturel*. I was mesmerized and showed it. That weekend, Uncle Charles took me to Paris and left me in the most exclusive brothel in Pigalle. He came and got me two days later. I think my voice had dropped three octaves."

Maggie laughed.

"That was the beginning of five years of Uncle Charles's idea of an ideal education. It was obvious that I couldn't live with him on his yacht, so he just kept me bouncing from country to country—and he gave it all a lot of thought. Amsterdam, Paris, and Vienna to study art. Berlin for three months a year to keep up with my math. Oxford to sit in on literature classes taught by his old professor. Switzerland in the winters to ski. I learned to climb in India and ride in Ireland, and how to hunt in Africa. I didn't like killing, so I haven't done that again. When I was sixteen, we rented an apartment in New York and I attended symphonies, operas, and plays."

"Wasn't it lonely at times?" Maggie asked.

Eric pondered the question for a moment, able to recall only good times and adventures with his uncle. Then, telling himself that most people instinctively remember good and conveniently forget unpleasant experiences, he answered, "I guess it was, but most childhoods are lonely in one way or another. If I felt depressed, I'd call and Uncle Charles would fly in and we'd go off on some quest or journey." Eric's eyes lit up when he recalled, "Once he acquired title to a monkey farm in the Amazon and we got lost for two weeks trying to find it. Never did."

"That's incredible," Maggie whispered. "You didn't go to school?"

"Not a day since I was fourteen. I learned history and geography on location, religions and cultures from the people practicing them, science, language, and math from people using it, and art from the people who created it."

Maggie stared at him for a minute and said, "You and your uncle are still very close."

"We are," Eric replied, watching her reaction carefully, but he saw nothing unusual.

"Does he live in Princeton too?"

"Uncle Charles lives on his yacht, currently in St. Tropez."

"What brings you to Salzburg?" she asked.

"He's recuperating in a nearby clinic," Eric said.

"I'm sorry," Maggie said. "Is he seriously ill?"

"He was injured in a skiing accident in Davos on my birthday. Traditionally we meet on my birthday to take care of family matters. We usually ski. There was an accident on the lift, Uncle Charles went through a series of operations, and now he's here regaining his strength."

"The accident—is that how you hurt your leg?"

Eric looked down and nodded, wondering whether or not he was telling her something she already knew.

The waiter interrupted to set the food on the table, and

he asked if they wanted another bottle of wine. Eric looked to Maggie. She nodded.

"Now tell me all about Maggie McCabe," he said.

"I was raised in Tampa, Florida, and met the man of my dreams when I was eighteen. We lived together while we were in college and later while he was in med school. I thought that after seven years of paying all the bills and washing all the clothes, it was time to at least buy an engagement ring. Without telling Carl, I took a morning off, withdrew money from our joint bank account, and then stopped back at our apartment to ask him to come along. I found Carl bouncing around the bed I'd paid for, with two candystripers. I walked over to my closet and packed all my clothes, took them to a girlfriend's house, and then went to a travel agent and bought the ticket for this trip."

Eric started to laugh. Maggie stared at him, her Irish temper rising.

"You think that's funny?" she demanded.

"Sorry, but I'm picturing you calmly folding clothes into a suitcase with three naked people tangled on your bed."

The tightness on Maggie's face lessened, and she tried to smile.

"What did Carl say?" Eric asked, hoping to sound sympathetic.

"He looked up and said that it wasn't what I thought."

Eric exploded into laughter.

"He said he was tense and he was just letting off steam," she added, shaking her head, and finally she began to laugh too.

The laughter felt so good to Maggie she hoped it wouldn't stop. It was the first time she had been able to think objectively about the bedroom incident, and now it seemed so distant, almost unimportant. They ate, drank, talked, and laughed for two hours.

When the waiter brought Sachertorte and hot brandy, Eric took Maggie's hand and stroked it gently. They devoured the chocolate cake and ordered more brandy. As he leaned closer to smell her perfumed hair, his nearness sent a shiver of desire through Maggie.

The walk to her hotel was silent. In the distance, the Hohensalzburg Fortress, illuminated from below, looked like a storybook castle. The intoxicating magic of Salzburg had cast its spell. Maggie McCabe was floating.

Eric followed her into the hotel room without invitation. Her token protest dissolved with the first kiss. He cupped her face in his hands and kissed her lightly. Maggie reached up and ran her fingers into his thick hair, pulling him down to her. As he kissed her, he peeled her dress away from her shoulders. It slipped down over her hips to the floor. Maggie pulled him tighter, kissing him hard. Braless, her breasts rubbed against the fabric of his shirt, and the friction felt good. Maggie moaned and pulled his head from her neck to her chest. She threw her head back and sighed as he sucked her nipples. Encouraged by her response, Eric tore her panties down her legs and continued exploring her with kisses. She recklessly pushed his head lower and then arched backward as he nuzzled her thighs. Tumbling over, she sank into the thick featherbed, grinding to accommodate his eager kiss. She cried out through clenched teeth as a rhythm started to build. With each thrust and kiss, the pleasure spread through her.

Reaching down, Maggie pulled at his shirt. Eric stood, and Maggie lay gasping, animal lust burning in her eyes. He stretched out of his shirt, and as he unbuckled his belt, she reached up and pulled open his slacks. He was hard, excited. Maggie slowly wrapped her fingers tightly around him, hesitating for a moment. She closed her eyes and brushed her lips across his tight smooth skin, savoring his masculine scent.

Wetting her lips, she kissed him gently. Eric closed his eyes in pleasure. She sucked him softly into her mouth, tracing him with her tongue. Pushing himself to her, Eric gently cupped her face, and Maggie took him deep. The warmth of her kiss and her soft moans excited him even more. Pulling away, he ran his hands down her neck to her delicate shoulders, then leaned to kiss her. Wrapped in each other's arms, they fell side by side back onto the bed.

Climbing over his huge body, Maggie straddled him, and with eyes closed, reached down and guided him into her. She lowered herself cautiously, wincing as he filled her. With her head thrown back, her long hair swaying, Maggie began to feel the first flash of orgasm. She gasped when he leaned up and passionately kissed her breasts. She rocked back and forth, and Eric pulled her down, driving himself deeper. Maggie shuddered, her face tight with ecstasy. She felt his huge body stiffen and his deep thrusts quicken. Maggie fell forward, holding his rhythm. He pulled her tighter and tighter until he could hold her no closer. She kissed him savagely, almost biting into his neck.

With his teeth clenched, Eric turned her on her back, driving her again and again down into the soft featherbed. Digging her fingernails into his thick shoulder muscles, she groaned with each powerful lunge. The wanton abandon of Maggie's responses, the exciting pain of her nails raking his back, pushed Eric over the edge, and he let go, his climactic thrusts lifting her across the bed.

Sated and glistening with perspiration, they lay forehead to forehead, panting on the rumpled sheets. Even as their breathing returned to normal, they did not speak. Comfortably entwined, Eric gently caressed Maggie until she fell into a deep contented sleep.

Maggie woke in the morning to the sound of a running shower. She smiled, stretched, and called Eric's name. There was no answer. She slid out of the bed and knocked on the bathroom door. Receiving no response, she pushed open the unlocked door and found the bathroom empty. As she looked around her room, she noticed that her camera bag was open. A panicked check revealed that her cameras had been emptied and all of her film stolen.

CHAPTER 3

Eric took the turnoff too fast, spraying gravel against the stucco gatehouse wall. He jerked the BMW's steering wheel to the right, jammed the gearshift into second, and pushed the gas pedal to the floor. The blue sports car shot forward, its Michelin tires pounding over the cobblestone drive that wound through the grounds of the Kurhaus Clinic.

At the clinic's front entrance, he slid to a screeching stop and, leaving the car's door open, ran into the building. He stormed down the hall, past the receptionist, and into the doctor's office. The startled physician looked up from his desk.

"What happened?" Eric demanded, his jaw set in anger.

"He's not a young man," the doctor explained. "The strain . . ."

"But you said he was doing well!" Eric said with bitter edge to his voice.

"I said that he was doing remarkably well considering the extent of his—"

"But he was recovering!"

The doctor shook his head and led Eric into the hall. As they walked down the quiet corridor, the young Austrian physician explained, "There is just too much damage to the liver and kidneys. We can arrange to operate again, but . . ."

"Then arrange it," Eric ordered.

The doctor stopped walking, touched Eric's arm in sympathy, then said, "The patient has refused."

Eric blinked, remained silent for a moment, then said,

"I'll talk to him. Get ready to have him transported." He continued walking toward his uncle's private room.

"If Herr Ivorsen is sleeping, let him sleep. He's had a bad night," the doctor cautioned, "and is very weak. Please do not upset him with an argument."

At the door to his uncle's room, Eric stopped and looked down at the fairhaired young doctor, wondering why a more experienced man wasn't caring for his uncle. He pushed open the door and started in, but froze when he saw his uncle lying on the bed. Charles Ivorsen, with his eyes closed, his mouth hanging open, and his skin the color of ash, looked very old and terribly near death.

Except for a vase of fresh flowers on the small metal table next to the window, the room was devoid of decoration. A clear plastic tube snaked up from a machine next to the bed and disappeared under a strip of white surgical tape that covered most of Charles's dapper white mustache. His normally thick and wavy white hair lay matted against his head, and his left hand rested open on the crisp white bedsheet. The heavy bandages of his upper body were covered by a single pale-blue blanket. An unsavory combination, antiseptic odor and fresh flower scent, filled Eric's nostrils, reminding him of the death of his parents. For a brief moment, the horror of seeing their broken bodies wrapped in sheets came flooding back to him.

Fear emptied the anger in Eric's heart as he looked down at the man to whom he had turned on that day. He tried to swallow away the thickness lumped in his throat and blink away the tears that misted his eyes, but the possibility of losing his uncle was incomprehensible—unacceptable. He pulled a chair next to the bed, sat down, and gently lifted his uncle's hand into his own. It felt cold and too light. Clasping it, Eric rubbed gently, hoping to bring back some warmth. Unconsciously biting his lower lip, he watched the blue blanket slowly rise and fall. The young doctor leaned into the room and quietly closed the door.

Eric stared helplessly at his sleeping uncle and recalled his own stay in a very similar room when he was fifteen. Even though the best clinic in Geneva had diagnosed simple tonsillitis, Uncle Charles had insisted on flying in a specialist from Boston. As soon as the routine operation had been completed, a troop of clowns, imported from an Italian circus, began a performance that lasted three hours in the clinic and reportedly went on for two days in the nightclubs of Geneva. Uncle Charles, two nurses, and the Boston doctor had apparently joined the troupe. Charles later claimed that he had paid for it all with the winnings from a San Francisco poker game.

Smiling sadly at the memory, Eric stared at the floor.

"What's eating you?" Charles whispered when he opened his eyes and saw his nephew's despair.

Snapping to, Eric studied his uncle. Even on the verge of death, the light of life sparkled in the old man's eyes.

"They tell me that they're going to do one last operation and then you'll be ready for anything. . . ."

Charles smiled weakly, closed his eyes, and shook his head.

Eric began, "KLM stewardesses—two of them—here on a two-week layover. I met them yesterday, told them all about you. We have a date for dinner."

"We have things to discuss," Charles whispered, ignoring the banter. Weakly, he wrapped his fingers around Eric's hand.

Eric fell silent, and his hopeful smile slowly faded.

"There will be no operation," Charles insisted, gazing up at his nephew.

"Why not?" Eric asked. "You'll rest for a few days and they'll have you as good as new."

Charles moved his head back and forth on the pillow. "This is it for me, Eric."

Eric, unable to reply, closed his eyes to hide the tears.

"We've been like this before," Charles said softly. "You holding my hand—afraid to let go, remember?" He coughed, and his breathing quickened. Gripping Eric's hand and slowing his breathing, he continued, "Chamonix—your first climb. Those skinny legs sticking out of your boots looked like two toothpicks knocking together. It was the north face . . . we were doing pretty well until we came around the overhang. You wouldn't let me go to set the piton. I couldn't come back around you, and so we clung there until I convinced you that I knew best. I believe it took almost two hours. Let's not go through that again." Charles smiled.

"You haven't kept your promises," Eric said in desperation. "What about that trip down the Nanpan Kiang River that you're always putting off?"

"I'll have failed you there—you have a point," Charles admitted, and then remained silent for several moments, resting.

"And that saloon we're going to buy in the Yukon . . ."

"There are some matters I'd like taken care of," Charles said softly. "Please don't sell the yacht. I want Lady Barbara to have full use of her for as long as she cares to.

"You know all my bank accounts. Please settle my bill at the Ruhl Casino in Nice. And I think I still owe nine hundred thousand lire for damages to that hotel in Capri. Pay the owner off and tip the staff a hundred thousand each—that was a helluva party." Charles sighed.

Eric swallowed hard, trying not to cry.

"No funeral service. I don't want anybody to see me this way. Please have my remains cremated, and if you can get away with it, deliver the urn to the Players Club in New York. Have Lou put me up on the shelf next to Booth's dagger from Macbeth. Then buy the house a round and you get drunk for both of us. A simple last request."

Eric stared at his uncle.

Charles turned, looked at Eric, and whispered, "I've loved you like a son, Eric, and even though I haven't been much of a father, I've taught you how to take care of yourself."

"Oh God, this can't happen," Eric pleaded.

"You have to be extra-careful now," Charles said, tightening his weak grip on Eric's hand. He tried to sit up but could barely move his head on the pillow.

"Rest," Eric said, "I'll get the doctor."

Charles was breathing fast but would not rest. "No," he gasped. "Listen. The people who did this will be watching you. Waiting for you to find your father's work. I was just a pawn—taken off the board to force your move. You must be careful." Grimacing, Charles squeezed his eyes shut and began to breathe in short gasps. Eric stood up over him and helplessly brushed the white hair from his pale forehead.

Charles Ivorsen opened his eyes as his breathing slowed and, looking up at his nephew, winked once. His grip relaxed, the sparkle in his eyes faded, and he was dead. Eric leaned over, hugged his uncle, and cried, "God, no!"

CHAPTER 4

The temperature in Tampa was eighty degrees. Delta flight 404 eased up to Airside Terminal 3 and the passengers disembarked. Maggie carried only her camera bag, but her luggage, finally discovered in Atlanta, was waiting in baggage claim.

"Well, how was your little trip?" Carl Millbank asked sarcastically.

"What are you doing here?" Maggie shrugged wearily and continued walking toward the automatic tram that shuttled all passengers to the main terminal building.

"What am *I* doing here? What are *you* doing here?" he demanded.

"I'm going to get my luggage, go home, and go to sleep. Don't bother to tag along."

"Hey, you left, not me." Carl followed Maggie into the shuttle.

"The lease is in my name. I was hoping you'd have your stuff out by now."

"I'm not movin' anywhere, honey," Carl declared, his voice rising. Several other passengers stared at him. Maggie did not respond. The shuttle arrived at the main terminal building and the doors opened.

Maggie, staring straight ahead, walked to the escalators and rode down to the baggage-claim area, where she picked up her other luggage. Still following, Carl watched her try to juggle her camera bag and carry the two heavy suitcases.

"You can't even run away without my help," he whispered angrily, grabbing for the luggage.

"Leave it alone," she snapped.

Carl threw up his hands and backed away. Maggie called a redcap and had her bags loaded into a cab. Then she got into it alone, leaving Carl at the curb. She rode most of the way to the apartment with her head buried in her hand.

Afternoon sunlight, shimmering on Tampa Bay, filled the stark apartment with light. Carl had insisted that all the walls be white and the furnishings either green or brown. The result was striking but cold. Maggie carried her bags into the bedroom and dropped them on the floor next to the closet. She heard the door being unlocked and looked up to see Carl come storming through.

"Okay, Maggie," he declared. "If that's the way you want it, that's how it's gonna be. We'll just see how you like living alone."

He walked over and removed some of his belongings as Maggie silently unpacked her unused clothes. She paused for a moment when she pulled the wrinkled green evening dress from her camera bag. A tear ran down her cheek, but she made no sound. Carl slammed the door as he went out carrying an armload of suits, jackets, and slacks.

"I'll be back for the rest!" he called through the door.

It took a week for Carl to remove all his belongings, and with each run-in, he escalated his attacks and accusations. On Friday afternoon he found that his key no longer opened the apartment door. He banged until Maggie unlocked it. He pushed his way in, not bothering to close the door behind him.

"So what happened on your little fling? Did you get even? Is that it? And now you're ashamed 'cause you jumped in the sack with some horny businessman?"

"It's not what you think, Carl," Maggie answered calmly. "I was tense and just letting off steam." She smiled to herself.

"So you did do it!" Carl screamed. "You fucked some stranger!"

Maggie did not answer. Carl turned red with rage, the veins in his neck and temple pulsing. He unballed his fist and cocked his arm to slap her. Maggie backed away as he started to swing.

"I wouldn't do that if I were you."

The voice was deep, calm, sincere.

Carl checked his swing and spun around to the doorway. Eric Ivorsen loomed like a mountain behind him.

"Just who the fuck are you?" Carl snarled.

"I'm the man who's going to reduce you to a small ball of fuzz if you even think about hitting that beautiful girl," Eric said convincingly.

Sensing the wisdom of retreat, Carl turned to Maggie and demanded, "What's this pituitary case doing here?"

"I'd like to know the same thing," she said, staring in disbelief.

"I'm returning these photographs," Eric said, holding up a manila envelope. "And this film. I took the liberty of having it developed by an expert in New York. I think you'll find that it's in perfect condition. Also, I think the pictures are terrific."

"Carl," Maggie said without taking her eyes from Eric, "get out."

Carl stared at her, cursed under his breath, and made his way around Eric.

"Could you get the door, Carl?" Eric called after him.

Carl turned at the doorway, glared up at Eric, then leveled a lethal stare at Maggie and spat, "You whore." He spun around and swaggered down the hall.

"So that's Dr. Carl? What a charmer," Eric said as he looked back at Maggie. "It must be his kind nature that you found attractive."

She stood with her hands on her hips, her strong Irish chin set in defiance, and anger in her beautiful green eyes.

"Why?" she demanded.

Eric's expression changed. He walked to her, searching her face with his eyes, and said softly, "I knew a lot about you after dinner and bed. I knew that you were even more beautiful than I had imagined. I knew that you had a splendid sense of humor. I knew that you were a wonderful lover." His tone became serious. "But I did not know why you had been taking photographs of me in the square."

Maggie's mouth fell open.

"Why didn't you just ask?" she stammered.

"I can't tell you, and it would be best if you didn't know," he replied.

"I thought you were rather attractive, that's all," she said. "I take pictures for a living. You just happened to be in a couple of them."

Eric smiled sadly and said, "I know that now, and I wanted to apologize personally."

Maggie shook her head and sighed. She turned and walked out onto the balcony overlooking Tampa Bay. Eight stories below, sailboats and small pleasure craft rocked in their slips. A warm breeze from the Gulf carried the briny scent of the sea. The huge orange sun sank slowly behind a purple cloud, and the first stars of the night began to twinkle in the sky above.

Eric, relying on the walking stick to ease the discomfort in his leg, walked up behind her and gently touched her shoulder. Maggie pulled away and turned. The anger in her eyes were gone, replaced with tears.

"I'm not having the best time in my life," she said. "The last thing I needed was to be hurt more. Please go—go away."

Eric reached down, lifted her hand to his lips, and whispered, "I'm sorry. Goodbye, Maggie McCabe."

He walked out the door, closing it softly behind him. Maggie picked up the manila envelope he had left on the table. He had had all of her photos enlarged to 8 × 10s. The last four were the shots she had taken of him. She stared at the full-face close-up and thought of the look in his eyes when they had made love.

The phone rang, making her jump. She was sure it would be Carl.

"Miss McCabe?" the voice asked.

"Yes?"

"May I speak please with Mr. Ivorsen?"

"I'm sorry, he's left," she said. "Who is this?"

There was only silence at the other end.

"Who is this?" she demanded.

The caller hung up without identifying himself. Maggie, upset by the fight with Carl, the unexpected visit from Eric, and now this mysterious call, poured herself a glass of sherry, heaved a deep sigh, and took a gulp.

After a hot bath, she climbed into bed and fell into a restless sleep, strange dreams waking her repeatedly throughout the night. When she heard loud knocking at 6:30 in the morning, she wrapped herself in a bathrobe and padded across the apartment, fully expecting another row with Carl. She opened the door but kept the security chain in place.

"Miss McCabe?" a man in a gray suit asked.

"Yes," she answered, blinking the sleep away.

"FBI. We'd like to ask you a few questions," he said, briefly holding up a badge and government identification.

Maggie unbolted the chain and let the two men in.

"We'd like you come with us. Please get dressed."

"What's this about?" she asked, frowning.

"You have a relationship with a Mr. Eric K. Ivorsen, is that correct?"

"We've met," she answered defensively.

"Yes, well, we'd like to talk to you about that."

"Can't we talk here?"

"Afraid not," he said gently.

"But I have things to do today. Will this take long?" she asked.

"Not at all. We'd like you to look at some pictures and then you're free to go. We really need your help," he added sincerely."

"Is Eric in trouble?" Maggie asked.

"Please get dressed," the other agent said with a smile.

Maggie closed herself in her bedroom and put on a pair of khaki slacks and a madras blouse. Wondering to herself what Eric had done that would involve the FBI, she considered calling her parents to tell them what was happening. She had just picked up the phone when the FBI man rapped on her door and said they had to go immediately.

Somewhat reluctantly, she followed the two men into a Chevrolet Caprice. They drove her to the marina at John's Pass and escorted her into the cabin of a fifty-two-foot Hatteras luxury cruiser.

"What's this?" Maggie asked, frowning, when they approached the dock.

"We'd like you to meet someone," the agent said.

* * *

"Mr. Ivorsen?"

Eric, waiting in line at the Eastern Airlines check-in counter, turned and looked down at a heavyset man. The man motioned him to step out of the line.

The man's tone was businesslike. "We have your Miss McCabe. You know what we want in return. You give it to me and the girl will not be harmed. Understand?"

Eric was silent.

"I asked you if you understand," he said patiently.

"I need time," Eric said. "And I pick the place and method."

"Mr. Ivorsen, we're callin' the shots."

"No you're not. I'm the one with the code sequence," Eric said matter-of-factly.

"We have the girl right now. She's on a boat and could disappear without a trace. Her demise would be most unpleasant. We'll discuss the exchange."

"It's simple," Eric explained. "I talk to Maggie before I give you anything. You get half the access sequence then and the rest when I know that nothing, and I mean absolutely nothing, has happened to her. I wouldn't want to be in your shoes when you explain to whoever you work for that you didn't get the sequence because you had to prove that you're tougher than I am."

The man pondered for a moment and then nodded.

Eric continued, "Call me in two hours at the Don Cesar hotel and let me talk to Maggie. You'll get the access intro. We'll arrange the exchange and you don't give her up until you have the other half. You'll have enough time to check out the sequence."

The man looked up at Eric, considered his options, and then, consoling himself with the knowledge that he had insurance in place, agreed.

Two hours later, Eric was sitting in a room that overlooked the Gulf of Mexico. He picked up the phone on the third ring.

"Eric?" Maggie's voice was weak, terrified.

Eric remained calm. "Have they hurt you in any way?"

"No."

"Have they threatened you?"

"They said they'd kill me if you don't give them what they want."

"I'm going to give it to them right now."

The bogus FBI agent ripped the phone out of Maggie's hand and spoke into it. "She's as pure as wind-driven snow. Now give me the sequence."

Eric spoke slowly. "Write this down. 'Open file, Ivorsen, quote XXX close quote, seven nine one, six six two eight zero zero, enter, scan level one, enter, sort, enter, display.' "

"This better work," the man answered.

"Run it. It'll get you in and display numeric database. You need the second half to complete the run and translate the document. Bring Maggie up to the beach in front of the hotel. When I see her wave and smile, you get all but the last three entries. When I see her climb out onto the beach, you get the last three."

"Forget it. We're not coming in to shore. You come out and get her. We'll be five miles out, due west from John's Pass. Radio us on Channel 68 and we'll set her adrift in a life raft. When you give us the whole sequence, we pull away and you can pick her up."

"No good," Eric said. "I want you far enough away that you can't get back to her after I've given up the code."

There was silence at the other end of the line.

"I'll come out on a sailboat. When I see her in the raft, you get all but the last three entries. You head back up the coast and when I feel that you've put a safe distance behind you, I'll radio the final entry."

"You got a deal," the negotiator said quickly and hung up.

Eric set the phone on the cradle and looked down at the sparkling pool on the beach below his room. Squinting out at the blue-green horizon, he thought about the rapid-fire acceptance of his terms. He knew what would happen.

The late-morning sun was strong, the air still, and the Gulf's surface flat and oil-slick. On the port side of the *Hatteras,* away from the shore, Maggie's captors quietly dumped bucket after bucket of bloody fish guts into the sea. Plopping into the warm green water, the slimy entrails disappeared beneath the surface and sank, leaving behind a cloud of billowy dark stain as they spiraled downward. The dinnerbell had been rung.

The radio crackled and the two men turned, looking to their leader. Red Delahunt sat up on the flying bridge with a Piña Colada sweating in his hand. He sipped as Eric's voice boomed over the speaker.

"*Hatteras*, this is Ivorsen, over."

Delahunt smiled as he lifted the mike. "This is *Hatteras*. We are ready to copy, over."

In the stern, one of the men scanned the horizon with binoculars and stopped when he saw an approaching sloop. There was no mistaking its direction and purpose.

"When I see her wave from the life raft," crackled Eric's voice.

Delahunt nodded, and Maggie was brought up on deck. The man with the binoculars dragged out an inflatable raft and pulled the charge cord. The resulting whoosh made Maggie jump. The yellow boat began to grow, popping into shape. When it was fully inflated, they dropped it over the stern. It splashed onto the surface with a hollow thud. Fifty feet away, a gray fin sliced the surface.

Focusing his binoculars, Eric watched Maggie climb down a small aluminum ladder into the bobbing craft. She fell to her knees, bracing herself on the gunwale as the rubber boat heaved under her weight. Then suddenly she began frantically looking around at the nearby surface. The man in the stern said something to her, pointing directly toward the sailboat. Maggie raised her arm in a slow wave.

Eric pushed the button on the side of his microphone and said, "*Hatteras*, please copy. 'Open R, file quote Viking Cipher close quote, one three three, enter, suppress database, enter, display result, enter, password equals . . .' "

Eric paused. He raised his glasses and saw the Hatteras begin to move. It circled around, and the life craft disappeared behind it. The radio in Eric's boat crackled, "*Hatteras* copies, we await final entries, over."

Eric brought the mike to his lips. "When you are far enough away."

He quickly raised his binoculars.

* * *

The man in the stern leaned over the side and, dropping out of sight, grabbed the life raft's edge. Aiming a rusty icepick at the glistening yellow underbelly of the raft, he made two quick thrusts, and the rubber hull began to bubble and hiss. Then dropping the shiv overboard, he moved away. Delahunt pushed both throttles ahead, and the huge craft surged forward, leaving Maggie in a deflating raft amid a boiling whirlpool of bloody water, mangled fish, and hungry sharks. Several small butterfish were sucked into the propellers, adding to the aquatic carnage.

Maggie waved frantically at the sailboat as the life raft's gunwale dimpled. The slashing sounds of feeding frenzy became more audible as the heavy Johnson and Towers diesel engines carried the *Hatteras* farther and farther away. A fin sliced by, and Maggie could see a shark's black eyes as it turned and ripped apart a competitor. She gasped in panic, and shock began to take control of her breathing. The big cruiser droned in the distance and the sailboat seemed as far away as ever. The crease in the yellow life raft deepened.

Eric spoke as he watched the *Hatteras* cross the horizon. "The final three entries are as follows. 'Final password equals Copernicus, C-O-P-E-R-N-I-C-U-S, enter, document use equals location, enter, execute solution, enter."

"Is that it?" Delahunt asked.

"Yes. If you're running it, it'll take a few minutes to display the final screen. Stand by," Eric explained.

"Oh, we're running it, all right," Delahunt assured him.

"Is it working?" Eric asked.

There was no reply.

Eric raised his glasses and watched the cruiser slow, its bow lowering. The *Hatteras*'s starboard side rose and its stern swung around in a powerful turn. Eric had his answer. They were heading back toward the sloop—full-throttle.

A trickle of salt water spilled in over the deflating gunwale of Maggie's life raft. The undulation of the water below became more and more perceptible as the rigidity of the boat diminished. Surrounded by chopping splash and churning gore, Maggie turned in terror toward the distant slow sailboat. She saw the big cruiser bearing down on it and realized that her last chance was about to be destroyed.

A five-foot tiger shark broke surface six feet away, and the splash of bloody brine sprayed Maggie's face. She crawled to the other end of the foundering boat, but water poured over the edge, so she moved back to the center, where the deepening puddle soaked her. Terrified, she looked up in time to see a snow-white Donzi ocean racer skid full-speed around the sloop.

The boat's hull barely touched the surface as its roaring inboard/outboard engines hurtled it across the flat water, a roostertail of spray arcing in its wake. The cruiser changed direction to pursue, but the lumbering luxury boat was no match for the competition racer. Then a man with a rifle scrambled to the cruiser's bow.

As one edge of the raft caved in, Maggie cried out and grabbed at the sagging rubber, trying to pull it up. The tattered head of a kingfish floated out from beneath the raft, staring at her. She felt a sharp bump through the rubber, and at the same instant the fish head disappeared in the gaping jaws of a small tiger. Water flooding over the gunwale behind her filled the raft, and Maggie's weight pushed it under. Sinking into the churning frenzy, she panicked and began to thrash.

Eric was fifty yards away when the first bullet struck the surface. A second later, the distant pop of the rifle reached the boat. Slowing into a turn, Eric reached over the side and grabbed for Maggie's hand. She screamed when she felt the dull thud of the shark on her right thigh. It hit her once to see if she was edible, then turned to begin feeding, but by then its prey was out of the water.

"C'mon, Irish, or you'll be a helluva dessert," Eric said as he pulled her aboard. Maggie was like jelly. She sagged to the deck.

A foot from the bow, a pencil-thin column of spray shot up into the air. Then another right next to it. The third shot splintered into the fiberglass hull. With Maggie lying low, Eric punched the throttle forward. The engines roared and the boat leaped. A shot slammed into the instrument panel, missing Eric by less than six inches. The Donzi planed off and rocketed along the surface, bouncing to starboard and port. The cruiser attempted to follow, but it was a token effort. Eric and Maggie were gone.

Delahunt watched the Donzi skip across the green horizon toward John's Pass. He lifted the cruiser's radiophone from its cradle and had the marine operator place a call to a motel in Indian Rocks Beach. The phone rang only once.

"Yeah," a voice answered.

"Wire it," Delahunt growled.

CHAPTER 5

Maggie took a deep breath and looked up at Eric standing at the helm.

"Are you okay?" he yelled over the roar of the engines.

Maggie climbed up onto the seat, and the blast of wind in the fast-moving racer filled her thick chestnut hair. Squinting into the bright sun, Eric piloted the Donzi full-throttle down the intracoastal waterway toward Tampa Bay.

"What the hell is going on here? Who were those people?" Maggie yelled back. She was breathing fast.

He turned, shrugged, and replied, "I don't really know."

"Oh that's great—just great!"

Eric smiled.

"Don't tell me that you're enjoying this!" she yelled, anger replacing some of the fear on her face.

He didn't admit it, but the excitement of the rescue had temporarily replaced the heartache of losing his uncle.

"Who was in the sailboat?" Maggie demanded.

"I hired a charter. I told the two guys who own the boat that we were making a movie and needed a scene with a sailboat. I thought it worked pretty well." He smiled.

"They could've been killed," she pointed out.

Eric shook his head. "No. Not when our friends saw me in this." He patted the Donzi's wheel.

Maggie shook her head and looked back at their wake—a spreading ripple in the flat water foaming below a glistening rainbow cast in the misty spray of the roostertail.

Two hundred yards ahead, a bridge tender waved for them to slow down. Eric glanced up and then returned his stare to the waters ahead as they shot under the bridge and rocketed off into Tampa Bay. Turning, Eric waved at the irate man.

"Shouldn't we call the police?" Maggie asked.

Eric shook his head.

"Why not?" she demanded.

"We have things to do," he replied.

"Like what?" she yelled.

"Pick up your passport," he answered.

"Now just hold on," Maggie said, wagging her finger. "I want to go home."

"That's where we're going. You tell me where in your apartment I can find your passport—"

"What?"

"I'll run in and grab your passport. We've got to get in and out as fast as we can," he said as if describing a trip to the supermarket.

Maggie was too stunned to respond, but decided to just play along until she could lock herself in the apartment and call the police. Watching Eric as he calmly steered his speeding boat across Tampa Bay, she wondered what kind of maniac she had gotten involved with.

When they pulled up to the dock in the marina of Maggie's apartment complex, Maggie scrambled up onto the bulkhead and headed for her building.

"You better let me go in," Eric began.

"Forget it," she said and continued walking. "I'm calling the police."

"I don't think—"

"I don't care what you think. I'm calling the police."

Eric spoke slowly and deliberately. "Grab your passport, come back out to the boat, and then we'll call the police."

Maggie ignored him. She ran into the building, rode the elevator to the eighth floor, and then remembered that her keys were in her pocketbook and her pocketbook was still in the cruiser. She rode back down to the super's apartment and rang his bell.

"Oh, hiya, Miss McCabe," the elderly man said with a grin.

"Could you let me into my apartment, Mr. Moran? I lost my key," she explained.

"No need," he replied. "It's open. I just let your TV repairman in."

Maggie's face paled, and she backed away. She hesitated for a minute and then headed back out to the marina.

"Did you get it?" Eric asked.

"I think there's someone in my apartment," she whispered, white with fear.

Eric nodded and climbed up onto the dock.

"Stay here," he said. "Where's your passport?"

"Uh, in the kitchen. In a basket of bills and papers, next to the telephone. I was going to take it to my safety deposit box."

Eric looked up at Maggie's balcony as he strode with a slight limp toward the building's entrance. He rode to the eighth floor and found the door to Maggie's apartment unlocked. He turned the knob carefully, pushed the door open, and found the living room and kitchen empty. Walking softly to the half-closed door of the bedroom, he peeked in. The room looked normal—until he glanced down at the bed, where he saw a man's legs extending into the room next to an open toolbox full of small electronic parts.

As he heard the distinct click of wire snippers clipping through wire, Eric backed into the living room and crossed silently to the kitchen. Discovering the passport under a pile of papers, he stuffed it into the back pocket of his slacks and started for the door. Pleased with himself, Eric tiptoed across the room toward the hallway entrance. Smiling as he passed the half-closed door of the bedroom, Eric glanced in. But there were no legs under the bed. Then the door flew open and a fist crashed into his face.

Eric tumbled back and hit the wall, breaking the impact with his left arm. Pushing off, he swung his huge fist into his attacker's neck. The man caved sideways, stumbling over an end table near the couch. But undaunted by the powerful punch, the man crouched, sneered, and then launched a savage kick at Eric's groin. Eric turned so the blow glanced off his left thigh. Pain screamed through his body. Falling backward, he caught himself on the bedroom doorjamb. The attacker took immediate advantage of Eric's awkward position, spun, and stamped down. The kick knocked Eric to the floor just inside the bedroom.

The attacker lost no time trying to duplicate the devastating blow, but this time Eric caught his foot and twisted savagely. The man's knee popped, and he screamed a cry of pain that Maggie heard down at the dock. Struggling out of the twisting grip by kicking at Eric's face, he crawled quickly into the living room.

As Eric pulled himself up on the doorknob, the man launched a vicious kick that caught Eric in the side, lifting him off the floor. Grunting like a wounded bear, Eric took the pain and managed to stand. But the man kicked again and connected. The blow knocked Eric over onto the bed. He landed heavily, bouncing. Vulnerable and open to attack, Eric braced himself for the next blow. But it did not come.

Wired into the box springs beneath the bed, a two-minute timing mechanism began a silent countdown. A device intended to provide a safety margin in case of premature triggering, the small electronic switch had served its purpose and saved the installer's life.

Snapping around, Eric saw his attacker backing away, wide-eyed in terror—scrambling to get out of the apartment and down the hall. Eric frowned, looked down at the bed, and suddenly realized the reason for the hasty retreat. Pushing himself off the headboard, he bolted through the living room, slammed the door behind him, and got to the elevator in time to see that the car and his attacker had reached ground level. He pushed through the emergency-exit stairway and began leaping down the steps. He left the building in a limping run to the boat and Maggie.

"Was there someone?" she asked.

"Yep," he gasped, out of breath.

"Is he gone?"

"Yep." Eric sat down quickly on the bulkhead to board the boat.

"Well then, I'm going in to call the police," Maggie said with determination.

"No you're not," Eric said trying to catch his breath.

"Yes I am!"

"No you're not."

A blinding flash of light and an earsplitting roar from the eighth floor knocked Maggie to the ground. As the apartment exploded out through the balcony's sliding doors, a huge ball of fire blasted the doors and windows into a thousand shards of razor-sharp glass that rained down on the water below. The echo rolled across the bay, and black smoke boiled out of the gaping charred holes in the concrete. Maggie slowly looked up at Eric.

"You about ready?" he asked.

Maggie scrambled down into the Donzi, and Eric pushed the throttles forward. As they pounded across Tampa Bay, she looked back up at the smoldering hole that had been her home and then at Eric. Staring at the open water ahead with his head slightly tilted, he seemed distant, as if distracted by the memory of another place and time. Maggie thought she even saw him smile.

Ten minutes after the wheels of Air France's flight 77 kissed the tarmac at Kennedy International, two cabin attendants lifted an elegantly dressed Gunter Toombs into his wheelchair. His aide Katrine pushed the vehicle out through the cabin door, then into and along the jetway.

Katrine, although only twenty, was the oldest and most beautiful of Toombs's recent companions and the one he chose to keep. Her hair was long and Scandinavian white. Her eyes, glazed and sleepy, were a pale blue. But of most importance to Gunter Toombs, her tight blouse did little to hide the fullness of her breasts. She acted as his nurse, bathing him in the mornings; his secretary, handling his menial business affairs during the day; his recreation, fulfilling his perverse fantasies at night.

As usual, they passed quickly through customs to the waiting Mercedes limousine and were in their suite at the Pierre by six.

"Bring me a drink, Katrine," he said, raising his left hand. "And the telephone."

Katrine poured out exactly two ounces of Boodles gin, added a splash of lime juice, and placed it along with the telephone on the antique cherry desk in front of Gunter Toombs.

He sipped the bitter cocktail unaware that a trickle had leaked from the right corner of his mouth. Bending over him, Katrine gently wiped the small line of liquid from his chin. As she did so, his eye dropped down and scanned her deep cleavage. He reached his bony left hand up into her blouse, cupped her breast, and squeezed.

"That's a good girl, Katrine," he whispered, tightening his grip.

Her expression did not change. When he released her and reached for the phone, she sat down to await his next command. Toombs stabbed at the buttons of the instrument with his carefully manicured middle finger, dialing the number of a farmhouse located in the bucolic hills of New Jersey's Hunterdon County. The English-speaking assassin from Davos answered.

"Seton Wynn 'ere."

Gunter Toombs spoke slowly. "Where is he now?"

"Left for Florida yesterday with Gregor on the tail. Visited the bird."

"The woman from Salzburg?"

"Right. And it looks like we've got competition, mate. Somebody popped her flat—bloody awful job," Wynn said.

"Was Ivorsen hurt?" Toombs whispered, his left eye wide.

"Not at 'ome when it blew."

Gunter Toombs pondered this new information for a minute and said finally, "Have Mr. Gregor return to New York. I don't want to come out to the farm. I want bōth of you here." He hung up the phone and motioned Katrine by flicking his index finger. As she stood, she began mechanically unbuttoning her blouse.

The voyage up to Cedar Key had taken all afternoon. Eric brought the Donzi into the small marina on the island's Gulf side. As he tied up in an overnight slip, he informed the dockhand that he would be leaving the boat until someone from the mainland could pick it up. Then he gave the man a hundred-dollar bill from a fat stack.

"Do you always carry so much cash?" Maggie asked as they walked into the little fishing village.

"Whenever I'm not sure what I'll need," he replied.

"Are you going to tell me what's going on?" she asked.

"Let's get a shower and some fresh clothes for you, and

I'll tell you everything I know over a dinner of crab and wine."

"How can you even think about eating?" she said through her teeth.

He shrugged and opened his hands. "We have to eat. We might as well do it in style."

Maggie closed her eyes and shook her head. They walked to a small general store near the marina, found a pair of jeans that fit Maggie a little too well, according to an admiring Eric, and then headed off to a cluster of vacation cottages tucked into the dunes near the deserted side of the island.

Maggie felt better after the hot shower had washed away the salt and smell of fish. She stepped from the shower, wrapped herself in a towel, and found Eric stripped to the waist. He was examing a five-inch black bruise on his side. Maggie winced.

"A present from the guy who rearranged your apartment," Eric explained. "But I got the passport." He grimaced when he put his weight on his left leg.

"You're not in very good shape, are you?" she teased.

Eric stared at her for moment and then continued undressing. There was an equally large bruise on his left leg. He stepped out of his slacks and into the shower. Maggie watched him lather himself and remembered their torrid encounter in Salzburg. Her predicament did not seem quite so bad.

She turned her back to him and leaned to the mirror. Without warning he lifted her effortlessly back into the shower. He pulled her towel away and tossed it out onto the floor. Running his wet hands down her shoulders and around her back, Eric crushed her to him. Standing on her toes to meet his kiss, Maggie reached up and gripped his shoulders. Under the sensuous pulsing stream of hot water, the long embrace excited them both.

"Dinner or dessert?" he asked, relaxing his hug just a bit.

"Dinner," she replied.

He hesitated but released her. Maggie stepped from the shower. As she dressed, she caught Eric admiring her in the mirror. Seductively raising an eyebrow, she smiled back.

The evening was warm and the sky absolutely clear. A huge yellow moon, just surfacing, shimmered thin moonglades on the black water. As they walked into the village, Maggie decided that the stars appeared brighter there than when seen from the mainland. Frowning, Eric stared up at the stellar clusters as well—but he was doing more than just stargazing.

When they reached the Cedar Key Hotel, the terror of the day was gone from Maggie's mind. She and Eric sat at one of the tables on the porch and ordered two plates of stone crabs. Eric whispered something to the young waitress, and she returned with an iced bottle of Taittinger champagne.

"Champagne?" Maggie asked. "Are we celebrating?"

"It's good to be alive," Eric said as he raised the goblet of sparkling wine. Maggie touched his glass with hers and drank.

"Now let's have it," she whispered with a smile. "Who are you and what the fuck is going on?"

Eric smiled and replied, "Could you be a little more direct?"

Maggie stared into his eyes.

Eric took a deep breath, sighed, and explained, "I am who I said I am. Two months ago, my uncle and I met in Zurich to sign papers that transferred funds from a trust set up by my father, just as we had every year, but it was to be the final and largest transaction of the fund. Uncle Charles and I took the weekend to ski in Davos. He was shot on the ski lift. I don't know by whom, and I only think I know why. I lost him ten days ago."

"Oh God," Maggie stammered. "I'm sorry, Eric."

"I thought he was going to make it, but he didn't."

She reached over and laid her hand on his. Eric sipped the cold champagne and continued, "When we met at the bank, I was given an unexpected document, written by my father. It contained a complex random code based on an astromathematical system that he taught me as a child."

"What does 'astromathematical' mean?" Maggie asked.

"It was just an exercise in ancient astronomical mathematics. Loosely based on the work of Copernicus. My father taught me to analyze all things according to some mathematical order—either absolute or random. This particular system worked well for children, because it's based on star and planet position. Kids love to look at the heavens, and my father showed me how to solve simple calculations based on the sidereal and the synodic period of a random planet."

"That's what you do for a living?" Maggie asked, confusion wrinkled across her brow.

"No, no." He smiled. "It was a game we played to learn mathematical theory. It's all quite obsolete."

Maggie shook her head but listened intently.

"My father did his research at the Institute for Advanced Study in Princeton. After World War II, he developed a philosophy that he hoped would prevent further warfare. He began gathering or visiting the world's best minds—the beginning of a ten-year program of research. Scientists, religious leaders, philosophers, economists, historians, all the best, from all over the world. The result of that research was a computer model—a complex formula sequence which if applied to data gathered by my father's group would produce accurate forecasts of potential change. Political, economic, religious, social, cultural, etcetera."

"Your father could predict the future?"

Eric had never thought of it in quite those terms. He paused for a moment and then answered, "In a sense, that's exactly what he hoped to do. Forecast and institute appropriate action for improvement."

"And did it work?"

"No one took him seriously. He first published in 1958. The Ivorsen Forecast, as it was called, was politely ignored. 1959—same thing. In 1960, though, the forecast caught the attention of some in the academic world. The previous publications had been right on the money. In 1961 he published a three-year forecast that suggested the beginning of a shift in world economic power to the oil-producing nations in the Middle East. Everyone laughed. The forecast also included an ominous warning that in early 1963, events could take place that would make it politically advantageous for the upcoming Kennedy administration to be terminated. One week after publication, my mother and father died in an avalanche on a mountain on the Swiss-Italian border. The computer model, its database, and all of his unpublished work disappeared at the same time."

The waitress brought out two plates piled high with stone-crab claws. Eric cracked the claws expertly, set the chunks of sweet meat in front of Maggie, refilled the two goblets, and continued, "Well, I was too young to know what was happening. Uncle Charles didn't explain it until I was twenty, and it just seemed far away and in the past. I didn't even really think about it—until the bank officer handed me an envelope sealed by my father. I translated the document and found it as confusing as the code it was written in. So far all I have is five series of equations that translate to five series of irregular concentric circles. I don't know what they mean. I keep staring at the stars, but I just can't figure it out."

"Why was your uncle killed?" Maggie asked.

"I think they were gunning for both of us, but he managed to warn me. I jumped from the lift."

"That's what happened to your leg," she said.

Eric nodded. "For certain powers, the best thing other than having a device that can accurately forecast change is making sure that no one else does. I think this document pinpoints the location of my father's work. Someone knows that I've come into possession of the document, and now the race is on."

"Now what?" Maggie asked. She stabbed a forkful of delicious crabmeat and took a sip of her champagne.

"We have to get to Vienna," Eric stated.

Maggie swallowed hard. "Excuse me?"

"There's a man there who might be able to help."

"I can't go to Vienna," Maggie said emphatically.

"You can't stay here."

Maggie blinked at the table and touched Eric's arm. "You don't understand. I can't just leave."

"We'll make a decision tomorrow," he said and filled her glass.

Maggie buried her face in her hand and sighed.

When they walked back along the deserted beach, the moon was high and silver. A gentle breeze, sweet with the scent of Confederate jasmine, wafted across the island. The second bottle of Taittinger had left them both a little light-headed. Eric put his arm around Maggie, and they wandered slowly back to the little cottage, each eagerly anticipating the next hour.

"Remind me to call the guy I rented the Donzi from," he said. "I'll have him pick it up."

"And how are we getting back to the mainland?"

"I'll rent a plane."

"You fly too, of course," she said with a hint of sarcasm.

"Summer of '70. Uncle Charles thought it best."

"You're going to fly us to Vienna?" Maggie was ready to accept anything.

He laughed. "No. We have to go to my place in Princeton first."

Dressed in a khaki suit, button-down oxford shirt, and striped tie, Lawrence Tilton would have looked perfectly normal in the university town—except that he had no eyebrows. As he took the registration slip from the desk clerk at the Nassau Inn, he requested a room on the top floor with a southerly exposure, explaining that he liked to work in the afternoon light. He lifted the clerk's pen, neatly signed a fictitious name, and carried his own luggage up to the room. Once inside, he locked the door, and before touching anything, extracted a pair of latex surgical gloves from the pocket of his jacket. Stretching them onto his hands, he gazed around the room mentally noting every aspect that might concern him.

Then he pulled all the covers from the bed, exposing one single sheet and one pillow. The rest of the bedclothes he carefully folded and placed in the closet. He walked into the shower, removed his clothes, wig, and latex gloves, and washed himself thoroughly. Reapplying the gloves, Tilton got down on his hands and knees in the shower and made sure that no telltale body hair had washed from his person. To make sure that he left no trace, he poured lye from a small tin into the drain and ran hot water to wash it down while he dressed.

Confident that he'd taken every precaution, Tilton flipped open his velvet-lined attaché case and extracted the various parts of a broken-down Ruger M77 hunting rifle. He carefully locked the 3-9X Diavari-C telescopic sight into the custom Suhl claw mounts and walked to the lightswitch. With the room dark, he could see easily into Eric Ivorsen's apartment on Palmer Square. For a moment, he centered the cross hairs on the bed illuminated by an outside streetlight. Then he took his weapon apart, picked up the phone, and asked for a Florida marine operator.

In the cabin of the *Hatteras*, Red Delahunt answered the call.

"I'm home," Tilton announced.

"He'll be with a girl. Shoot both."

CHAPTER 6

When she heard the running shower, Maggie opened one eye. She reached over for Eric, felt only sheet, and sat bolt upright, blinking into the morning sun. Wrapping herself in a sheet, she tiptoed into the bathroom, gripped the shower curtain, and pulled it aside. When she saw the empty stall, her mouth fell open and a worried frown wrinkled her forehead.

"Good morning!"

Maggie jumped, spun around, and saw Eric grinning at her from the doorway.

"Where were you?" she said, forcing a smile.

"I stepped outside to check the weather. It looks like a perfect day for flying," he replied innocently. "I ran the shower to bring up the hot water."

"Oh," she replied with a suspicious look.

"You didn't think I'd run out on you?" He smiled as he stepped around her into the steaming spray. Grabbing the soap, he turned away and began lathering himself.

Maggie smiled sweetly, reached into the shower, and turned off the hot water. She stepped back and waited. It took only a second for the water to turn cold. Eric's hand shot up, grabbing the nozzle to deflect the excruciating spray. Gritting his teeth as he turned the hot-water handle, Eric leaned out and rasped, "In the future, I'll wake you before leaving the bed."

"The future is something we have to talk about," Maggie said flatly.

"Okay. Let's get some breakfast and we'll talk."

The conversation during their walk into town was stilted. Something was bothering Maggie. Eric, looking forward to an afternoon of flying, squinted up at the billowy white clouds and blue sky. After several attempts to break the tension with levity, he sensed Maggie's discomfort and answered each of her questions directly, without elaborate explanation.

"What were those code numbers you radioed yesterday?" Maggie asked.

"The code is the opening sequence in my father's letter."

"And now those men have what they want?"

"Not quite. Now they have the same set of concentric circles that I have. If I don't understand them, they don't understand them."

"Why did they try to kill us, then?"

"Not sure. My guess is that they think they have the ability to decipher the Viking Cipher location from what I've given them."

"The what?" Maggie asked, trying to sort it all out.

"Viking Cipher—a cryptonym for the computer program."

"And now they don't need you?" she asked.

"Apparently not," Eric admitted. "Which means that they have access to some very sophisticated hardware and talent."

Maggie stared out over the Gulf, rubbed her forehead, and asked, "Will they try to kill us again?"

"I'm the only danger to them now," Eric replied. "As far as they're concerned, you've served your purpose—to get me to reveal the code sequence."

"I don't understand how they can solve this Viking Cipher if you have the only copy of your father's letter."

Eric stopped walking, shrugged, and replied, "I don't understand that either."

As they sat down at a sunny table in the Cedar Key Rest, Eric looked content—still enjoying the adventure. But Maggie looked sad, as if about to perform an unpleasant task. Biting her lip and staring down at the scratched Formica tabletop, she traced the deeply etched initials of a previous customer with her fingernail and sighed.

"Listen, Eric," she said finally. "I want to go home—

back to Tampa. I'm not used to this sort of thing. You seem to thrive on it."

Eric smiled understandingly and listened as Maggie explained her feelings.

"I like you very much and I wish we could have met under normal circumstances, but this is sheer lunacy. One minute people are feeding me to sharks and the next they're blowing up my apartment. In the middle of all this, we're making love and I'm discovering thrills I didn't even know were possible." Maggie looked up directly into Eric's eyes, shook her head slowly, and said, "It's too much. When I woke up in the middle of the night last night, I couldn't tell whether yesterday had really happened or if I had just had a bad dream. Then you woke up and the next minute I was on my back again headed for never-never land."

Eric nodded and said, "You're right, of course. It was selfish of me to expect you to abandon your world to run off to Europe with me. If you have a safe place to stay in Tampa, we'll arrange transportation when we reach the mainland."

Maggie took a deep breath and, searching his face, wondered if she was making the right decision. The look in his eyes did little to convince her that she had.

"Will I see you . . .?" she began.

"The very minute I've straightened out this situation," he assured her, laying his hand on hers.

Maggie smiled and sank back against her chair, relaxing for the first time. "Viking, huh?" She smiled, looking at him sideways. "I thought Vikings were blond."

"Run-of-the-mill, garden-variety Vikings," he retorted. "My mother was a raven-haired French beauty. I inherited her coloring and my father's size."

"Not a bad combination," Maggie admitted.

"You're not afraid of flying, are you?" Eric asked nonchalantly.

Maggie sat back up. "I've never been in a small plane, but I'm not afraid of heights, if that's what you mean. It's confined places that terrify me."

"You're claustrophobic?" he asked, surprised.

"I don't know why," she explained, "but I can't take

small spaces. When I was twelve, I was playing with a couple of kids building an underground fort in the woods near our neighborhood. They thought it would be fun to close me in for a while. When I didn't make any sound, they thought I was just fooling around. So they ran away, assuming that I'd push the plywood sheet away when I was tired of playing. My mother and father found me hours later, frozen in shock. The memory still terrifies me."

"Well, you'll like flying. It's relaxing," Eric said with a smile.

Cedar Key Airfield was little more than twenty-five hundred feet of oiled-sand runway, two weatherbeaten old hangars, and a field of assorted small aircraft in varying degrees of decay. Eric and Maggie walked into the ramshackle shed leaning against the larger hangar and found Charlie "Pops" Burwell draining the last few drops of a bottle of Orange Crush.

Sitting at an old oak desk covered with yellowing outdated flight charts, coffee-stained maintenance records, and various parts from several carburetors, Pops looked right at home. His hands were black with grease, his arms muscled from sixty years of hard work, and his chin fuzzy white from three days of not bothering to shave.

"Aahhhhh," he sighed, wiping his mouth with the back of his hand. He looked up, tossed the soda bottle onto a pile of rags, wrenches, and spark plugs, and grinned. "Howdy do!"

"Hi," Eric said.

"Wanna take the little lady flyin', right?" Pops asked with a grin that showed his gold tooth.

"I'd like to rent a plane," Eric said.

"That's too bad," Pops replied.

"Why's that?" Eric smiled patiently.

"Ain't got none to rent ya."

"Your sign says rentals," Eric said, pointing through the dirty window at a faded hand-lettered billboard advertising Cessna planes, flight instruction, rentals, and charters.

"Old sign."

"I see," Eric said.

"Sell ya one cheap, though," Pops offered. "Got a real beauty out back."

"How much?" Maggie asked.

Pops looked sideways up at Maggie, frowned for a minute, and then asked, "Who's buyin'? You or Stretch, here?"

"Why?" Maggie asked.

"Ten percent off fer pretty girls." Pops laughed again. "I can let-ya have the whole shebang, with full tanks, for say five hundred."

"Five hundred dollars for a plane?" Maggie whispered, gripping Eric's arm.

Eric shrugged, Maggie rolled her eyes, and Pops belched.

"Okay. Let's take a look," Eric said.

Pops, mumbling about Stinson being the most dependable plane in the sky, ambled out of his office with Eric and Maggie following. They came around the corner of the hangar and Pops headed off across the tiedown field.

They passed a new Beachcraft, two Cessna 150s, and a Bonanza before Pop's destination became obvious. At the very edge of the field, a battered-looking 1955 Stinson, listing decidedly to the right, sat by itself. The plane's tires—one bald and the other flat—sat cradled in clumps of overgrown grass. A huge dent in the plane's aluminum fuselage bore the scars of ballpeen-hammer restoration. The engine cowl, like a replaced fender of an auto wreck, had clearly been salvaged from an aircraft of a different color. It was solid pale yellow; the contrast with the faded blue stripes on the aluminum of the rest of the plane made the craft look unbalanced.

The left tiedown rope dangled unattached over a cement block buried in the sand. The right rope, frayed to a thread, hung limply to a block of its own. A two-foot rip in the fabric had been hastily repaired, leaving the right wing looking scarred. In the small cabin, the dual controls had been removed from the passenger's side and only the pilot's control wheel remained.

"Lemme jest cut 'er loose here," Pops said as he fumbled with the two lines.

Slightly open-mouthed, Maggie began circling the plane. The windshield was scratched and streaked with sparrow droppings. A tiny brown head popped out of the engine cowl, chirped angrily, and then disappeared. As Eric approached the dilapidated craft, the sparrow hopped out onto the propeller, relieved itself, and fluttered away.

"No charge fer the bird," Pops said as he unlocked the cockpit door. He reached across the cracked seats and opened the passenger door for Maggie. As she cautiously poked her head into the cabin, a tree frog hopped across the crumbling brown foam rubber in the split of the seat and attached itself to the glass lens of the airspeed indicator.

Maggie followed its progress, looked slowly up at Pops, and said, "Surely you jest."

"Now don't be worryin 'bout the critters. I'll clean them suckers outta here no problem."

"Does it fly?" Eric asked softly.

" 'Course she flies. Guaranteed!" Pops declared. "I just gotta get her over to the hangar there, chuck on a coupla tires, and fire 'er up."

Pops rolled up the sleeves of his washed-out green workshirt, revealing on his right arm an ornate tattoo: "Marge—My One and Only." Beads of sweat formed in the deep wrinkles of his forehead as he strained trying to rock the plane out of the grass. Turning beet-red, he began to wheeze. Eric and Maggie pushed on the wing struts and the plane reluctantly began to roll, its bad tire thumping over the grassy sand.

When they reached the hangar, Pops didn't rest. He went right to work replacing the worn tires with two that looked not much better. Eric studied the Jacksonville sectional chart. Maggie sipped a Coke and hoped that the engine wouldn't start.

"Climb in there, will ya, Stretch?" Pop's muffled voice called out from inside the engine cowl.

Eric eased himself into the cramped pilot's seat. Pops straightened up, pocketed several rusty spark plugs, and closed the cowl.

"Ready?" Eric called. "Step back and I'll try it."

Pops squinted and replied, "Boy, fer five hundred dollars, you don't get no self-starter. We gotta prop 'er."

Maggie closed her eyes as if in pain, Eric nodded, and Pops gripped the propeller.

"Prime 'er twice," Pops yelled, "Master on. Ignition on both. Half throttle. *And stand on them brakes, boy!*"

Pops pulled down, the propeller jerked, and the Lycoming engine coughed and spluttered once. Pops straightened up and grabbed the prop again. With his yellow teeth clenched, he ripped down with all his might and the engine roared to life, blue smoke pouring from the exhaust pipe. Maggie jumped back, and Pops stepped out of the range of danger. Eric throttled back, and Pops climbed in the passenger seat.

"Get out, Stretch! I'm gonna take 'er for a test ride," he yelled.

Pops slid across the seat as Eric unfolded himself and climbed out. Eric and Maggie watched the plane bounce across the field, turn to the middle of the runway, and begin to roll. The engine roared and the plane picked up speed. The tail wheel rose off the ground and Pops pulled up steeply, clearing the trees at the end of the field by less than ten feet. Banking hard, he circled the field once and came in hot. The plane hit the runway, bounced four feet into the air, and then settled smoothly onto the oil-packed sand. When he rolled back up to the hangar, Pops left the engine idling, leaped out, and motioned Eric over.

"Good as new. I tested the tires there too. Whaddya say?" he shouted.

Eric peeled off the cash and climbed in. Maggie hesitated. Eric looked up. Closing her eyes briefly, she took a deep breath, shook her head, and climbed into the passenger seat.

"Let me getcha the ownership certificate," Pops yelled and disappeared into his shed.

"Is this thing safe?" Maggie asked. "You barely fit!"

"Guaranteed!" Eric shot back with a grin.

Maggie remained unconvinced.

"Here ya go, Stretch," Pops called, waving the certificate. "Ya can fill it out yerself. Say, you do know how to fly, don't ya? No matter, we'll all find out in a minute."

Eric winked, Pops backed away, and Maggie asked, "You do, don't you?"

"Like the man says—we'll find out in a minute," Eric replied, advancing the throttle. The engine grew louder, the plane began to vibrate, and Maggie held her breath. When they reached the end of the runway, Eric applied the brakes for a run-up check. The plane responded surprisingly well, considering its condition. Eric scanned the sky for incoming planes, saw none, released the brakes, and pushed the throttle to full open. The plane shuddered and began to roll, taking on speed. When the airspeed reached seventy-five, Eric eased back on the yoke and the Stinson rose, easily clearing the trees at the end of the runway. On the ground, growing smaller, Pops grinned and waved. Maggie breathed out.

When he heard the knock, Lawrence Tilton pulled the surgical glove off his right hand and met the room-service waiter at the door. Concealing his left hand, he tipped the waiter three dollars and wheeled the food cart into the room himself, careful not to touch anything with his right hand. After replacing the rubber skin, he divided his attention equally between his meal and the room across Palmer Square. Although there had been no sign of activity, he remained diligent in his surveillance. A professional, Tilton had trained himself to accept the boredom of the stakeout as occupational necessity. He used the time to calculate optimum angles and to reminisce about previous assignments.

With his eyes riveted to Eric Ivorsen's windows, he lifted the gooey Reuben sandwich to his mouth and remembered a similar view in Brussels. The target was Japanese—small in stature. Difficult angle from a warehouse across the alley. The first shot eliminated the window. The second eliminated the man's right eye, ear, and jaw. Immediately following independent confirmation, Lawrence Tilton's net worth had jumped ten thousand dollars.

Climbing through twenty-five hundred feet, Eric banked slightly to the right, around the base of a mountainous cloud.

"I think we need a trade-in," he said suddenly.

"Why? What's wrong?" Maggie asked with alarm.

"Nothing. We're too slow. It'll take all day and night for us to get to Princeton in this bucket of bolts. We'll land in Jacksonville and arrange a flight for you to Tampa."

"What about you?" Maggie asked.

"I'll take the next scheduled flight north."

Maggie leaned forward and gazed at the billowy mountains of white that soared thousands and thousands of feet.

"Beautiful, aren't they?" Eric said as they began climbing up, around, and through the towering shifting bluffs.

"Incredible," Maggie whispered.

They topped the clouds twenty minutes later and, cruising five hundred feet above the ocean of puff, did not descend until Eric estimated that they were approximately fifteen miles from Jacksonville. Without the aid of navigation radios, they were forced to descend for visual reference. The descent was even more breathtaking than the climb as they banked and glided in slow gentle turns, spiraling down through the gray-and-white cotton canyons.

They entered the pattern at Jacksonville at a thousand feet, landed without incident, and followed a small courtesy jeep to the general aviation terminal. Eric taxied to a tiedown space, pulled out the mixture knob, snapped off the master switch, and as the engine choked, turned the ignition switch to the off position. The plane fell silent, and an attendant wandered over, staring at the decrepit craft.

"Ya'll need service?" he asked, squinting at the hammered fuselage.

"No thanks," Eric said as he stepped down.

The skinny young attendant wore a Flight Line Services cap, mirrored aviator's glasses, and a crisp tan shirt with "Bob" embroidered on the breast pocket. He looked up at Eric and frowned.

"Say, don't I know you?" he asked.

"I don't think so." Eric shrugged.

"Excuse me," Maggie said, "where can I find a rest room?"

"Oh, right over there," the attendant said, pointing at the terminal entrance. A troubled frown wrinkled across his brow, he gazed again at Eric and mumbled, "Damn, I could swear . . ."

"I'll be back to take care of the plane," Eric said as he turned with Maggie toward the glass doors.

Once inside the terminal building, Maggie headed off for the rest rooms and Eric inquired about the next available flights to Tampa and Newark. As Maggie passed the newsstand near the Hertz counter, she glanced down at the morning edition of the *Florida Times Union* and saw on the front page her full-face photograph of Eric under a headline that read "Princeton Mathematician Sought in Tampa Kidnapping/Bombing!"

Maggie's eyes widened, and she tore the paper from the rack. She scanned the story with her mouth hanging open in disbelief. Anonymous sources reported Eric Ivorsen's involvement in the crime, and Dr. Carl Millbank confirmed that the victim had last been seen with Ivorsen and seemed distraught. The cover photograph, salvaged from the blast, was the most recent known photograph of the suspect. Maggie spun around, desperately searching the crowd for Eric.

"Hey, lady," an unpleasant voice called from behind her.

Maggie snapped around. The vendor, with a cigar crunched in the corner of his mouth, stood with his hand extended, palm up. "Fifty cents, hey."

Maggie tossed him the paper and ran back toward the airline counters. Eric was in the middle of a conversation with the reservations clerk. Maggie grabbed his elbow and tugged hard.

"Excuse me," Eric said to the pretty clerk. He looked down at Maggie, tried to read the expression on her face, and said, "Yes?"

"Can I talk to you for a minute?" she said through her teeth, forcing a smile.

"Sure," Eric smiled.

"Over here," she said, pulling him toward the glass doors. "Alone."

Turning to the girl behind the counter, Eric joked, "She gets so jealous whenever I talk to other beautiful women."

The young girl giggled, blushing and batting her eyes up at Eric.

"Come on!" Maggie whispered sternly.

Eric followed, and his smile faded as Maggie explained what she had just seen. He listened carefully, and when she finished he said nothing.

"Well?" she demanded.

"It's too fast," he stated finally.

"What's too fast?"

"The information hit the papers too fast. It's a setup. Our friends have cleverly decided to let the Florida police do their hunting for them."

"But Carl . . ."

"They lucked out with Carl. He just confirmed my presence and identified the photo," Eric said, his mind racing.

"I'd better tell the police that I'm okay and you had nothing to do with— "

Eric grabbed Maggie by the shoulders and looked down into her wide green eyes. Maggie, startled by the gesture, trembled in his grip.

"I need you, Maggie," he said, squeezing her gently.

"What?" she whispered, her eyes searching his face.

"Even if we convince the police that you haven't been kidnapped, they'll have to hold me for questioning in the bombing. I'll be a sitting duck."

Maggie blinked. Eric looked up across the terminal and saw the skinny attendant walking toward an Airport Authority guard.

Eric continued, "We have to get back to the plane. Bob just remembered where he's seen me."

The attendant spoke to the guard, thumbing toward the tiedown area. The guard listened for a moment and then lifted his transceiver to his mouth. The alarm was going out.

"I need you," Eric repeated desperately.

Maggie nodded, and they pushed through the doors, running toward the sad-looking plane. When they reached it, Maggie scurried around to the passenger's side and climbed in.

"Uh . . ." Eric began.

"Well, let's go," Maggie said excitedly.

"Yeah, uh, one thing, Maggie," Eric said. "Remember how we had to start the plane on Cedar Key?"

"Yeah, so?" she replied, nodding for him to hurry.

"Well, you're going to have to take the controls."

CHAPTER 7

Two Jacksonville Airport Authority officers bolted out of the security office, across the terminal, into the milling crowd of waiting passengers, well-wishers, and airport workers. Running with their hands on their guns, they caught up with the security guard and the flight-line attendant, Bob, at the glass doors that opened onto the general aviation service area. Three hundred yards away, Eric Ivorsen was hurriedly explaining to Maggie McCabe how to prop-start a 1955 Stinson airplane.

"Don't worry about a thing, Irish," Eric said, "Just keep your feet pressed down on the tops of those pedals and pull that throttle back as soon as the engine starts."

"Which one's the throttle?" she cried in panic, staring wide-eyed down at the various knobs, dials, levers, and switches.

"The red one!" Eric called as he scrambled under the wing strut to the front of the plane.

At the sound of leather slapping across tarmac, Eric looked up to see the three policemen racing toward him. Bob was not far behind.

"Freeze!" two cops yelled in unison.

"Contact!" Eric shouted and ripped down on the prop. The engine spluttered and died.

Gritting his teeth, Eric grabbed the blade and yanked again. The engine exploded to life and the propeller blast split the air, sucking the two-thousand-pound plane forward. Eric was gone, and Maggie screamed, letting go of both the throttle and the brakes.

Eric, hugging the ground under the deadly cyclonic blur, rolled to the side and came up running. He reached the wing strut on the passenger's side just as the plane was gaining enough speed to pull away. In a desperate dive, he caught the strut and was dragged across the tarmac. Maggie, desperately reaching across the seat, opened the door and watched helplessly as Eric strained to pull himself aboard.

Clawing at the doorframe and ripped leather seat, Eric managed to drag himself up into the plane's cramped little cockpit. Out of breath and bleeding from both knees, he fell back, sucking wind.

"Nice work, Maggie," he gasped. "Now all you gotta do is take off and fly us outta here."

As the creaking craft pulled away, the three cops stopped running. Winded and breathing fast, the tallest of the three turned back to Bob and asked, "You got a plane on the line?"

"Yessir," Bob replied, a smile of enthusiasm spreading across his face.

"You wanna help me track that sonofabitch?"

"Yessir!" Bob was bursting.

The tall cop turned to the other officers. "Contact the tower. They probably can't stop them, but they can keep an eye on them until we're in the air."

Bob sprinted over to a brand-new Cessna 172, quickly untied it, and jumped into the pilot's seat. The cop climbed in next to him, gave a thumbs-up, and asked, "Think you can catch 'em?"

"I can fly this plane through a chicken coop and fry the eggs with my exhaust," Bob said with a cocky smirk. "And I can sure as hell outfly some damn girl in a Stinson."

The cop nodded, and Bob hit the ignition switch. At the same time, two security cars fishtailed onto the airfield, speeding toward the Stinson.

Bouncing across the grass between the taxiway and the runway, Maggie managed to take out three runway lights and a direction marker. She wrenched the control wheel right and left, but the plane did not respond.

"Actually," Eric said calmly, "you don't steer by turning

the wheel back and forth. You have to push your feet down on the pedal in the direction you want to turn."

"Then what's this fucking wheel for?" Maggie demanded angrily as they bounced out onto the active runway, forcing the tower to divert an incoming Eastern Airlines 737.

"That's for later when we want to bank left or right."

"Why don't you just tell me how to stop this thing and you run around and take over the controls?" Maggie said, trying to make the stubborn craft do what she wanted.

"Because by then those well-meaning policemen will have caught up with us," Eric replied, pointing to the two cars racing toward them from across the airfield. "Now push down on the left pedal."

The plane rolled left, lining up on the runway.

"Now push on the right until we're rolling straight."

Maggie did as she was instructed, and the plane straightened out. Eric reached over and pushed the throttle open. The engine roared and the old plane began to vibrate, accelerating. Maggie stiffened, her knuckles turning white as she gripped the control wheel. Unconsciously stepping on the rudder pedals, Maggie started the plane zigzagging back and forth across the runway. Breathing faster and faster, she was starting to panic.

"Easy with the feet," Eric said, matter-of-factly.

The plane straightened again and reached lift-off velocity. The tail wheel rose and the vibrations ceased. Maggie didn't realize it, but she was airborne by inches.

"What happened?" she gasped when the vibration stopped.

"You took off."

"Oh my God," she whispered and pulled back on the control wheel.

The plane's nose shot up and they pitched skyward, instantly losing airspeed. Eric dove across Maggie and pushed the wheel forward before the plane stalled out of the air. The nose dropped and the plane leveled out thirty feet above the runway, gaining speed. Below, the two security cars paced along, the police drivers waving for them to land. When the airspeed indicator reached seventy-five, Eric sat back and Maggie was in control again.

"Don't let go!" she said desperately.

"It's okay. You've got it," he said reassuringly and waved back to one of the policemen.

Maggie sat rigid, a deathgrip on the wheel.

"Relax," Eric said. "This is the fun part."

As the old silver Stinson rattled off the far end of the runway, Bob brought the Cessna whipping around for a quick run-up check. Jolting to a stop at the end of the runway, he ran the engine up to fifteen hundred rpm, checked the magnetos and carburetor heat, and then, gunning the engine, rolled to the edge of the tarmac, at the same time grabbing the microphone. "Six nine eight nine Sierra ready for takeoff," he advised in an officious tone.

The radio in the Cessna crackled and the tower controller's voice filled the small cabin. "Six nine eight nine Sierra, cleared for emergency takeoff."

"Roger," Bob answered, jamming the throttle in. The blue-and-white plane began to roll, and fifteen seconds later it lifted into the sky, tracking the distant Stinson.

"As you turn the wheel left, just step down on the left pedal and we'll turn left," Eric said calmly.

Maggie, with her tongue curled to her lip and a frown of concentration locked on her brow, tried it, and it worked.

"Try one to the right," he suggested.

The plane responded perfectly.

"Ease back on the wheel."

The nose lifted.

"Push in," he said.

Maggie pushed in and the nose dropped.

"Piece of cake—right?" Eric asked.

Maggie nodded and tried several gentle turns on her own. Eric glanced through the rear window and saw the Cessna climbing up behind them. He guessed their distance to be no more than half a mile and muttered, "Uh oh."

"What? What?" Maggie cried, her eyes wide.

"Nothing."

"Jesus, don't do that!" she sighed and returned her concentration to the controls of the plane.

Eric looked again and saw the chase plane growing,

gaining fast. A quick check of the altimeter told him that they were just climbing through two thousand feet. He knew that there was no chance of outrunning the newer plane and decided on the only course open to them.

"Keep the nose up a bit," he said, pointing at the airspeed indicator. "We want to keep a steady climb at seventy. If we drop below, just ease the nose down a bit by pushing the wheel in. If we go faster, then ease back."

"Can't I turn?" Maggie asked, a little disappointed.

"Not just yet. Wait'll we reach those clouds and then you can turn all you want."

The Cessna caught the Stinson at twenty-six hundred feet, climbing alongside. Maggie glanced left and blinked. Staring back from the passenger window of Bob's plane, the angry-looking policeman was emphatically pointing at the ground.

"Oh no," Maggie murmured. "Look."

Eric leaned forward, saw the policeman, and smiled at him. The officer glared back, pointing at the ground and mouthing something Eric didn't bother to try to figure out.

"There is only one way to handle this," Eric said to Maggie. "Keep flying."

"What's the point? They'll just follow us until we land."

"Not if they don't know where we are."

Maggie blinked at Eric, then turned toward the Cessna. With the base of the towering clouds hanging only five hundred feet above, the Cessna inched closer and the policeman jabbed his finger toward the ground, mouthing an unmistakable *Now*.

"How do you propose to lose—" she began to ask.

"When we reach that cloud, you fly right on in," Eric interrupted.

As the two planes approached the slowly swirling white wall, they were only yards apart. At seventy-five miles per hour, both craft disappeared into the mist.

In the cabin of the Stinson, the sun was suddenly gone and the windshield turned a milky translucent gray. The plane began to jump and bump.

"What's wrong?" Maggie gasped, trying unsuccessfully to control the motion.

"It's just that the air is a little less stable inside the cloud. Don't worry—you're doin' fine."

"How do I know which way to go?"

Eric scanned the instrument panel and replied, "I'll tell you what to do, and we'll lose them sooner or later."

Gripping the wheel, Maggie peered into the gray windshield and the Stinson continued its climb. Eric watched the instruments.

Bob banked left.

"Whaddya doin'?" the policeman barked.

"I'm sure as hell not flyin' around in some cloud with another plane."

"Then how the hell are we gonna catch 'em?"

"We'll wait outside and keep looking."

The Cessna broke out of the cloud, a wisp of mist spiraling in its wake. Bob brought it around hard and continued climbing, several hundred feet away from the side of the cloud, but another even larger cumulus formation was converging above. Forced to turn again, back toward an opening between the two mountains of white, Bob banked the Cessna hard. By maintaining visibility, he gave up altitude.

As the Cessna shot through the closing gap, the Stinson slipped from one cloud into the other, three hundred feet above. Sunlight glinted in Bob's mirrored sunglasses as he looked up in time to see the Stinson's silver tail swallowed by the cloud.

"Aw, shit," he growled as he wrenched the Cessna around in an uncomfortably tight turn. He banked hard to the right and jammed his foot down on the rudder. The Cessna's left wing whipped skyward, and the policeman drew breath as he found himself staring out the window straight down.

The plane bumped once as they passed quickly through the edge of a cumulus swirl. Turning to get a better view of the north side of the huge cloud, Bob squinted up and saw the Stinson break out and immediately bank around behind.

"There they are," he snapped and began to follow.

By the time he made it up and around the shifting puff, the Stinson was just starting to turn toward another cloud.

* * *

Maggie pushed the wheel, banked right, and stepped down on the right rudder. The plane's nose dropped, its left wing rose, and they plunged into the side of a cloud. Once inside, Maggie eased back on the wheel and leveled the wings.

"How was that?" she asked proudly.

"Damn good," Eric said with a smile.

Bob banked away and continued to climb.

"This ain't no good," the policeman pointed out. "You gotta second-guess 'em."

"Let's take a chance and climb on around behind this mother," Bob grumbled, turning the Cessna.

The climb took almost five minutes, but when they leveled off, they were in a patch of clear sky that stretched almost a thousand feet between towering peaks. They had an uninterrupted view of the two clouds and guessed that the Stinson was somewhere in the left. Bob trimmed the Cessna for slow flight and banked gently left and right, waiting. But he began getting nervous as they closed the distance on the left peak and the Stinson did not appear.

"Shit," he spat. "We're gonna have to come around."

He turned right, heading directly into the other misty peak.

Maggie looked up at the gray windshield streaked with condensation and pushed the wheel in, diving the plane. Their airspeed increased, the wind outside howled, and the Stinson burst from the cloud. Dead ahead, less than one hundred feet away, Bob and the policeman looked up through the Cessna's windshield. The image of the diving Stinson was a growing double reflection in the sunglasses of the pilot.

Bob threw his hands up, covering his face with crossed wrists. The cop tried to push himself into the Cessna's back seat, a mask of horror gripping his face. Eric winced, turning his head away from the inevitable collision. Maggie ripped back on the wheel. A split second later, the planes met.

The propeller of the Cessna slammed into the aluminum

underbelly of the Stinson like a jackhammer, gashing out chunks of metal and rivet. The staccato thunder lasted only seconds and ended when the Stinson's tail wheel was blasted away by the Cessna prop's mangled tip.

Bent by the wrenching impact, the Cessna's engine shaft began to grind. A second later, Bob and his passenger were earthbound, gliding powerless.

Maggie held the Stinson's control wheel to her stomach and the plane shot straight up. The airspeed dropped to zero, the right wing snapped over, and plane plunged into a violent spin.

Eric slowly opened one eye and peeked through the windshield and then over at Maggie frozen watching the earth rotate below.

"Push in the wheel," Eric commanded, "and work the rudders."

Maggie didn't budge. Wind began to howl through the gashes in the fuselage. Coupled with the bellow of the racing engine, the increasing roar in the cabin was deafening.

"Maggie," he said sternly, "*Right rudder!*"

The old plane shook and the rip in the fabric of the wing started to open.

"Right rudder!" Eric yelled again, pointing at her foot.

Maggie hesitated but finally did as she was told and the plane slowly stopped spinning. But they were pointed straight down in a full-throttle power dive, nineteen hundred feet from the ground. The earsplitting noise of the wind and engine forced Eric to shout instructions as he watched the ground growing rapidly closer. Shaking violently, the plane's frame began to creak.

"Ease back on the wheel!" he shouted.

At six hundred feet, Maggie pulled back and the plunging Stinson, its engine screaming, swooped out of the dive. As the airspeed dropped to ninety and the noise in the cabin lessened, Eric turned and looked at Maggie. Her expression was completely blank—neither fear nor relief. She sat silently staring ahead, holding the plane steady in straight and level flight.

"You did it," he said with admiration.

Maggie took a deep breath and released it slowly through puffed cheeks. After a moment of silent reflection, a devilish grin spread across her face. She turned to Eric and with childlike surprise in her voice, exclaimed, "I did—didn't I?"

Eric nodded. Maggie beamed. Banking right, she executed a perfect turn and they began to climb back up to the safety of the clouds.

CHAPTER 8

Seton Wynn and his associate, Josef Gregor, waiting for an elevator, looked out of place in the Pierre's lobby. Several of the hotel's guests glanced at the two men as they stepped into the elevator and turned. Wynn looked like any tourist, but Gregor, with his cruel eyes and bad teeth, looked wrong somehow—nervous and uncomfortable. His eyes darted across the crowd, and the people that met his stare were happy to see the elevator doors close.

Wynn and Gregor did not speak as they rode to Gunter Toombs's floor. Gregor didn't like Toombs but liked his money and his young voluptuous friend. Even if his English had been better, he would have let Wynn do all the talking just as he had in Davos and earlier in Zurich. He knew his job and his reward. He had spent the flight up from Florida thinking about the reward.

The doors opened on the fourth floor, and the two men strode to Toombs's room. Katrine answered the door and dropped her eyes when she saw Gregor. Gregor's tongue flicked out across his pointed teeth.

"Hello, love," Wynn said, pushing past the girl.

"Ah, Mr. Wynn," Gunter Toombs whispered from his wheelchair. "I see your associate has returned from his mission."

Gregor grunted.

"Report," Toombs commanded, leaning his head back.

"Gregor 'ere tells me that our oversized friend up and disappeared with the bird. Like I said, mate, looks like someone else has got interested in your little project."

"This girl is the same one he met in Salzburg?" Toombs asked, his good eye wide, nearly the same size as his paralyzed right eye. For a moment, he looked almost normal—then the left eye narrowed. Toombs was plotting.

"Right—McCabe's 'er name," Wynn replied.

"It appears that this woman means something to Ivorsen," mused Toombs.

"Hard to say for sure. Thought enough of 'er to take 'er along," Wynn commented as he strolled across the room. Pulling the drapes away from the window, he gazed out over Central Park and the lights of the Manhattan skyline.

"This bombing was meant to kill her or him or both?" Toombs asked.

Wynn turned to Gregor.

"Bot," Gregor grunted in his thick accent.

"The only reason someone would want to eliminate Ivorsen would be if he had extracted from him all necessary information, thus rendering him useless," Toombs concluded, his eye flashing back and forth as his mind raced. He looked up and hissed, "This is not good."

"You want us to bring 'im in?" Wynn asked.

Toombs hesitated before answering. "Yes, it's time. I think you'll find him at his residence. I suspect he's there or will be shortly. And if the girl is with him, bring her as well—the girl might be useful as a tool of persuasion."

Gregor started to grin, his thin lips pulling away from brown teeth, but stopped suddenly when he saw Gunter Toombs's eye fix on him. A moment of uncomfortable silence followed.

"Princeton, isn't it?" Wynn asked, to break the tension.

"Yes," Toombs replied and snapped his fingers. "Katrine will give you the address."

Katrine obediently crossed the room and extracted a slip of paper from the antique desk. Gregor followed her with his eyes riveted on her thighs. Gunter Toombs studied Gregor's unblinking leer.

"You like to look at my Katrine, Gregor?" he asked in a baiting tone that left Gregor unsure whether to answer or not.

Gregor looked nervously at Wynn. Wynn nodded without trying to hide his disapproval.

"Ya," Gregor answered flatly.

"You've seen this McCabe woman?" Toombs asked.

"Ya." Gregor nodded.

"Do you want to do to her what you do to my Katrine?"

Gregor sneered. Seton Wynn turned again, gazing out the window—he knew what was coming, and it was the one aspect of working for Gunter Toombs that even he couldn't quite accept. Gregor, on the other hand, considered it part of the compensation and probably wouldn't have worked for the Toombs under any other terms.

"Good, Gregor—then she shall be yours. You'll get what you want when I have what I need," Toombs said, the left side of his face pulled back in a smile.

"Say, mate," Wynn said suddenly. "any guess who we're competin' with?"

Annoyed at the abrupt return to business, Toombs twisted in his wheelchair to look at Wynn. His eye narrowed, and he spoke slowly, menacingly. "I know exactly whom we are competing with, and should it become important for you to know as well, then you shall."

Seton Wynn was not intimidated by the grotesquely crippled creature that sat immobile before him. Wynn's motivation was monetary, and he was businessman enough to know that his profession carried with it certain compromises. He nodded and smiled at his employer. "Whatever you say, mate. Just thinking of the job."

Toombs was not placated by the flip reply. Without removing his stare from Wynn, he snapped his fingers at Katrine and ordered, "Bring me ten thousand, Katrine. Five for Mr. Wynn and five for Mr. Gregor. The other half will be available on Monday. By then, the assignment will be completed, won't it, Mr. Wynn?"

Wynn met the evil stare for just a moment, nodded, and looked down.

Raising his bony left forefinger at Wynn, Toombs warned, "You secure Ivorsen and this McCabe girl and then call me at the farm. I want answers."

Katrine did as she was told and placed the stacks of hundreds in front of Toombs along with a petty-cash voucher for signature. He reached out with his left hand and gripped the pen, clawlike, scrawling out his name in tight little characters. Looking up, he held out Wynn's stack. "I assume that you will not be staying for the festivities."

"Not my cup o' tea," Wynn said. "I'll be waitin' downstairs."

He tucked the money in the inside breast pocket of his jacket and left the room. Toombs picked up the other stack and handed it to Katrine. "Gregor wants his reward, Katrine."

With her head bowed, unable to look into Gregor's cruel face, she crossed the room and offered the money. Gregor took the stack of bills and set it on the desk. He reached up and gently took Katrine's chin in his hand. Katrine continued staring down. Gregor, breathing through his rotted teeth, reached around behind her and twisted her arm until she cried out. Gunter Toombs watched transfixed.

Forcing her to her knees, Gregor reached down and lifted her chin until she was forced to stare at him. Grunting in German, he slapped her face once in each direction. Then, kneeling next to her, he began tearing away her clothes.

Toombs watched each humiliation, each indignity and violation, with a small bubble of saliva blowing in and out of the corner of his smiling mouth.

Lawrence Tilton rubbed his eyes and peered through the scope at Eric's apartment. It remained unchanged as it had for the previous twenty hours. He rubbed his eyes again and decided that he could no longer maintain constant surveillance. It was a particularly upsetting decision, because it meant that he would have to rely on a piece of electronic equipment rather than just his own skill. The percentage of probable success diminished.

He locked the door to his room, exited the Nassau Inn, and crossed Palmer Square. Entry to the apartment was simple—the pick worked on the second try and he was in. He noted the layout of the rooms, smiling because his assumptions had been correct. Placing the device was easy. It was disguised as a well-worn textbook, and he simply set it in Eric's bookcase next to a similar-looking volume. The device, like the receiver Tilton carried back to his room, had been designed, manufactured, and tested in an electronics laboratory in Minsk, USSR.

Upon reentering his room, Tilton set a small alarm clock on the nightstand. A small green light glowed on the dial, illuminating the numerals and signaling the reception of an undisturbed signal from the transmitter hidden inside the book across Palmer Square. Confident that the slightest commotion in Eric Ivorsen's room would alter the signal and activate the alarm, Lawrence Tilton stretched out carefully on the bed and closed his eyes to rest.

"This is fun," Maggie exclaimed as Eric studied the sectional chart looking for a place to ditch the plane. With dusk closing in and the Stinson's fuel tanks getting dangerously low, the necessity of landing had become urgent.

"Excuse me?" Eric said, looking up from the chart.

"Flying is fun," she repeated.

"Right," he replied. "But landing is ecstasy."

Maggie, although not sure what he meant, nodded and banked the plane.

Eric looked down and saw a huge empty parking lot—a regional shopping mall just outside Charlotte, North Carolina, in the final stages of construction, had apparently just been paved.

After making several passes, Eric, with a confident smile, said, "Okay, Maggie . . . in we go."

Maggie, unaware that she was about to land an airplane with no tail wheel and slashed tires, grinned back. "Right. How do we do it?"

"Well," he said, "First we descend to one thousand feet."

Maggie pulled back the throttle knob. Eric pulled out the carburetor heat.

"What's that for?" Maggie asked, eager to learn as much as possible.

"That keeps the fuel flowing through the carburetor even if too much moisture starts to freeze the line. Always apply carburetor heat when you cut the power."

Maggie nodded.

"Bank right," Eric instructed.

Maggie, leaning into the turn, brought the plane around smartly. They settled to one thousand feet, running parallel to the parking lot. Eric eased the throttle in, maintaining straight and level flight.

"I can do that," Maggie stated.

"Oh—sorry."

The parking lot, two thousand feet to their left, ended, and Eric said, "Okay . . . crank down ten percent flaps."

Maggie, with absolutely no idea what he was talking about, shot back, "Copilot, crank down ten percent flaps."

Laughing, Eric reached down and did as he was told. The plane slowed.

"Nicely done," Maggie said without smiling.

"Thanks," he replied. "Now bank left and pull the throttle back just a bit."

The plane turned and began to descend. Eric lowered the flaps further and the plane's airspeed fell to eighty.

"Bank once more until we're lined up on that parking lot."

Maggie banked again and then leveled the wings. Brand-new and as yet unoccupied, Belk's, Sears, and J.C. Penney buildings sat ahead to the right, and four thousand feet of empty asphalt stretched out before them.

"Pull the throttle back all the way and keep your airspeed at seventy."

With the throttle back and the nose of the plane sinking on the horizon, Eric lowered the flaps all the way. Maggie had to push the wheel in to keep the airspeed constant. The Stinson glided downward, settling toward the end of the lot outside Sears's automotive department.

At one hundred feet, they soared past the Belk's side entrance. Maggie held her steady. At twenty feet, Eric, trying to appear as calm as possible, folded his arms and casually glanced at the ragged rubber tire on the wheel to his right.

"Flare out," he said in controlled voice.

"What does that mean?" Maggie asked calmly as the plane sank rapidly toward touchdown.

Eric, sitting up and leaning back, said, "Ease back—ease back!"

"No problem," Maggie replied, pulling back on the wheel. The nose lifted and the the plane floated along at ten feet for what seemed to Eric like an eternity. Finally, the Stinson mushed and hit the pavement at fifty miles an hour, directly in front of J.C. Penney. Bouncing along, the plane shook and rattled. The tires slapped along for a second and then ripped away in black shards. The earsplitting screech of metal scraping asphalt filled the cabin. The tail fell to the ground, trailing sparks and chunks of aluminum. Shuddering and creaking violently, the plane slid two hundred feet before the bent right wheel seized up. Fortunately, they had slowed enough that the Stinson did not flip over as it whipped around and stopped.

Having no experience with which to compare her performance, Maggie looked over proudly and asked, "How was that?"

Slowly opening one of his closed eyes, Eric scanned the cabin, convinced himself that they had come through unscathed, and turned to Maggie. He released the deep breath he'd been holding and replied, "Smooth—very smooth."

As the Lycoming engine spluttered and died, a pink '61 Chrysler Imperial, with a young black man at the wheel and his girlfriend wedged against his side, rolled out of the shadows behind the half-completed Mecklenburg County Bank building. It crossed the parking lot and eased to a stop as Eric climbed out of the Stinson.

"Say," the young man called out to Eric. "Now whatchyall doin' landin' in a parkin' lot? Airport's down the road."

"Ran a little low on fuel," Eric replied.

The young man got out of the rusty car, his head bobbing. He circled the plane as Maggie climbed out.

"This here's one bad-lookin' machine," he observed.

"You've got a classic of your own," Eric replied, nodding toward the Chrysler.

"Naw, that ol' boat ain't worth spit," the young man said. "But this here . . . this here is transportation. With a plane, you could up and fly away anytime you want." He shook his head in admiration and ran his brown hand along the aluminum fuselage.

"A bit banged-up," Eric said.

"Shoot hell, I could fix that," he dismissed the comment.

Eric smiled at him, and the young man smiled back.

"Ya'll mind?" he asked when he reached the pilot's door.

"Not at all. Jump in."

Grinning with pride, he called out the passenger side, "Hey, Lashonda! Come on over here, girl—lookit this here!"

Lashonda shyly climbed out of the car and approached the plane, hesitating when she got to the passenger door.

"Climb right on in, Lashonda," Eric encouraged her.

Lashonda plopped down in the seat, Eric glanced at Maggie, and Maggie grinned.

"What's a plane like this cost?" the young man asked, staring at the controls.

"This one was cheap," Eric admitted. "Because of its condition."

"Shoot, nothun a coupla hours in my shop wouldn't set right."

"I'd be willing to trade you for your car," Eric said suddenly.

The young man froze, then turned, frowning, and asked, "You ain't funnin' me, is you? You'd trade me this plane for my car serious?"

"Sure as I'm standing here."

The young man turned to Lashonda, who giggled and looked down, embarrassed. He squinted back at Eric.

Eric patted the cowl and said, "You'd need to put on new wheels, tires, and tail-wheel assembly and you'd have to replace the underside of the fuselage."

"Even trade?"

"Even trade," Eric replied.

"Deal," the young man said.

Eric reached into the side pouch next to the door, pulled out Pop's ownership certificate, and handed it to the young man. "You just have to write your name on the line at the bottom, and this plane belongs to you. The previous owner already signed it over and I haven't bothered to fill it in."

The young man reached into his back pocket, extracted the Chrysler's keys, handed them to Eric, and said, "Say, will ya'll be kind 'nough give me 'n' Lashonda a lift to my place in your new car? Gotta get me the flatbed to haul my plane home."

"Hop in." Eric grinned.

"Ya'll be careful where you drive 'er, hear? These plates are a little out of date and I lost the registration," he admitted.

"She's not hot, is she?" Eric asked.

"Naw . . . junked. I got the title back at the house."

Ten minutes later, Eric, Maggie, Lashonda, and the young man wheeled into a dirt driveway, scattering chickens and startling two puppy bloodhounds that had been sleeping underneath an ancient flatbed Ford. A skinny old black man, sitting on the sagging porch of a ramshackle farmhouse, looked up as his grandson and Lashonda got out of the car. Bounding across the porch, the young man disappeared through a rickety old screen door and returned a minute later with a dog-eared piece of paper that turned out to be the title for the Chrysler.He handed it to Eric, threw two planks into the back of the truck, and then helped his grandfather climb up into the cab.

Eric backed out of the driveway with the young man following in the truck, the chickens trotting in circles, and the puppies tumbling over one another in their wake. Once on the road, Eric pulled to one side with the intention of following the flatbed back to the shopping center to lend a hand. But during their absence enough of a crowd had gathered that he didn't have to assist in the loading of the Stinson. When they reached the plane, Eric and Maggie pulled up next to the young man and sat with the Chrysler idling.

"Take some flying lessons," Eric said, holding his left palm extended.

With one cracking slap, the young man acknowledged the advice and said goodbye. He climbed up onto the truck's bed and called out instructions to the eager crowd pushing the battered plane up the makeshift ramp. Once the plane was secure, his grandfather drove proudly home with the young man sitting at the controls of the Stinson, lost in a fantasy of flight.

The rusty pink Imperial, its muffler rumbling and shocks squeaking, bounced across the parking lot with Eric Ivorsen at the wheel and Maggie McCabe wedged against his side.

CHAPTER 9

"I have to call home," Maggie said. "My parents will be worried."

"I just saw a sign for a truck stop in ten miles," Eric replied as he wheeled the long heavy car into the fast lane of Interstate 85. "And I could use some food."

"I think my father will speak to me," Maggie mused, thinking out loud.

"Is that so unusual?"

"Daddy and I haven't spoken since Carl and I . . ." Maggie left the sentence unfinished.

"Your father is somewhat conservative?" Eric understated.

"My father is a retired Marine Corps drill instructor," Maggie answered. "He thinks Carl Millbank is not man enough for me."

Amazed at the prospect of a father's not speaking to his child, Eric asked, "How long has it been since you've spoken to your family?"

"Oh, I speak to my mother and sisters all the time. It's just that Daddy doesn't come to the phone or visit."

"Do you visit your mother?"

"Sure, they live only about six miles from my . . ." Maggie caught herself. ". . . . from what used to be my apartment. Mother tells Daddy that I'm coming, he asks her if I'm still seeing Carl, she says yes, and he goes fishing."

Eric laughed, shaking his head.

"Didn't you ever fight with your parents?" Maggie asked.

Eric's smile disappeared, and he tilted his head, reminiscing. An uncomfortable silence filled the car. Maggie bit her lip, suddenly remembering the story of Eric's parents' death.

"No," he answered finally.

"I'm sorry," she began, "I forgot."

"No, it's all right," Eric said, smiling sadly. "I was just thinking about how good it had been for fourteen years. I guess I was too young to have become rebellious."

Maggie turned and stared through the windshield at the road, the lights of oncoming headlights occasionally sweeping through the car.

"What were your parents like?" she asked with a softness in her voice that made Eric want to tell her everything he could remember about his mother and father.

"They were warm, loving, and civilized. My favorite memories are of the all too infrequent reunions between my father and Uncle Charles, who would always show up unexpectedly, always stay for just two or three days, and then disappear for months to parts unknown. I remember one December in particular, I think I was four or five years old. Anyway, it was just a day or two before Christmas. Charles rolled in at midnight, my mother made a five-course dinner, and we sat in front of the fireplace until dawn listening to my father and Charles tell stories. At seven o'clock in the morning, Uncle Charles, still going strong, had polished off one bottle of cognac and just started on another when Einstein came trudging through the snow looking for a ride to the Institute—"

"Hold it," Maggie blurted out. "Einstein came trudging through the snow looking for a ride to the Institute?"

"Yeah," Eric replied matter-of-factly. "He used to do that whenever he missed his ride with Oppenheimer."

"Albert Einstein?" Maggie was astounded.

"Einstein worked with my father at the Institute."

"Albert Einstein," Maggie whispered reverently. "What was he like?" she asked, leaning forward.

Eric frowned for a minute, trying to remember. "He was always nice to me. Most of the time he would just eat dinner and then wander off into the library with my father. Every once and a while we'd play checkers. He was good at checkers, but I could beat him at chutes and ladders."

Maggie shook her head.

"At any rate," Eric continued, "there we were, snow piling up outside, Uncle Charles, drunk, telling us a story about two Tahitian native girls he was supposed to marry, Einstein and my father are laughing like hell, and my mother is starting to prepare a breakfast.

"In the middle of the story, Uncle Charles suddenly remembers that his Chinese business partner, Quong Wing, is in New York buying a Matisse. He got up, put on his coat, and walked out of the house. We didn't see him until the next summer." Eric laughed at the memory, sighed, and added, "Other than those crazy reunions, life at the Ivorsen household was secure, friendly, and fairly normal. I miss the warmth," he admitted.

"Do you still have the house?" Maggie asked.

"I rent it to university faculty. I live in an apartment in town. It's big enough for my needs, and I travel so much—it's convenient to be able to just lock the door and leave."

They rode in silence for a minute and then Maggie said, "Einstein rarely dropped by our house."

Eric looked over and laughed.

Maggie smiled back, adding, "But I did see Pinky Lee once."

Barreling along Interstate 85 in the big pink Imperial, Eric reached over and took Maggie's hand. "Tell me about your family," he said.

"Let's see. Daddy is built like a human refrigerator—strong jaw, crewcut, and believes the world was better when men were men and women were sex objects. Blessed with the misfortune of fathering three girls, he nevertheless treated us like recruits. Push-ups at the drop of a hat. Laps whenever we did something wrong. It worked until we reached puberty. Then we would just cry and he would wander off muttering.

"My mother is the typical Marine wife. Loyal, loving, and feminine. I used to think she was far too good for him, but I grew up and realized that they were perfect for each other. She keeps him up to date on me and he pretends not to listen. But if she lets a week go by without mentioning me, he finds some excuse to complain about Carl and me and then she tells him how I'm doing and he quiets down. I love them both."

"What are your sisters like?"

"My older sister, Emily, is married, lives in Arizona with her husband and two kids. She's a lot like my mother. My younger sister, Susan, is in her last year at Miami University. She is crazy, no question. If my father had even the slightest idea of her life-style, she'd be doing push-ups and laps until the year 2000, puberty or no. She cleans up her act when she comes to visit.

"I'm the big disappointment. What it comes down to is that I'm my father's favorite. Always was and always will be. We were the closest. I would go to him with my problems. My sisters would go to my mother.

"It hurt him that I didn't follow his advice when I told him about my plans to live with Carl. While the moral issue is the argument he used to forbid the relationship, I think it was more his dislike for Carl than his concern for my spiritual well-being."

"He was right," Eric observed.

A little stunned by the blunt remark, Maggie did not respond. She thought about being angry for a moment and then realized that her father had been right and if she hadn't lived with Carl she wouldn't have broken up with him and if she hadn't broken up with him she wouldn't have gone to Europe and she wouldn't have met . . .

"So you think I should've listened to him?" she said, setting the trap. Cocking her head, she waited for Eric's reply.

"Obviously not," Eric smiled, and then added, "I'm a mathematician, McCabe—logic is my strong suit."

Maggie wrinkled her nose at him, slid across the seat next to him, and gently ran her fingernails back and forth across the inside of his right thigh. Eric gasped in pleasure, and Maggie whispered, "How long before we get to Princeton, big fella?"

"Uhhhh," he gritted through his teeth. "About six or seven hours."

"I can hardly wait," she responded, nibbling on his ear.

"Uh, Maggie dear," Eric protested, "don't tease the driver."

"Oh, come on," she breathed. "Let's find a motel. It's this car—it does something to me."

Eric, barely holding in a grin, turned and whispered, "We could always just pull off to the side of the road right here. . . ."

Seton Wynn, with Josef Gregor at his side, turned the rented van off the New Jersey Turnpike at Exit 8. They drove along the Princeton road looking for a place to eat, found nothing open, and continued on into the university town. Settling for the all-night market near the train station, they ordered sandwiches and coffee. Wynn then drove around the streets of the university for thirty minutes, familiarizing himself with possible escape routes. Satisfied, he parked the blue panel van in the municipal parking lot behind Palmer Square, opened the bag of food, and waited.

"We'll eat first, mate," Wynn stated, "and then visit our boy's flat. I hate to snatch a bloke on an empty stomach."

Watching guests in the Nassau Inn's outdoor café across the street, Gregor sank his pointed teeth into a bloody-rare roast-beef sandwich and tore away a mouthful. A small glob of mayonnaise squeezed out of the roll and dribbled onto his chin. He didn't notice.

Wynn ate quickly, tipped back his Styrofoam cup, and drained a last swallow of bitter black coffee. "Wait 'ere," he ordered and casually walked across the sidewalk, scanning the addresses of the street-level shops. When he reached the entrance to Eric Ivorsen's apartment he climbed the stairs and walked up and down the hall outside Eric's door. Returning to the panel van, he tapped on the dark window of the passenger side. The window lowered and Gregor stared back through half-closed eyes—dead, uncaring eyes.

"Going to ring 'im up, mate. Keep a look at those rooms there," Wynn said, pointing at the apartment. He crossed the grass in front of the Princeton post office, picked up a pay phone, dropped in a quarter, and dialed Eric Ivorsen's phone number. The phone rang once.

The green light on the alarm clock next to Lawrence Tilton flickered and the tiny receiver emitted an urgent beep. Tilton snapped up, spun around, and gripped the stock of the Ruger rifle. Peering through the telescopic sight, he panned quickly back and forth across the dark rooms. There was no change. The beep ceased, then a few seconds later beeped again. Then again. He realized from the pattern that it was simply the ringing phone. Rubbing his eyes, he looked up from the scope and down at Palmer Square. Because of its position, the blue van was out of view. Tilton saw nothing unusual.

When the flickering green light turned steady and the alarm beep ceased, Lawrence Tilton laid his bald head back on the pillow and closed his eyes again. Folding his gloved hands on his stomach, he looked like a reposing hairless corpse. The familiar pig dream drifted into his mind as he wavered between reality and sleep. Chasing him again, stopping to urinate like a dog, every few feet. Eating garbage and tracking mud into the house. Snorting. Humping other pigs and the dogs. Leaving stains. Bleeding on everything. Squealing and sweating as he chopped it apart with the ax. Gold coins falling from its belly.

Smiling, Lawrence Tilton fell asleep.

Returning to the van, Wynn stated the obvious. "No answer. See any lights?"

Gregor shook his head.

"You take the first watch, mate. Wake me if they show." Wynn opened the sliding side door of the van, closed it behind him, and stretched out on the floor.

Gregor sat back against the van's high vinyl seat and stared at the sidewalks, empty shops, and nearly deserted streets. Two couples eating ice-cream cones strolled through the square, window-shopping. As the last guests left the café, the parking lot emptied. Several cars passed through the square, but when a borough police car swept around the corner, flooding the van with light, Gregor slid below the blinding beam. The car stopped outside the entrance to the apartment. An officer got out of the passenger side and walked into the building.

After checking Eric's apartment for the third time that shift, he walked back out to the car, shook his head, and declared to his partner, "If this guy's as hot as the FBI says, he's not gonna show up here. No way."

The partner, pushing his hat back on his head, shrugged. "They tell us to check it—we check it. When they tell us to stop—we stop. Besides, you got something better to do?"

The car pulled away from the curb, and Gregor, undetected, rose snakelike as it turned out onto Nassau Street. A smile of satisfaction stretched his thin lips away from his pointed brown teeth.

He spent the rest of his watch thinking about his reward. Not the one he'd just had; that was over and forgotten. Rather he thought long and hard about the one to come. What he would do and how he would do it.

The small glob of mayonnaise began to yellow on his chin.

Sitting at a booth in the Greensboro Truck Stop Diner, Eric watched Maggie reach up and drop a coin into the pay phone. A bleached-blond waitress, cracking gum, wiggled over to the table, glanced down at the bloodied torn knees of Eric's slacks, and asked, "Ya'll crawl here?"

Eric looked up and smiled. "Yeah, and I hope your food is worth it."

"House specialty is chicken-fried steak with collard greens."

"Gee, I can't remember the last time I had a good chicken-fried steak," Eric claimed, trying to sound sincere. "But I was thinking more along the lines of a couple of omelets."

The waitress, smiling, nodded and scribbled across her order pad.

Eric continued, "Two coffees with the meal and two to go when we leave."

"Grits or home fries with those omelets?" she asked.

"Home fries," Eric replied with conviction.

The waitress turned and flipped the order slip through a window to the cook. Eric turned and listened to Maggie's end of the phone conversation.

"Hi, Mom," she said cheerily when she heard her mother's voice above a suddenly hushed conversation in the background. Instead of calling out Maggie's name, Mrs. McCabe lowered her voice and asked sweetly, "Why, hello, dear, where on earth are you?"

"Oh, I'm in North Carolina."

"That's nice," Mrs. McCabe replied in a carefully controlled voice. "Are you all right?"

"Yes. I'm fine. What's going on there?

"You don't sound as though you're kidnapped."

"I'm not."

Maggie heard her mother turn to whoever else was present and say, "It's Maggie. She's not kidnapped."

Returning to the phone, her mother said, "The FBI is here, and Carl and your father and Susan flew up when she read the newspaper."

"I'm sorry for all the trouble, Mother."

"The newspaper and Carl said you were kidnapped by someone named Ivorsen."

"No. We're kinda taking a little trip north together."

"Carl is very upset, dear. He's been here all day and cried through dinner."

"I'll bet Daddy loved that."

"Your father went fishing," Mrs. McCabe said. "But he's back now."

"I want to talk to him."

There was silence at the other end of the line.

"Mother?" Maggie said.

"Yes, dear, I'm here."

"Put Daddy on the phone."

A long silence followed, and Maggie heard Carl's excited voice in the background. Another voice, official-sounding, said something about keeping the recorder running in case it was a trick. There was a clicking sound on the line, and finally Maggie heard her father's voice.

"Hello," he said.

"Hi, Dad," Maggie said. "I need your advice."

No answer, but she knew he was listening.

"I can't explain what's going on—I'm not even sure I know. I haven't been kidnapped and I had nothing to do with the explosion at my apartment. I have to make a decision and I need your help."

Maggie quickly ran through the events of the past few weeks and then said, "I want to go with Eric."

Her father remained silent for a moment and then said, "Put this man on the phone."

Maggie turned to Eric and motioned him to the phone.

"My father would like a word with you," she said, smiling. Eric took the phone. "How do you do, Mr. McCabe."

"Ivorsen, eh?" McCabe asked in a no-nonsense tone.

"That's right."

"The feds here tell me you're some kind of brain boy."

"Maggie here tells me you're some kind of Marine."

Eric couldn't tell for sure, but he guessed correctly that McCabe was smiling at the other end of the line.

"You tough?" Mr. McCabe asked curtly.

"I can take care of myself," Eric shot back.

"I don't know what the hell is going on, but tell me something, man to man," McCabe said. "And don't bull-shit me. Can you take care of my little girl too?"

"No question," Eric stated.

"Let me talk to Maggie."

Maggie took the phone. "Hello?"

"I say go with him—anything's gotta be better than the sniffling pup," McCabe said, referring to Carl.

Maggie heard Carl in the background. "Is that my Maggie? Let me talk to her—let me talk to her . . ." And then her father said, "Judas Priest, Millbank, calm down, she's awright fer Chrissake . . ."

"Maggie?" Carl cried into the phone. "Are you all right, baby?"

"Yes, Carl."

"Maggie, listen . . . we've all been through a lot. What we have to do now is get back to normal and pretend that none of this ever happened. Listen carefully, baby. Come home right now—we'll go downtown tomorrow, buy that engagement ring, and start planning that wedding you want so badly," Carl said, and after a dramatic pause, added, "And Maggie . . . don't worry . . . I forgive you."

Maggie blinked, looked up at Eric, and dropped the phone onto the cradle. After devouring the spicy omelets, collecting their two containers of coffee to go, and paying the check, Maggie and Eric climbed into the big pink Imperial and continued their journey north.

CHAPTER 10

After eight hours of nonstop driving, a bleary-eyed Eric Ivorsen turned the Imperial onto Nassau Street, drove to the private lot behind his apartment, and parked. At 4:30 in the morning, Princeton was virtually deserted, and the crunch of the big car's bald tires on the gravel surface echoed off the stone buildings behind Palmer Square. The drive had taken its toll on Eric and on Maggie, who was slumped against the door, sound asleep.

Eric parked near the pedestrian tunnel leading to Palmer Square. He walked around the car, pausing for a few moments to appreciate the tranquillity of the silent courtyard. The cool night air was still, peaceful, and Eric felt a sense of uneasy sadness. At that precise moment, he realized for the first time that his life would never be the same. The boredom-breaking adventure had somehow become permanent. He couldn't just plunk down a handful of cash, buy a ticket home, and go back to work. Home was now dangerous, friends potential enemies, and the only person he could always count on dead and buried. Eric stared up at the heavens, and the mystery of the concentric circles seemed as indecipherable as ever. He looked down at Maggie sleeping and smiled. As he opened the door, she fell into his arms.

"Home sweet home," he said, gently kissing her cheek.

Maggie sat up, working her lips. She opened her eyes and looked around at the new surroundings. "Are we here? When did I fall asleep?"

"Around Baltimore," Eric grunted as he stood, stretching

some of the stiffness from his back. Maggie climbed out and fell against the car.

"I need bed," Maggie slurred, leaning her head on the roof. "And the use of a bathroom."

"Listen, I have to get some things from the apartment. You can use the bathroom while I grab the papers we'll need, but I don't think it's a good idea to stay here," he said as he searched for his keys under the glare of an overhead lamp. Passing through the stone pedestrian tunnel to get to the building entrance, Eric carefully checked to make sure that no official welcoming committees waited for them. The tunnel, the street, and the building were empty. He and Maggie hurried through the passage, along the street, and into the entrance without noticing the blue van parked in the shadows only fifty yards away.

Seton Wynn saw them come through the tunnel. Reaching down, he shook Josef Gregor's leg to wake him. Gregor rose slowly in the back of the van, his eyes narrowing on Maggie's chest.

When Eric and Maggie disappeared into the apartment entrance, Wynn and Gregor quietly exited the van and crossed the street to follow. They caught up at the top of the stairs.

"Easy, mate," Wynn said, a .357 Magnum in his hand.

Eric turned and looked down at the powerful gun. Gregor smiled as he jabbed the long silencer screwed to the barrel of his .45 in Eric's back, forcing him down the hall. Shrinking from Gregor's clawlike reach, Maggie backed down the hall behind Eric.

"Open the door," Wynn commanded.

Eric inserted his key in the deadbolt and turned. The door popped open. Gregor shoved Maggie past Eric into the darkness. She stumbled, falling to her knees. Eric followed and helped her stand.

"Move away," Wynn said as he closed the door to the apartment.

Gregor circled around toward Maggie. Eric, his lips pulled back in anger, started toward the ugly man.

"Easy, mate, or I'll put a nasty 'ole through the lady—we don't need 'er," Wynn warned. Eric stopped moving, his fists balled. He was debating the chances of a successful attack when Wynn, pointing to one of the windows that overlooked Palmer Square, demanded, "Lower that shade."

Gregor continued slowly across the room, backing Maggie into the corner near the small kitchen area, directly in front of the other window. Wynn stepped between Eric and Gregor, motioning Eric to the window with the barrel of the gun. Eric, watching Gregor carefully, pulled the shade down and the room grew darker.

Gregor sneered at Maggie, reaching for her chin.

At the sound of the alarm, Tilton was up and swinging the scope to the left window of the apartment. With no lights on inside, he could not see clearly, and when the shade lowered, he panned right. He squinted hard but saw no one. Then the silhouette of the couple moved into the light and Tilton watched the man raise his hand to take the woman's chin. The intimate gesture confirmed that he had his prey.

He centered the cross hairs on the back of the man's head. He knew the first shot would be a kill and was almost certain that the second would take out the woman. Lawrence Tilton squeezed the trigger three times.

Seton Wynn watched the rage on Ivorsen's face as Gregor reached for Maggie. And he was about to call Gregor off when he heard the chink of breaking glass and the muffled report of the Ruger. Wynn turned toward the window in time to see Josef Gregor's head blow apart. Seizing the split-second opportunity, Eric rammed his fist into Wynn's face, cracking the Australian's jaw. The .357 flew across the room. Wynn, unconscious when he hit the floor, landed on his back, and Eric came down hard, smashing nose cartilage and cheekbone.

The impact of the first shot snapped Gregor into Maggie, who crumpled under his weight. The second shot, deflected by the protruding bone of the dead man's shattered skull, slammed into the plaster wall just above the kitchen cabinet. The third shot passed harmlessly overhead, imbedding itself in the refrigerator door just above a glistening glob of brain matter stuck to the handle.

Diving to the floor, Eric scrambled to Maggie, who lay limp under Gregor's corpse. Carefully avoiding the assassin's line of sight, Eric reached out and dragged her across the floor. Away from the window, he took her in his arms and brushed her hair from her face. Except for a splatter of Gregor's blood, Maggie was unmarked. She moaned, opened her eyes, and winced. Reaching gently to her forehead, she groaned, "What happened?"

Eric looked over at what was left of Gregor and pulled Maggie away from the nauseating sight without letting her see. He climbed over Wynn, picked up the .45, and reached up to his bookshelves. Pulling away five books revealed a small wall safe. He spun the tumbler, opened the door quickly, and extracted an envelope, his passport, and several bank books.

Crawling, Eric led Maggie into the the safety of the bathroom. Then, sitting in the darkness, he washed away the streak of crimson from her chin and cheek.

Still dizzy from the blow, Maggie shook her head and asked again, "What happened?"

"The gentleman with the applecore teeth developed a rather sudden headache," Eric said in an urgent whisper. "I'm going to pack some clothes. You freshen up, but don't turn on the light until I've closed the door. You'll have to hurry. We don't have much time."

Closing Maggie in the bathroom, Eric moved catlike across his living room and pulled open Wynn's jacket, looking for identification. He found five thousand dollars, but no wallet. Gregor's pockets yielded another five thousand and nothing more. Eric dropped Gregor face down on the floor, except there was no face, only an empty cavity dripping mucus and blood.

Maggie rubbed her eyes and stared into the mirror over the washbasin. Her skin was pale, her hair stringy, and her eyes red. Splashing water on her face made her feel better, but she knew she couldn't go much further without sleep. She snapped off the light and opened the bathroom door.

Lying flat on his back in a spreading puddle of blood, Seton Wynn moaned. Eric, in a fresh pair of tan slacks, was carefully peering out the side of the window shade that he had been ordered to lower.

"Do you see anything?" Maggie breathed.

"Our benefactor, intentional or otherwise, seems to have moved on," Eric observed.

"Shouldn't we call the police?" she asked.

"We can't. I'll have the same problem here that I had in Florida. We can't afford to hang around trying to explain something I don't fully understand myself," Eric said as he placed his wallet in Josef Gregor's back pocket.

"What are you doing?" Maggie asked, frowning.

"Buying a little time, I hope."

Tilton snapped the latches on his rifle case shut, opened up his overnight bag, and folded in the pillowcase and bedsheet, making certain that no nose or anal hair fell onto the carpet. He scanned the room, assuring himself that he was leaving no traces.

His job was done, and he had precious little time to make good his escape. He stepped into the hallway only after he was sure it was empty. After hanging the "Do Not Disturb" card on the knob, Tilton turned and walked calmly to the emergency-exit staircase. Exiting the building through the north doors, he was seen by no one.

The first sirens became audible as he crossed Witherspoon Street to the municipal parking lot and made his way to the car he'd rented two days earlier in Camden, New Jersey, directly across the Delaware River from his home in Philadelphia's Society Hill.

Telling himself again that it was okay to have taken an assignment this close to home, he noticed a parking ticket clamped under a wiper blade on the car's windshield. Tilton froze, staring at the rectangular card. A slow rage began to build deep within him, and he balled his fist so hard that his entire body began to shake. With police cars approaching from all directions, Lawrence Tilton stood rigid, temporarily insane in the Princeton Public Library parking lot. Then the crisis passed and he got into the brand-new automobile.

The first police car skidded to a stop on the street outside the apartment entrance seconds after Eric and Maggie had dropped to the ground from the heavy iron fire escape that led from the back of the building to the private parking lot. Bathed in the pulsing sweep of flashing red and white lights, two Princeton Borough police officers, guns drawn, ran into the building and up the stairs, then stepped carefully into Eric Ivorsen's apartment. One knelt next to a moaning Seton Wynn, the other squatted beside Josef Gregor. Gripping Gregor's shoulder, the young cop pulled him over, blinked at the shattered half head, and promptly vomited.

"Jesus Christ," the older cop whispered. "The feds shouldn't have pulled out after all."

As the young cop gasped for breath, his partner tugged Eric's wallet from Gregor's pocket. Flipping it open, he read the driver's license, shook his head, and said, "And we can tell Tampa to stop looking for Eric Ivorsen."

Eric eased the door of the Imperial closed, turned the key, and winced when the Chrysler's big engine roared through the rusted-out muffler. He pulled the gearshift into forward and drove slowly through the parking lot without benefit of headlights. A police car swept around Chambers Street on its way to Palmer Square, but it was moving so fast that the officers inside did not see the big pink car gliding slowly through the shadows in the dark private parking lot. Bouncing over a cobblestone curb, Eric drove into the service alley leading to Nassau Street along the back of the buildings. Maggie, biting her lip, sat looking out the rear window.

Eric slowed to a stop when he reached the end of the alley and looked up and down Princeton's main street. Seeing no cars, he rolled out onto Nassau Street and turned on his lights. Almost immediately, flashing lights appeared in the rearview mirror and the scream of a quavering siren grew loud.

"Damn," Eric spat, watching the lights coming up fast.

He debated trying to make a run for it but quickly dismissed the option as impossible. The lights were right behind them, and Eric pulled to the side of the road, all too well aware that a check of the Chrysler's plates would result in a lengthy visit to the police station, and in the revelation that the corpse in his apartment was that of a stranger. But the lights suddenly turned and the night-piercing shrillness diminished.

"Whew," Maggie whistled in relief as the ambulance fishtailed into Palmer Square.

As the big pink Chrysler rattled away from the pandemonium, a new pair of headlights appeared in the rearview mirror.

Rolling past the Palmer Square plaza, the driver of the car glanced down the street. The scene outside Eric's apartment was an eerie landscape of haphazardly parked police cars, emergency vehicles, and milling policemen, illuminated by the stroboscopic blaze of red and white flashes casting grotesque shadows on the square's stately stone buildings.

The traffic light at the corner of Nassau and Mercer streets was red, and Eric braked. A brand-new Buick Century pulled up alongside, heading straight toward Interstate 95 and the fifty-minute drive to Philadelphia. The driver looked over at Maggie, and she glanced back, briefly holding his stare. The light turned green and he looked away. Eric turned left and Lawrence Tilton continued straight.

Once they were rolling along Mercer Street and it was obvious that they were not being followed, Maggie turned and asked, "What just happened back there?"

"I would say that a very fortunate case of mistaken identity just contributed significantly to our longevity."

"Where are we going now?"

"The Institute," Eric answered.

"What exactly is this Institute for Advanced Learning?" Maggie asked in a tired voice.

"Study," Eric corrected her. "Institute for Advanced Study. It's a facility for independent research. There's an emphasis on physics, math, and science."

"Is tuition high? I mean, who goes there?"

"The financing is private. Mostly grants, trusts, and fellowships. A committee selects individuals who show extraordinary potential and then they extend an invitation. The visiting fellows pay nothing."

Maggie was silent for a moment, trying to understand. "Are the classes hard?" she asked finally.

"No." Eric chuckled. "There are no classes—you simply

have an an opportunity to converse with people with similar interests."

"No classes?"

"No."

"Assignments?"

"Never."

"You mean they just sit around and think?"

"That's about it. But they have thoughts that change the world."

Maggie shook her head, astounded. As they drove onto the Institute's campus, along the sprawling lawns, and into parking lot B near the meticulously landscaped frog pond, she became even more amazed.

"Why are we here?" she asked as Eric got out of the car.

"I need the notes in my father's office."

"I thought you said your father is dead."

"He is. But they keep his office for my use," Eric said. "You can stay here. I just want to pick up the mag tape and notes."

Maggie was too tired to ask what a mag tape was. Listening to the croaking frogs, she watched Eric open a locked back door and disappear into the contemporary concrete building. Several seconds later, a light came on in one of the offices. Maggie saw shelves of books, a blackboard with an impossible formula stretching from one side to the other, and a video display terminal in front of Eric. The light went out and he returned to the car.

"Aren't there any security guards?" Maggie asked, amazed at his easy entry of the building.

"Nope. No need. The real value here is in the minds of the people walking around."

Maggie nodded politely. Eric drove back out onto Mercer Street and headed for U.S. 1 and the New Jersey Turnpike.

"Where to now?" Maggie yawned.

"New York. We'll get a room tonight, do a little vacation shopping tomorrow, and try to get the first available flight to Vienna. If we're lucky, I'll be presumed dead until we're out of the country. If not, they'll probably pick us up at the airport. Either way, tonight you get a nice hot shower, a king-size bed, and the world's greatest backrub."

"I still want to know what happened back in your apartment," Maggie insisted. "But you can explain it all tomorrow."

"Apparently there's more than one party interested in the Viking Cipher," Eric replied and then asked, "Did you recognize either of those two?"

"No." Maggie sighed. "Never seen them before." She slumped back against the seat and closed her eyes to rest.

Eric drove along in silence, trying unsuccessfully to analyze the events of the past month. With his brow knitted and his tired eyes narrowed in a squint of concentration, he stared out at the road. He knew that his father's work had been important in its day, but since then at least a dozen companies had developed computer models capable of similar projections.

"Logically," Eric mused, "this just doesn't make sense. Financially, it's insane—the expense of hiring people to kill my uncle, kidnap you, and eliminate me must be unbelievable." Eric shook his head slowly. "It just doesn't add up . . . unless, of course, the Viking Cipher is much more than a fifty-year forecast program."

Maggie fell against Eric's side, sound asleep.

CHAPTER 11

Snowfield Farm, in the rolling hills of New Jersey's Hunterdon County, was listed in the East Amwell Township tax records as being owned by Arpel Limited, an international real estate holding company with headquarters in Zurich. The three-hundred-acre farm and elegantly restored farmhouse had been purchased only one month after Gunter Toombs confirmed that young Eric Ivorsen would make his home in Princeton. The reason for the purchase was simple and singular. It provided an excellent base from which to keep constant watch on the young mathematician.

Although all the buildings had been modified to accommodate his handicap, Toombs was careful to spend very little time at the property. He had never been seen by townspeople, and local rumors about Arpel and its owners ranged from speculation that the company was a front for the Mafia to a more recent belief that the Saudis were landbanking American farmland.

Managed entirely by a local real estate broker, who had never met Toombs personally, the farmland was rented to local farmers and the house kept exclusively for the use of Arpel employees. Explaining that their employer was not a well man, the employees kept to themselves, allowed no one in the farmhouse, and revealed no information concerning the company. The nine Arpel employees had all been recruited in Europe; they were all well paid and all absolutely discreet. Only five knew the connection between Gunter Toombs and Arpel Limited. One was now dead, one was on his way to the Princeton hospital, two were sound asleep in their rooms at the farm, and the fifth, Katrine, was sleeping in a bed next to the paralyzed body of the chairman of the board in their suite at the Pierre.

After his morning sponge bath, Toombs was lifted into his wheelchair by one of the hotel bellboys. With no communication from Wynn, Toombs was unusually cranky and sat eating his scrambled eggs in a cold silence broken by an occasional order barked at Katrine.

"Get the limousine. We're going out to the farm," he growled. "And find out if anyone has heard from Wynn."

Katrine called the farm and was told by one of the two security men on duty that Wynn had not yet arrived.

The ride out to the farm was silent. Toombs, propped up in the back seat of the car, spent the time thinking about Eric Ivorsen, as he had every day of the past fifteen years.

The long silver Mercedes rolled onto the farm lane that led to the farmhouse. A cloud of dust swirled in the wake of the elegant car. Surrounded by huge maple trees, the restored house and barns looked serene, bucolic. The old horse barn, freshly painted red, was in picture-perfect condition. Although its doors looked as if they would slide away to reveal stalls and hay lofts, actually they were bolted shut and the only access to the building was through an underground passage from the computer room in the main house, fifty yards away. Instead of tractors and horses, the barn contained a braid of cable attached to a ten-meter dish antenna pointed at a communications satellite twenty-four thousand miles in space. Receiving daily transmissions from all over the world, the system made the farm one of the most sophisticated information centers in the Northeast.

Toombs was lowered into a battery-powered wheelchair kept at the farm for his infrequent use. He grabbed the polished steel lever with his left hand and jabbed forward. The motor hummed and he rolled up the ramp onto the farmhouse porch and into the center hall. Jabbing right, he rolled around the corner toward his private office.

He glided around behind his desk and waited for the two men who were responsible for operations at the facility.

As they walked into the room, Toombs looked up and hissed, "I don't like to be kept waiting."

"Sorry, Mr. Toombs, but we stopped by communications to pick up last night's download, when this came across our tap on the Princeton police wire," one answered, handing Toombs the transcript of an official request for information from Princeton police to the Tampa sheriff's office.

Toombs's left eye dropped to read the printout; his unseeing right eye continued staring forward at the two men. The transcript revealed that in response to Tampa's request for surveillance on Eric Ivorsen's residence, a homicide was discovered at 3:42 A.M. The fingerprints of the murder victim and the prints of another critically injured victim had been transmitted to the FBI National Crime Information System computers in Washington, D.C., for a positive identification on Eric Ivorsen. Now that a felony had taken place within its jurisdiction, the Princeton Borough Police Department was requesting all background material on Maggie McCabe.

Toombs looked up and whispered, "Did we get copies on those prints?"

"Yessir, in last night's recorder."

"Was it Ivorsen?" Toombs whispered, his eye wide—terrified.

The man slowly shook his head and replied, "Gregor and Wynn. Gregor's dead and Wynn is in the hospital. The FBI will be able to identify Wynn, but Gregor is not on file."

Toombs leaned forward, pushing the intercom buzzer on the desk next to the phone. "Katrine, get in here."

Speaking for the first time, the other man asked, "How do you want to handle Wynn?"

Toombs thought for a moment before answering. "We need independent counsel. This morning, if possible. Through the Canadian firm—they're reliable. I'll wire the retainer."

The man nodded and explained, "We have no idea where Ivorsen is. There was a flurry of communication back and forth yesterday when Tampa issued its warrant, but the FBI suddenly backed off early last night. Tampa called Princeton an hour later and yanked the kidnapping charge. My guess is that the girl contacted the authorities and told them that she hadn't been kidnapped. With the FBI out of the picture, the local police made only sporadic checks."

"What about the tap on Ivorsen's phone?" Toombs asked.

"His phone rang seven times last night at nine o'clock. There was no answer. It may have been Wynn or Gregor trying to determine whether or not Ivorsen was home. If only we had been allowed to wire the apartment . . ." he began.

Toombs stared up, and the deadly stare of his left eye silenced the comment. Toombs had considered placing a permanent bug in the apartment but ultimately dismissed the idea, fearing that its discovery would alert Ivorsen to the growing interest in his activities. As a result, the constant surveillance became more difficult and far more expensive. The cost did not bother Toombs, though. He already had more money than he could spend, and if he succeeded in forcing Ivorsen to locate the Viking Cipher papers, he would have billions more. In fact, the money meant nothing—it was a hunger far more powerful that Gunter Toombs was driven to satisfy.

Arrangements had been made quickly. The retainer had been wired from Zurich to Quebec City by ten o'clock. After departing an Air Canada flight at La Guardia and riding a limousine bus into New York City, the well-dressed independent counsel took an Amtrak express to Princeton and shortly after 1:00 presented his card to the officer assigned to watch Seton Wynn. The card, printed only hours before, looked genuine, and the officer had no reason to question its authenticity. It bore the name of a Princeton law firm, and the attorney who presented it looked like any of fifty other attorneys in town. He insisted that he be allowed to see his client alone.

Wynn had regained consciousness, but his jaw was wired, his nose broken and reset, and his cheekbone crushed. He looked up from the hospital bed without moving his head. The lawyer drew a chair up next to the bed and sat down.

"Who're you?" Wynn whispered.

"I've been retained by your employer to handle your case," the well-dressed man said, opening his briefcase on his lap.

He pulled out a file folder, extracted an envelope, and shook the contents over his hand. A small needle, its tip stained a bluish brown, fell into his palm.

Wynn, staring at the ceiling, said, "It's a 'elluva mess, mate. Don't know what 'appened. . . ."

The lawyer, ignoring the conversation, leaned over, pricked Wynn's neck, and calmly put away his folder.

"What the fuck?" were Seton Wynn's last words. His eyes bulged, his throat closed, and his heart stopped.

The lawyer stepped from the room, told the guard that he'd be right back, and left for Newark Airport in a car left parked outside the hospital by one of the Arpel security men.

Kashmar Kashan, one of several hundred international students at Princeton, was reading in his room at Holder Hall when the phone rang. The caller claimed to be a friend, but Kashmar had never met the man. His instructions were clear, as always: Find out as much as possible about the incident at Palmer Square, but above all, determine the identity of the man killed. Once determined, call a Florida phone number and ask for Red.

Kashmar's major was English, and everyone who knew Kashmar also knew that Kashmar planned to be an investigative journalist. What they did not know was that Kashmar's education was financed by the KGB and whenever Kashmar asked a question, the answer, if important enough, could well reach Moscow within hours.

After an hour of questioning Eric Ivorsen's neighbors, Kashmar Kashan strode past the George Washington monument at the end of Nassau Street, into the Princeton Borough police building, and directly to the desk sergeant, who recognized him as that pain-in-the-ass kid from the university who asked too many questions.

"Aw, shit," the sergeant muttered to a detective standing next to the desk.

"What?" the detective asked, looking up.

"This fuckin' kid," the sergeant whispered before Kashmar was within earshot.

"Excuse me," Kashmar said in his meticulously pronounced English. "I wish information concerning last night's shooting in Palmer Square."

"Sorry, Kashmar," the sergeant smiled.

"But freedom of the press gives me the right to inquire . . ." Kashmar broke right into his usual constitutional-rights speech.

"Yeah, yeah, I know all about your rights and the right of the public to be informed and so on and so on, but we don't have anything to give you, Kashmar."

"This is not in accordance with the Constitution of the United—"

"Easy, Kashmar," the sergeant said, holding up his hands in mock surrender. "I'll let you talk to Detective Platt here."

Platt looked down at the smiling sergeant and sneered, "Thanks a lot."

"Anytime, ol' buddy, anytime." The sergeant grinned back.

"Okay, whaddya wanna know?" Platt asked Kashmar in a tone of bored resignation.

"What is the identity of the man shot through the window?" Kashmar asked, with his notepad open and his pen poised to write.

"Positive ID not yet established," Platt responded flatly.

"Was it not the mathematician Eric Ivorsen?"

"Who told you that?" Platt asked, suddenly looking down his nose at the short, slight Kashmar.

"It is his apartment, is it not?"

"Yeah, well, we haven't made positive ID."

"Has the medical coroner made a report?"

Platt, suddenly uncomfortable at the thorough questioning, squinted at Kashmar. He cocked his head and asked, "Whadda you care?"

"I am a writer for the newspaper, and I am writing this story."

"Yeah, well, the coroner made his report and it's not available yet."

"You have seen his report?"

"Yeah, so?"

"Since you have not made positive identification, will you answer for me four questions?"

"Depends on the questions."

"What was the approximate age and weight of the victim?"

Platt shrugged and looked down at the desk sergeant, who shrugged back. Platt figured he couldn't get in trouble answering the question.

"About fifty years old and weighed one-eighty."

"What was the victim's height?"

Platt chuckled, wondering whether he should quote the "as-is" height or the estimated height before partial decapitation. He opted for the latter. "Approximately five ten."

"Color of hair?"

"Hair?" Platt said, wiping his nose, "He didn't have much hair left when they found him, but I think the report said the pubes were light. How's that?"

"What means this word 'pubes'?" Kashmar asked in a serious tone.

Platt looked up and out of the side of his mouth answered, "The hair around his balls, ya know? Pubic region?"

The desk sergeant started to laugh, and Platt broke up as well.

Kashmar flipped his notepad closed, looked across at the grinning policemen, and said, "This is very good. If I have other questions, I will come back." He turned and walked out the doors.

"Yeah, anytime, Kashmar," the sergeant replied.

Kashmar crossed Nassau Street and returned to his dorm. He placed a call to the number he had been given earlier and a dockside pay phone at the Pier House marina in Key West, Florida, began to ring. The man who had stabbed Maggie's life raft clambered onto the dock from the deck of the *Hatteras* and grabbed the phone. Delahunt came up from belowdeck.

"Yeah?"

"I wish to speak with Red," Kashmar said.

"Yeah, hold on," the man answered, nodding at his boss in the stern of the *Hatteras*. Delahunt slowly climbed up onto the dock and took the phone.

"You have information for me?" he said.

"A man was fatally injured at three forty-five in the morning at the apartment of Eric Ivorsen . . ." Kashmar began and then related all he had learned.

"Right," Delahunt answered. His face showed neither anger, disappointment, nor fear, although he felt all three. He replaced the phone on its cradle and climbed back aboard the luxury cruiser, heading directly belowdeck to the elaborate communications system built into the master stateroom. Sitting at the console, ready to set up a scrambled link with a receiving station ninety miles to the south, was the man who had convinced Maggie McCabe that he was an FBI agent.

"Contact Grand Cayman Trust and cancel the transfer to Tilton's account," Delahunt said. "And then get me a clean line to Nikolayev."

Ten minutes later, the radio cracked and a deep voice answered in Russian. Delahunt grabbed the microphone nervously and said, "This is Delahunt. There is some doubt as to the success of the assignment's completion."

"It is a good thing," the Russian replied. "Because there is also some doubt as to the success of the assignment's initial contribution."

Delahunt was stunned by this information. It took several moments for him to respond. "But we ran the sequence and it gave us a final screen."

"Ah, yes, Mr. Delahunt," Colonel Nikolayev said. "But so far we don't understand this final screen you are so proud of."

Delahunt stammered, "You said your people would be able to decipher the location with the final screen. This has been understood for years, and now you tell me that the final screen is useless?"

"I did not say useless, Mr. Delahunt. The final screen needs further decoding. Be assured that we are in the process of analysis at this very moment. Still, it is my superior's feeling that the mathematician's demise prior to satisfactory completion of the assignment would be premature."

A small bead of perspiration broke across Delahunt's brow. He could just see Pyatigorsk and Nikolayev sitting comfortably in Moscow waiting for him to screw up. If Ivorsen had been killed and the computer sequence useless, there would be no option to exercise and the ultimate responsibility for failure would be his to shoulder. He wiped the moisture away with a white handkerchief from his back pocket. His mind racing, he replied, "The man killed does not fit Ivorsen's description."

"Good. I suggest you keep an eye on Ivorsen until we have deciphered his code."

"I need your help," Delahunt croaked in a tight voice.

Now there was silence at the other end. Delahunt began to sweat more profusely, waiting for the Russian's reply.

"Why is that, Mr. Delahunt?" the Russian asked finally.

Delahunt cleared his throat before admitting, "We do not know where Ivorsen is."

"I remind you that we pay you to always know the whereabouts of Eric Ivorsen," Nikolayev said slowly, menacingly.

"And occasionally I need the assistance of your organization. This is such a time," Delahunt shot back.

"Very well," Nikolayev said. "We will broadcast his description to the appropriate operatives. I suggest that you and your friend plan to visit Vienna as soon as possible." The radio clicked, static crackled from the speaker, and the five-thousand-mile communication link was broken.

Delahunt wiped the water from his face, gripped the radio operator's shoulder, and dictated an ad to be placed immediately in the personal classifieds section of the *Philadelphia Inquirer*. "Larry, Papa is not well and needs to see us a.s.a.p. Love, Red."

CHAPTER 12

"Well here goes," Eric said to Maggie, putting a smile on his face. He walked ahead of her along the long corridor in the Swissair terminal directly up to the two security guards checking luggage for concealed weapons. Wearing a brand-new Kilgour navy-blue blazer, a white cotton shirt open at the collar, light slacks, and loafers, Eric looked distinguished and self-assured—more like a debonair epicurean on his way to an international wine tasting than a man running from assassins. Maggie, in her new Laura Ashley flower print and wide-brim straw summer hat, looked every bit as good. Having spent the day in New York shopping for clothes, luggage, and other necessities, they were well supplied for their escape.

Maggie had at first been reluctant to splurge on expensive items, but it did not take too much arm-twisting on Eric's part to convince her otherwise. After leaving Barney's men's store with Eric's new wardrobe, they took a cab to Lord and Taylor, where Maggie spent most of the afternoon on an unlimited buying spree. Eric paid cash for everything, including the limo ride to JFK International Airport and the two first-class tickets to Vienna.

"Hi, how's it goin'?" Eric asked as he ducked to get through the metal detector.

"Can't complain," one guard said, waving him through.

Eric wandered toward the departure waiting area. Turning, he watched Maggie place her new Lederer leather handbag on the X-ray scanner conveyor. The guard grabbed it and flipped it over so it could pass through the machine.

The latch popped, the bag opened, and Eric tensed. A few seconds later, it emerged on the conveyor, and the guard picked it up. Eric held his breath. Maggie looked totally unconcerned. When the guard handed the bag back to her without bothering to look inside, Eric breathed out. He continued on and selected a seat overlooking the waiting 747. Maggie wandered in and sat next to him.

"Well, that was no problem," Maggie observed coolly.

"So far, so good," Eric replied with a devilish grin.

A Swissair departure clerk picked up a microphone and announced, "At this time, we will begin preflight boarding of Flight 127 to Geneva and Vienna. Will all passengers requiring special services please come to the boarding gate at this time. All passengers with small children or who need assistance in boarding, please come to the gate."

The flight was way undersold, and no one came to the gate. The Swissair clerk waited for a few moments, then lifted the microphone and said, "Now that the preflight boarding rush is over, we will begin regular boarding for flight 127 to Geneva and Vienna." The small crowd of waiting passengers laughed. Except one.

He did not rise with the rest of the passengers. Instead he remained seated, watching Eric and Maggie preparing to board. When they passed into the jetway tunnel, he walked over to a phone booth and called Washington.

"This is Jenkinson. I'm at JFK on the Trinidad Project, but I just picked up a departure that might be of interest—Princeton Man just got on Swissair flight 127 for Geneva/Vienna," was all he said.

"Right, thanks, I'll inform the bureau," the man at the other end replied. Sitting at his desk overlooking a small flowered courtyard, he leaned forward and pushed the intercom button on his phone. "Bill, can you stop by? It's this Ivorsen thing again. We just picked him up leaving JFK."

Bill Scriven said yes and appeared in the office a few minutes later carrying a blank notepad. With the sleeves of his blue shirt rolled up to the elbows and his striped tie pulled open at the collar, he looked like an upwardly mobile young government worker who had just put in a tough day. He had.

Falling into one of two comfortable chairs in front of his boss's desk, he looked up and said, "I gotta tell ya, Pete, the last thing I needed today was a new puzzle."

Pete Burns chuckled and nodded knowingly. With twenty-five years of experience behind him, he knew the feeling all too well. He had earned his seniority at a variety of levels in the U.S. intelligence community, but he was happiest in his present position as operational division chief for the Central Intelligence Agency. He liked research work and was particularly good at data analysis. He laughed to himself whenever some "civilian" claimed that spycraft was glamorous.

"I just want to go over what we have to see if I'm missing something," Burns said.

"A week ago I'd never heard of Eric Ivorsen," Bill Scriven declared, opening his hand, "and now the name crosses my desk every day in the FBI briefs."

"Well, get used to it—he just stepped over into our territory. He's on his way to Geneva or Vienna."

"Any background?"

"Yeah, and it bothers me. Too many familiar names associated with this thing," Burns replied, opening a rather thin file folder that had been lying on the desk. "We used to keep a file on his father, Kyler Ivorsen. A professor. Did some early work on computer forecasting. Died with his wife in a climbing accident in the Italian Alps, in 1959. He was at the Institute in Princeton."

"Defense Analysis or Advanced Study?"

"Advanced Study," Burns answered.

"And the son?"

"Top-secret security clearance."

"He's at the Institute too?"

"And at Plasma Physics. He's been consulting on the Tokamak Project."

"Is that what all this interest is about?"

"I don't know. But I don't think so—his Tokamak work is fairly straightforward. Nuclear fusion physics. Certainly nothing to be killing people over."

"Maybe he convinced someone that he had a valuable commodity to peddle and once they paid, they found out differently. Now they're pissed."

"Maybe."

"You have a better idea?"

"I saw an FBI transcript of a recording made at Ivorsen's girlfriend's house. If her story is to be believed, she and Ivorsen don't know at all what's going on. And we've got a possible identification on the murder victim in his apartment. Seton Wynn was a positive. He was hit right after lunch . . . while under police custody."

"Somebody is covering tracks fast," Scriven commented dryly.

"Yeah, that's just it," Burns said. "That's what's bothing me."

"KGB?"

"Somewhere, but not Wynn and this Gregor character."

"Gregor?"

"Yeah—the possible identification for the d.o.a. in the apartment—Josef Gregor. Interpol shows Wynn working with Gregor on several occasions. Mostly Europe. There was a hit in Switzerland about six weeks ago that had their signature, and . . ." Burns paused to light his pipe. He drew three heavy puffs before the tamped tobacco glowed red. A swirl of blue smoke rose in the small room. "And the target was Charles Ivorsen—Eric's uncle."

"Uh-oh," Scriven replied with eyebrows raised.

"Right."

"So why are people popping the Ivorsens?"

"Why indeed?"

"How do you see KGB?" Scriven asked.

"The guy who hit Gregor cleaned his room."

"How clean?"

"Absolutely spotless. Took the sheets. Not one print in the room, and nothing had been wiped. What bothers me most is that he took out Gregor when Gregor was waiting to take out Ivorsen."

"Possibly a mistaken identity," Bill Scriven suggested.

"Possibly, but look who checked out the hit for confirmation," Burns said, tossing Kashmar Kashan's FBI dossier across the desk.

Scriven looked down, read quickly, and mumbled, "The plot thickens."

"So, just to summarize, we have one of our top

mathematicians either being hunted or protected by the KGB, two amateur hit men being taken out by the cleanest contractor I've seen in ten years, and absolutely no idea what's going on."

"I'll get on it tomorrow."

"Let's go back and take a closer look at the father and uncle."

"I'll see what I can dig up."

"Thanks, Bill," Burns said as the young man stood to leave. "And give Peggy my love."

As the stewardess refilled Eric's champagne glass, Maggie opened her handbag and buried her head, looking for her compact. She found instead two thick stacks of hundred-dollar bills. She snapped the bag shut, sat bolt upright, and slowly leaned over to Eric, who was listening to Beethoven's *Eroica* on his earphones. She tapped him on the shoulder and whispered wide-eyed, "There's money in my bag."

"Excuse me," he replied, pulling the earphone from his left ear.

With her lips tight, she whispered through her teeth slowly, "There is money in my bag—a lot of money—in this bag here—a lot of money!"

"Oh yeah, I know," Eric said matter-of-factly. "I put it there." He replaced the earphones, sat back, and closed his eyes.

Maggie pulled the plastic phones from his head with one quick jerk.

"Whaddya mean, you know?" she seethed, her green eyes blazing wide.

"Well, how else could we get it past airport security?" he answered.

"I don't believe you!" Maggie raged, trying to whisper.

"Listen," he explained. "I couldn't carry seven thousand dollars in my pockets, and if I'd told you that you were carrying it, you would've been nervous as hell and they would've picked you right out as a smuggler."

"Seven thousand dollars!" Maggie mouthed silently. She blinked and angrily whispered, "Where did you get seven thousand dollars?"

"Actually, it was ten thousand when we started. I found

it on those guys in my apartment. I figured they couldn't spend it, and we needed some new clothes."

"You stole this money from those two men?" Maggie was incredulous.

"I suppose you could look at it that way, or you could say I charged them five thousand each for getting blood on my oriental rugs. Uncle Charles and I bought that one rug in Karachi—and now it's probably ruined."

Maggie, speechless, stared up into Eric's eyes, and he took advantage of the lull in conversation to kiss her.

When he released her, she took a deep breath and sighed. "Will anything normal ever happen to me when I'm with you?"

"Oh, sure," Eric said sincerely. "Things will settle down once we're safe in Austria. We'll go to an old friend and colleague of my father's—Hans Schmidhuber. No one would know to look for us there."

"He'll go to Schmidhuber," Toombs slurred, staring at his wineglass. Tiny pinpoints of candlelight sparkled on the crystal glass of Pinot Noir as he clumsily sloshed the deep-red wine back and forth. Katrine sat silently eating her meal, as did the two men who ran the Snowfield Farm operation. The restored dining room of the stately colonial farmhouse was huge and dark, lit only by a twenty-candle chandelier over the massive oak dining table. For all its carved woodwork, carefully restored plaster moldings, and expensive draperies, the room was nevertheless devoid of warmth—almost forbidding, and as a result, used only when Toombs was in residence.

One of the two men glanced at Katrine as Toombs paused in his drunken display of self-pity. They had never seen this side of their employer before and probably never would again, but since he'd already consumed one bottle of wine and was well into the second, the abusive diatribe continued. He looked up at his three silent subservient companions and spat. "Baahhh." A trickle of burgundy dribbled down his chin. Katrine did not tend to it.

His head lolled to one side and he remained silent—reflective for a few minutes. Then he looked up and repeated, "He'll go to Schmidhuber and Schmidhuber will help him

. . . and my life will once again revolve around one of the three . . . the almighty three . . . Viking . . . baahhh . . ." The sentence trailed off into a desperate whisper that the other dinner guests could not understand. Toombs lifted the glass to his lips and drained it in an awkward gulp. He pushed the empty glass at Katrine, and she obediently refilled it.

"The Holy Trio . . ." he mumbled in an acrid tone that said more than his words. His unblinking cycloptic stare focused on nothing, and with his bitter pronouncements dripping with sarcasm, Toombs continued, "He thought he was so superior with all his theorem debates and Einstein accommodating him . . . when all the time, I could've applied it . . . used it . . .

"Ivorsen," Toombs snorted. "And the humble little Einstein. The Jews offered him the position . . . and he refused them—with the powers of heaven and earth at his disposal, he refused them!" His drunken smile disappeared, and he hissed, "And of course there was Schmidhuber—always going along with the grand scheme they all believed in like some divine mission . . . fools . . . Ivorsen . . . the damn fools . . ." He slurred off into spiteful unintelligible mumble. His head drooped, his eye closed, and Toombs fell asleep at the table.

Katrine finished her meal, pulled Toombs's chair from the table, and with the help of the two other men, put him to bed. She waited until he fell asleep, then wandered down and out of the house crying to herself. Her hatred for Gunter Toombs was surpassed only by her fear of losing what he provided. She walked out onto the porch and then across the moonlit lawn to the fence of a paddock that had been horseless since Arpel had purchased the property. As she remembered her parents' farm in Denmark and her innocent and happy childhood, tears rolled down her cheeks.

Her family home now too belonged to Arpel Limited, acquired only weeks after her parents died in an automobile accident that left her alone in the world. The men that came to the farm explained that Mr. Toombs also wanted to see Katrine provided for, and she was invited to stay at the Toombs chateau in Rambouillet until provisions could be made for her future. It was there that she stayed in a

state of confusion fueled daily by the medication provided by Arpel personnel—medication that made her forget until she woke up the next day. Days became weeks and then months. Nights disappeared in a blur of drugs and bright lights and naked people penetrating her. After six months, she had become hopelessly addicted to heroin and the unwitting star of a dozen pornographic home movies.

Then her medication was taken away. Three days later she was brought to meet Gunter Toombs for the first time. Sitting in his wheelchair, he calmly explained his needs for a personal secretary. With her guts twisting inside and cold sweat pouring from her tortured young face, she agreed to everything he demanded. Handing her a syringe full of salvation, he looked her up and down and sneered, "And get cleaned up. My women are always to look presentable."

She wiped the dampness from her cheeks, looked out once more across the rolling foothills of Hunterdon County, and returned to her room. Twisting a piece of elastic around her delicate arm, she located an untapped vein, pushed the needle through her flesh, and squeezed. A rush swept through her, and the room brightened. All at once she felt warmth, satisfaction, and a blissful serenity that sated the screaming monster inside her—for a while.

Colonel Yuri Nikolayev walked a half-step behind his superior, Yevgeni Pyatigorsk, in the cold morning sunlight bathing Moscow's Arbatskaya Square. The conversation, in Russian, was hushed not out of necessity but out of habit. Neither man smiled.

"The Ivorsen Program," Pyatigorsk said. "What is the status on the Ivorsen Program?"

"I spoke with Delahunt yesterday and advised him that we have not yet deciphered the data obtained three days ago."

"And how did he react to this?" Pyatigorsk asked.

"He was . . . upset."

"Good. It will keep him careful," Pyatigorsk replied sternly.

"He does not know Ivorsen's whereabouts. Accordingly, I have dispatched descriptions and photographs to our people in the most likely observation points. Ivorsen may be of use if we are not soon successful in deciphering these circles."

"Yes, of course." Pyatigorsk nodded. "But he is a liability the moment we do."

"I have so advised Delahunt."

"You know, comrade," Pyatigorsk mused, "this Ivorsen Program—it has been your responsibility since when? 1979?"

"1979," Nikolayev affirmed in a grunt.

"It is not your best work."

Nikolayev remained silent, looking grim.

"We should have known sooner that young Ivorsen would be the key to the location. But we waited until now. Why?"

"We had no way to confirm what the Jew, Nagorski, said was true. He spoke of Schmidhuber, not the son. It was most likely that he was lying about the entire matter."

"Apparently he was not."

"No. He was not," Nikolayev admitted.

"What worries me, comrade, is that the murder of the brother, Charles Ivorsen, is forcing us to act before we are completely prepared to do so. The men who committed this murder—they have been identified?"

"Two professionals. We know that they are now somewhere in America."

"Do they work for the CIA?"

"We will find out."

"Good. And maybe your computer experts will be more successful at finding out the meaning of the circles at the same time."

Nikolayev cleared his throat and promised, "It is only a matter of time. The circles are decipherable. It takes time."

"Perhaps Nagorski could have helped with these circles," Pyatigorsk commented dryly—a subtle suggestion of indirect guilt leveled at his sensitive subordinate.

"Perhaps," Nikolayev replied defensively.

In August 1979, Andrei Nagorski, a seventy-year-old physicist taken by the Russians at the end of World War II, was told by his doctor that he had six months to live. The terror of dying without seeing his son, imprisoned years earlier for the crime of practicing the Jewish faith, worked slowly on Nagorski, like the spreading cancer within his body. In October, he went to his superior at the nuclear laboratories in Smolensk, but the young Russian supervisor didn't like Jews and showed little compassion.

Nagorski had only one commodity with which to bargain: a twenty-five-year-old secret entrusted to him by Professor Kyler Ivorsen during the 1958 peace summit held in Vienna. With pain in his limbs and heart, Andrei Nagorski told what he knew to the KGB, in exchange for one last visit with his son.

Exhaustive research by KGB analysts quickly produced a program of passive surveillance that centered on Eric Ivorsen, Charles Ivorsen, and Hans Schmidhuber, an elderly colleague of both Nagorski's and Professor Kyler Ivorsen's.

However, nothing in the lives of these men seemed immediately connected with the story told by Nagorski. But the Russians would keep watching. For if what the ailing physicist had told them was true, they could not afford to do otherwise.

On a snowy night in November 1979, Andrei Nagorski was reunited with his son for thirty minutes. Then immediately upon returning home, he made his way to the cold damp basement of his modest home, climbed up onto an old crate, and stepped into the air with an electric cord tied from his neck to the floor joist in the ceiling above.

Andrei Nagorski went to his grave believing that he had betrayed more than his religion—he felt that he had betrayed the future of man. And he had.

CHAPTER 13

"*Danke schön*—thank you for flying Swissair," the stewardess said as Eric ducked to get through the aircraft door. Maggie followed right behind, clutching the strap of her handbag so tightly that her hand began to sweat. They walked to baggage claim with Maggie unable to get her mind off the money at the bottom of the bag. Her eyes darted around the terminal searching for suspicious policemen, security guards, or customs agents.

The luggage carousel sat motionless for what seemed to Maggie like hours. Finally it started to move, and eventually their two new pieces of luggage rose from the conveyor and dropped onto the revolving platform. Eric leaned over, picked them up, and walked ahead of Maggie toward the customs entry desk.

Leaning over to her before they were within view of the customs desk, he said, "Let me go through first. And don't look at me or let anyone know that we're together."

"But what if . . ."

"Not to worry," Eric said with a smile. "They almost never look in hand luggage, and even if they do, they probably won't look too carefully."

Eric walked ahead, greeted the severe-looking young agents in perfect German, and was passed through without incident. To Maggie, the two men with their leather boots, chest straps, and police caps looked like the SS officers she'd seen in a dozen B movies. Breathing fast, she wet her lips and tried to smile. Eric disappeared through frosted-glass doors and Maggie was alone in front of the two men.

"Guten Tag," one said without even a hint of warmth. *"Ihr Pass, bitte. Haben Sie etwas an zumelden?"*

"Uh . . . uh," Maggie stammered. "Huh? No spreakensee Deutch . . . I don't speak Austrian . . . uh, German." She started to push through toward the glass doors.

"Warten Sie!" the guard said. *"Ihr Pass, bitte."*

"Huh?" Maggie gasped. "Oh yes, of course, my passport. Here."

The young Austrian took his time reading the small blue book, occasionally glancing up at Maggie, who was beginning to tremble.

He whispered something to the other officer and then tapped his forefinger on the handbag. "Please. Open this."

"Nothing in here, just some things we bought in New York," Maggie said, trying to smile nonchalantly.

"Open this," he repeated.

Maggie swallowed and unzipped the bag. The officer slowly and methodically began unpacking the bag, and the line of exasperated passengers grew longer behind Maggie. As item after item was lifted from the bag and the customs agent got closer and closer to the stacks of money at the bottom, the terror of being arrested and left alone in a foreign country became more and more real. Maggie felt her stomach suddenly go cold.

Finally the pressure became too much and she blurted, "Look, let me tell you how this happened—"

"Danke schön," the officer said suddenly and handed back Maggie's passport.

She looked down at the various articles on the table. Everything except the two stacks of money had come out of the bag. She did not move.

"Bitte, Fräulein. Please to move along," the officer said, pushing her things to the end of the long table.

Maggie repacked the bag, but not before glancing deep inside to assure herself that they hadn't missed the contraband.

Eric was waiting on the other side of the glass doors. Maggie walked stiffly past him, and Eric followed. When they were well out of earshot and sight of the customs area, she whispered, "The money's gone!"

"No it isn't."

Maggie stopped dead in her tracks and turned to Eric. With her lips tight, she glared up at the smiling logician.

"Look," he said, "I knew you couldn't bring it through, so I removed it while you were in the washroom on the plane. It's all right here," he said, patting the pockets of his new blazer. "And you were perfect. You were sweating so much coming off the plane, a blind man could've seen you were smuggling. Those guards weren't going to bother me when they saw you coming. They thought they had a live one nailed. I thought it worked pretty well."

Eric's smile widened into a proud grin, and he tried unsuccessfully to hold in the laughter building inside. Maggie tried to look mad, but it didn't last long.

"Okay, Ivorsen," she said, raising her forefinger to his face. "I won't get mad—but I will get even. Keep it in mind."

"Fair enough." He smiled and they headed off for a Europacar counter.

After arranging the rental of a Mercedes 450 SL, Eric loaded the luggage in the trunk and they began the forty-five-minute journey up to the Vienna Woods and Hans Schmidhuber's home.

"Why again are we going to this man?" Maggie asked.

"He's the only person still alive who worked closely with my father—and his name was on the bottom of my father's letter as witness to the signing."

"Will he be able to explain all of this?"

"If not, I'm hoping he can at least explain the circles."

When they reached a little town on the outskirts of Vienna, Eric turned the car off the Heiligenstadterstrasse and parked in a small alley next to a wine garden.

"Hungry?" he asked.

"Sure," Maggie answered. "Where are we?"

"We are in Nussdorf," he declared. "And that river of brown behind you is the Danube."

Turning to the water, Maggie said, "I thought it was supposed to be blue."

"Not here," Eric replied. "But farther on, the Alte Danube is as blue as can be."

Walking behind a stone wall, they found themselves in a tree-shaded courtyard lined with long scrubbed-pine tables.

Choosing from a tray of cold meats, cheese, and fruit, they concocted a delectable midday feast and washed it down with a full bottle of Langenloiser wine.

Patting her stomach, Maggie sighed contentedly. "Have you noticed that our lives seem to be a succession of unbelievable gourmet meals, fantastic sex, and dodging bullets?"

"That has come to my attention, yes."

"Not altogether bad except for the dodging of the bullets."

Eric looked over and, smiling at Maggie's newfound sense of adventure, replied, "Careful . . . it can be addictive."

The rest of the trip up through the Vienna Woods to the village nearest Schmidhuber's home took only twenty minutes. When they neared the tiny hamlet of Durnstein, Eric stopped at a small vineyard house to ask specific directions to the home of Hans Schmidhuber. Fortunately, the proprietors knew Schmidhuber well, as he was one of their best customers.

Returning to the car, Eric said, "Apparently Herr Schmidhuber likes the grape."

"I can understand that if it's anything like that wine we just had in Nussdorf," Maggie answered.

"Actually," Eric replied, "Durnsteiner is better."

Maggie stared up at the mist-shrouded ruins of Durnstein Castle as Eric wheeled the Mercedes through a series of tight turns. The sleek sports car had no difficulty climbing the steep roads that wound up through the Wienerwald's vineyards and fields of heather. When they reached the dark forest, Eric hesitated at a crossroad for a moment and then turned right. Schmidhuber's home was only one kilometer further. Eric recognized the property from the description given to him by the vintner.

A two-hundred-year-old country house of timber and stone, it looked to Maggie like Hansel and Gretel's cottage. Towering pine trees shaded the entire grounds, and it was obvious that someone took great care in gardening—the flower beds and window boxes were aburst with blossom.

Eric and Maggie walked up the winding brick pathway to the home's heavy front door. Eric knocked, and after a short wait it was opened by an elderly little bald man with a full white beard and round rosy cheeks. His watery blue eyes twinkling, he blinked up at Eric and his mouth fell open.

"Mein Name ist Herr Ivorsen," Eric explained, assuming that Schmidhuber would recognize the name. Schmidhuber smiled broadly, nodded his head, and stepped out onto the small brick pathway.

"*Ya,* you are an Ivorsen. I was expecting *you,*" he said. "But I was not expecting such a likeness to your father. You are taller, *ya?*"

"Yes." Eric smiled. "Allow me to introduce Maggie McCabe."

"Kuss die Hand, gnädige Frau," Schmidhuber said, lifting Maggie's hand to his lips.

Maggie smiled, nodded, and as Schmidhuber turned to walk down the path, whispered to Eric, "I like that part."

"Please, excuse me, I am waiting for a magazine from America," Schmidhuber said as he ambled down to the mailbox at the end of the path. When he found it empty, he shook his head and walked back to Eric and Maggie, stopping briefly to remove a weed in the flower bed that ran along the brick.

"Did you say you were expecting me?" Eric asked with a frown of confusion on his face.

"*Ya.*" Schmidhuber nodded. "Your father said you would come one day this year, and here you are."

"My father told you I would visit you this year?"

"*Ya.* You have received your father's document?"

"A coded computer program."

"And you have deciphered this code?"

"Not completely."

"Of course not." Schmidhuber smiled. "Not without my half."

"I think I can break it without additional data, but I need a powerful system."

"Your father told me that it would take months to solve without my half."

This made no sense to Maggie and very little to Eric. "I'm afraid I don't understand what this is all about," Eric admitted.

Now Schmidhuber looked confused. "You have read the letter from Einstein?"

"No," Eric replied. "Just a sealed envelope from my father's estate."

Schmidhuber looked perplexed—worried. He said, "But you was supposed to receive letters. It was arranged to be so."

"The only letter I received was from my father's estate in Zurich. Shortly after, my uncle was murdered, and now someone is gunning for me. Your name was on my father's letter. I thought you might be able to help," Eric said, trying to explain.

"Your father's brother is dead?" Schmidhuber asked, his face dark.

Eric nodded.

"More death," Schmidhuber whispered. He stroked his white whiskers, stared at the ground, and said, "Then you do not know what you must do?"

Eric shook his head, more confused than ever.

"You do not know what is the Viking Cipher?"

"A computer forecast."

Schmidhuber's eyes widened in surprise. He moved to the door, looked sideways up at Eric, and said, "You have much to learn, young Ivorsen. But first, the time has come to speak of many things—of ships and fools and nuclear wars—and cabbage-headed kings—and why the world is so boiling hot—and how the bombs grew wings. . . ." Schmidhuber's eyes twinkled as he cast forth his version of the nonsensical Carrollian rhyme. He led Maggie and Eric inside.

In a gloomy gray windowless room in a four-story building in Moscow, a KGB programmer sat at a video display terminal. His face, illuminated from below by greenish light cast up by the computer graphic on the screen, looked ghostly, cadaverous. He slowly lifted his eyes up to Yuri Nikolayev standing in the dark shadows and nodded. He had solved the mystery of the concentric circles.

In the communications room at Snowfield Farm, a hung over Gunter Toombs snatched the telex printout from Katrine's hands. The Vienna office had acknowledged Toombs's transmission and was standing by for instructions.

"Tell the Mueller woman to watch for an unusually tall man. Make no contact. Report immediately if he turns up at the cottage," Toombs dictated, and the message was sent.

"Once he's spoken with Schmidhuber, he'll know," Toombs mused. He looked up at Katrine and snapped, "Reservations on the next available flight to Zurich."

Katrine picked up the phone as Toombs hissed to the man responsible for operations at Snowfield, "We have a key. Now it's just a question of how to use her to best advantage. I want a complete report on this Maggie McCabe."

Lawrence Tilton bought a copy of the *Philadelphia Inquirer* at a newsstand near New Market Square. He carried it along with a bag of food from the Happy Buddha restaurant back to his restored brick townhouse in Society Hill. He heated a bottle of saki and poured some into a small ceramic cup. After carefully spreading out the containers of food and the paper on a priceless Chippendale coffee table, he scanned the personal classified ads for the message confirming that his Grand Cayman Trust account had been credited.

When instead he read the cryptic note from Delahunt, he exploded in rage and smashed his fist on the two-hundred-year-old table, sending Chinese vegetables, noodles, and hot rice wine across the room. The terrifying display of insanity lasted only briefly, then he was suddenly calm—as if nothing whatsoever had happened.

Bill Scrivens leaned into Pete Burns's office and knocked on the open door. "Got a sec?"

"Sure," Burns replied. "Whaddya come up with?"

"The Russians are scurrying."

"How so?"

"Lotta questions about Wynn and Gregor. Apparently they think we might have been behind the Charles Ivorsen hit."

"What?"

"That's the word from Zurich." Scriven shrugged.

"Jesus, they don't learn." Burns sighed.

"Paranoia runs deep."

"What're we getting on Wynn and Gregor?"

"Zurich tells me that Wynn and Gregor work for Arpel Limited, an extremely low-profile firm with extensive real estate holdings. Information on current Arpel management is scarce indeed, but we do come up with one name—Gunter Toombs. Trying to confirm now."

Burns raised his eyebrows, flipped open the Ivorsen file, and said softly, "A puzzle in a riddle, a verse out of rhyme . . ."

"How so?" Scriven asked.

"Gunter Toombs worked for Professor Ivorsen, Albert Einstein, and several others from the Institute for Advanced Study. Lawyer—offices in New York and Zurich," Burns explained, and then smiled. "And so it all ties in except for one thing."

"What's that?"

Pete Burns glanced down at his desk and ran his index finger down a full typewritten page in the Ivorsen file, stopping about halfway down. He looked up at Bill Scriven and declared, "Gunter Toombs died fifteen years ago."

CHAPTER 14

"Please make yourselves comfortable," Schmidhuber said, opening the door to his home.

In his suspendered baggy corduroys and paint-smudged white shirt buttoned to the collar, Schmidhuber looked more like a working artist than a retired mathematician. Walking across the living room, he passed through a shaft of sunlight that flooded through the tiny-paned windows in the thick stone wall. His shadow passed over a bundle of gray fur that turned out to be his sleeping Persian cat, Bernadotte. Above the stone fireplace, a Kundo mantel clock slowly ticked a pleasing hypnotic tock.

The small living room was furnished modestly with a low table in front of a long couch, a well-used leather wing chair next to a wall of books, and an old desk covered with papers and manuscripts. Several paintings hung on the walls—two soft landscapes by Schmidhuber himself, an excellent copy of a Pissarro, and a Hogarth print. Schmidhuber's easel, covered by a piece of white fabric, stood between the living room and a small kitchen.

The soft strains of Mozart's Mass in C floated from the speakers of a stereo and combined with scent from the vase of fresh flowers on the table in front of the couch to fill the room with a feeling of comfort and warmth.

Maggie and Eric sat on the couch, and Schmidhuber sank into his wing chair. Bernadotte woke, stood up, and arched, kneading the rug. Looking up at Maggie, the kitten-faced Persian appeared drunk. Her left eye was partially closed and her right eye crossed. One lip, pulled up slightly, bared a tiny tooth and gave Bernadotte a constant silly smile. She mewed at Maggie and went back to sleep, covering her nose and eyes with her right paw. For Maggie, smiling like a little girl, it was love at first sight.

With a twinkle in his eyes, Schmidhuber sat back and asked Eric, "What do you think of the world?"

Eric, startled by the unexpected blunt question, hesitated before answering, "What aspect?"

"Begin with religion. Are you religious?"

Eric glanced over at Maggie. She raised her eyebrows, shrugging slightly. He looked back at Schmidhuber, who sat lightly pressing his fingers together almost as if in prayer.

"Not in a traditional sense," Eric replied. "I find most of the structured practices contradictory—some outright hypocritical."

Schmidhuber smiled. "Just like your father."

"Speaking of questions," Eric began, "I have a few I'd like to ask you."

"Do you believe in communism or capitalism?" Schmidhuber asked, ignoring Eric's attempt to cross-examine.

"I believe in both, since both obviously exist. Clearly, it would be sheer folly to say that I don't believe in a political system that encompasses two-thirds of the world's population."

"But which is better?"

"For me, capitalism. For a peasant starving in China, communism," Eric replied. "Why are you asking me these things?"

"Because it is important for me to know your views. If you had to choose between loyalty to your country and loyalty to civilization, what would be your choice?"

Eric hesitated, sensing a trap. "I would have to know more of the circumstances before I could answer such a question."

"Good," Schmidhuber said, smiling. "Good boy. But remember always, you are a human being first and an American second."

"What is this all about?" Eric asked with an edge to his voice.

Schmidhuber did not answer the question. Instead, he pulled himself up out of his deep chair and crossed the room. Extracting three wineglasses from the sideboard near the small kitchen end of the room, he went about methodically filling them from a chilled bottle of Durnsteiner.

Handing his guests each a glass, he returned to his chair and fell comfortably back. He made no toast but simply drank. Staring at Eric, his eyes carried a sadness, like the eyes of a parent wistfully acknowledging the innocence of a child—an innocence about to be destroyed by harsh reality.

"You remember your father?" Schmidhuber said finally.

"Of course," Eric replied.

"He was a good man," Schmidhuber said and then fell silent, reflective. His eyes started to glisten as he stared at the wine in his hand.

Eric said nothing, suddenly sensing something deeply wrong. It was not tears but the tone in Schmidhuber's voice that triggered the feeling.

"And your father's brother is now dead too?"

Eric nodded, and Maggie put her hands gently around his arm.

"As your father was good, so too there was evil. Like Vienna—a city that nurtured Brahms, Beethoven, and Mozart, so too did it nurture Adolf Hitler. And as my friends Ivorsen and Einstein gave man the ability to split atoms, so too did they give governments the ability to destroy the world."

Schmidhuber stared into his glass of crystal-clear wine. "I told them in 1940 not to cooperate, but the pressure was too great. The blitzkrieg—the Holocaust—it was simply too much. And so they helped build the bomb, and on August 6, 1945, one hundred thousand souls perished in ten seconds. The day of Hiroshima, I watched your father cry—because without him, the bomb never would have been built."

Eric never knew that his father had been involved in the Manhattan Project. Frowning, he stared at the floor. Maggie bit her lip as Schmidhuber continued.

"So your father decided to create a project to counter the destructiveness of nuclear power. And he turned to his colleagues. They came from all over the world to secret meetings. Those who could not come to the United States . . . we went to visit them. And so began the Viking Cipher."

"Computer forecasting is rather common today—"

"Computer forecast was only the research phase," Schmidhuber snapped impatiently. "It's what is to follow that is so dangerous."

Eric reacted with a skeptical frown. Schmidhuber saw it immediately and leaned forward to press his point. "The forecast is accurate to the year 2000. The data used can be updated, making the forecast accurate far beyond. Phases two and three comprise the work of the best minds in the world. The same minds that developed nuclear fission developed theories that are far more powerful. Theories that if applied to military purposes would quickly shift the balance of power."

Eric stared into Schmidhuber's eyes.

"Phase three is incomplete. But it is a blueprint—a program designed to institute change. Do you understand the power of such a program?"

"It doesn't seem possible," Eric declared, shaking his head. "They would have published—"

"Never!" Schmidhuber cried, pounding his fist in his hand. "*Nein!* Not after Hiroshima and Nagasaki! Never!"

Schmidhuber sat up on the edge of the chair, his right hand fisted. He whispered, "Don't you understand? Those first two nuclear bombs were toys compared to what exists today. Your father and Einstein knew that it was only a matter of time before they used them. Your father could never publish the entire Viking Cipher. You see what happened when he published a prototype three-year forecast. It cost him his life."

Schmidhuber rose, crossed the room, and sat next to Eric. He spoke with desperation in his watery blue eyes. "We hoped that the computer projection model would show us when the Viking Cipher could be delivered, but . . ." Schmidhuber paused, then gently laid his hand on Eric's shoulder and said, "But we soon learned that it could not be revealed. The world was far too volatile and would remain so. This we saw in the fifty-year projection.

"Things looked to grow worse instead of better. The projection said that in 1985 there would be four nuclear superpowers on Earth: the USSR, America, China, and Israel. When Israel asked Einstein to be prime minister, he could not accept. His responsibility was to all of man—not just one nation. He was a human being first and a Jew second."

Eric shook his head, but remained silent.

"Einstein died, I had no children, and so it was decided that you would have to carry on . . . but you were only ten years old. So in Vienna your father gathered trusted colleagues from all over the world. A select few were told of the project, and it was agreed that a plan be devised to survive all of us. Had I died as well, you would have received a letter from my estate to assist you. You would now have three letters—one from Einstein explaining his cooperation in the Viking Cipher, one from your father explaining the location of the Viking papers, and one from me explaining the choices you will have to make and when you will have to make them. I signed as witness on Einstein's letter and on your father's. Your father signed on mine."

"I have received only the letter from my father, and as you know, that is in code."

"Ya, all are in code that only a mathematician can decipher. But this Einstein letter troubles me. It was arranged very carefully, and I cannot understand why you have not received it."

"For whatever reason, I have received no letter from Albert Einstein. However, someone wants the solution to my father's letter and is more than willing to kill to get it. At least I know now why people are spending so much money. Do you know what the formulas in my father's letter translate to?"

Schmidhuber smiled and nodded. "Circles inside circles—four absolute sequences and one nonconverging."

"What are they?"

Schmidhuber looked a little disappointed. "Your father said you would recognize them. Don't you?"

"Not so far," Eric replied.

"I wouldn't either. Each aspect of the Viking Project was autonomous. But without all three, the project fails. You need my factor to solve the nonconverging-sequence formula and you need understanding of your father's circles to determine the place to apply it."

"What exactly is the nonconverging-sequence factor?" Eric asked.

Schmidhuber stood and walked to a cluttered desk. Returning with a pad and pencil, he began writing a series of numbers and equations that looked like hieroglyphics to Maggie. Eric nodded with each addition to the page. When the old man was finished, he straightened and took the pad away. He watched Eric for a moment and then said, "Whenever you have to make a choice, this formula will lead you in the right direction."

"That's it?" Eric asked, looking up as Schmidhuber returned to his cluttered desk with the pad.

"Not quite. You will have one decision to make that will come from your heart, not from a computer or a slide rule or a book. When you are ready to accept the possibility of making that decision, you may have this formula."

Emotionally, Eric felt confused by it all, but he knew what Schmidhuber meant. He didn't like being thrust into a situation over which he had no control. He didn't like thinking of his father's being potentially responsible for the end of mankind. But most of all, he didn't like shouldering the responsibility that went along with Schmidhuber's charge.

Eric sat silent, deep in thought. Schmidhuber watched him closely. After a few minutes of uncomfortable silence, Eric stood and walked to the door. Stopping, he turned to Maggie and said, "Um, I need a walk—some time to think. I'll be back in a little while."

Maggie, sensing his discomfort, nodded understandingly. Bernadotte jumped up on her lap and began to purr.

"Around behind the garden there is a path that leads to a stream. It is a good place to think," offered Schmidhuber.

Eric walked out the door with his hands thrust deep in his pockets and an expression of soul-searching concentration etched across his brow.

The woods thickened as Eric walked down the footpath, deep into the dark forest of evergreens. Passing half-buried boulders and trickling streams, Eric, preoccupied, did not notice the darkening skies above. When he reached the rushing stream he sat down and tried to organize his thoughts logically. The reality of the situation became more and more clear. Until now, Eric Ivorsen had viewed the potential of a nuclear Armageddon as something terrible, but not worth worrying about, as he had no control over its inception or outcome.

If what Schmidhuber said was true, however, the possibility existed that the scientific community could structure change, bettering world conditions to the point where nuclear threat was no longer effective. Without government sanction, the process would be delicate at best.

The collection of scientific data stored in phase two was a danger. Not in and of itself—but into whose hands would it fall? To what military use would the new power be put? Could he in good conscience hand over a power of this magnitude to any government? Even his own government made mistakes. And if the Russians had been in possession of such a power, would they have stopped in Afghanistan? Had his father asked the same questions of the Manhattan Project? And what would the result have been if he hadn't cooperated? Certainly one hundred thousand Japanese would have lived longer—but how many more would have died in a prolonged conflict?

There was, of course, one final option. Eric considered it for a moment and then, as a light drizzle began to fall, he stood and wandered back to the cottage. He carried with him more questions than answers. Knocking lightly and pushing the door open, he found Maggie on the floor playing with the long-haired odd-looking cat. Schmidhuber was busy pouring himself more wine.

Looking up, Schmidhuber said, "It is a pleasant walk, is it not?"

Eric nodded and then, looking deep into Hans Schmidhuber's wise old eyes, said, "I need time to think. Can we return tomorrow to speak more?"

Schmidhuber smiled, reached up, and patted the side of Eric's face. "*Ya*, of course. And perhaps pray to God for guidance, *ya*?"

Maggie reluctantly set Bernadotte on the couch and walked with Eric to the Mercedes. They drove in silence to the crossroads at the edge of the trees, but when he stopped at the road to Vienna, Eric turned to Maggie and said, "Do you realize what he's saying?"

"I haven't got the faintest idea what he's saying," Maggie replied honestly.

"If my father's Viking Cipher contains what Schmidhuber claims, it is probably the single most powerful collection of scientific data ever assembled. Certainly the minds that contributed to it were of the highest caliber."

"But its thirty years old," Maggie said.

"Therefore the forecast will be the acid test. If it proves to have been as accurate as advertised, then the program works and new data will extend it. Phase two and three are the mysteries. God only knows what they hold in store. Einstein's involvement alone means the possibility that his unfinished work may have gone further than is generally believed. He may even have unlocked the mystery of the unified field theory. Although as a scientist I find it hard to believe that he didn't publish his findings, on the other hand, as a pragmatist, I have to acknowledge the obvious reasons for not doing so."

"I think I understand that part," Maggie said, "but I don't understand exactly what's expected of you."

"They've pinned their hopes on my being able to apply the knowledge in a safe and useful way or else . . ." Eric stopped.

"Or else what?" prompted Maggie.

Eric looked over into her big green eyes and smiled at her innocence. Flipping on the car's windshield wipers, he pulled out onto the rainy road.

"Or else destroy it," he said softly.

As Colonel Yuri Nikolayev crossed Vienna's Rathaus Park, dark clouds rolled across the sun, turning the day gloomy. Upon entering the *rezidentura*, the KGB equivalent of a regional headquarters, he was advised that Ivorsen and McCabe had passed through customs at 9:53, rented a car, and proceeded to the home of Hans Schmidhuber. Ten minutes later the thick-necked Russian joined Lawrence Tilton and Delahunt at a table in the Café Sperl on the Gumpendorfstrasse. Delahunt spoke. Tilton did not. Nevertheless, the conversation was in English for Tilton's benefit.

"We have deciphered the circles," Nikolayev said without emotion.

Delahunt remained stone-faced but inwardly sighed with relief.

"Ivorsen is now a liability, as are the girl and Schmidhuber," Nikolayev pointed out. "This is to be taken care of immediately."

"Mr. Tilton has agreed to carry out this assignment without compensation in order to reestablish confidence in him by the Politburo," Delahunt offered.

Nikolayev nodded at the silent Tilton. "Very wise. You should find the job easy—they are all here in Vienna."

CHAPTER 15

Shifting down, Eric slowed the 450 SL to a safer speed on the winding wet road that led down out of the Wienerwald. A Volkswagen Westphalia sped by in the other direction, but with the rain slashing against the windshields of both vehicles, Eric and Maggie did not see the other driver. And he did not see them.

One hour later, at just about the same time Eric and Maggie carried their luggage into a small hotel in the Innere Stadt, Vienna's inner city, the Westphalia had reached the home of Hans Schmidhuber. Parking three hundred meters beyond the property, the driver walked back through the woods and approached the cottage without being noticed. The black rainy skies, heavy trees, and late hour combined to make the grounds forbiddingly dark.

Through the living-room window, Lawrence Tilton could see Schmidhuber working by the light of a lamp at his easel. Between strokes, he used his delicate paintbrush as a baton, vicariously conducting the Poulenc Concerto for Organ, Percussion, and Strings playing on his stereo.

Circling the building, Tilton was annoyed to find no evidence of Eric Ivorsen or Maggie McCabe. Returning to the front door, he reached inside his coat and extracted a Ruger .22 automatic with a three-inch silencer screwed to the barrel. He tapped the thick wood with the black butt of the gun and watched through the window as Schmudhuber set down his brush and palette. Tilton could hear the first crescendo of the Poulenc concerto build, but having no use for music, did not recognize the masterpiece.

Schmidhuber ambled toward the door, then, realizing that he had heard no car approach, hesitated and pulled aside the curtain of the window. He sensed danger immediately when he saw the ominous form standing in the drizzling rain. He quickly grabbed up Bernadotte, carried her to the back of the cottage, and pushed her through an open window. Straining, he climbed up onto the sill and squeezed through, falling to the soft muddy ground. As he started to pick himself up, he saw the shoes of Lawrence Tilton. He looked slowly up into the small black orifice at the end of the silencer and then into the killer's face. Hans Schmidhuber knew that his life had come to an end. He did not feel fear—only hatred for what the man represented.

"Where is Ivorsen?" Tilton asked.

Schmidhuber, with his wire-rimmed glasses askew and with mud dripping from his face, shook his head slowly.

Tilton trained the gun on Bernadotte, who sat fascinated, staring at the deadly instrument. She mewed and tilted her head.

"Where is Ivorsen?" Tilton repeated.

Except for the soft patter of falling rain, the only sound was the stirring strains of the concerto. Schmidhuber remained silent.

Tilton viewed the brilliant mathematician kneeling before him in the mud as simply a piece of meat, something to be processed into a corpse for compensation—or in this case, redemption. He started to squeeze the trigger.

Schmidhuber looked up at the hairless murderer and saw an agent of evil, the very thing he feared would fall privy to the Viking Cipher, the black soul of Satan personified. With every ounce of his being, the eighty-year-old scientist leaped from the ground, grabbing a surprised Tilton by the throat. Locking his fingers on the back of the killer's neck, Schmidhuber squeezed his brittle thumbs deeply into Tilton's soft flesh.

Tilton, with his lips ripped back in a fierce disgusted snarl, began jerking the trigger of the gun jammed against Schmidhuber's belly.

The thundering crescendo of the concerto was punctuated by the muffled *pfut* sounds of discharging cartridges. As the bullets tore into the old man's abdomen, the pressure in his hands ebbed. Falling dead, Schmidhuber slumped to the ground. In a wide-eyed insane rage, Tilton realized that telltale skin and hair follicles had been gouged from his neck. He threw back his head and screamed. Rivulets of bloody rain trickled from his throat.

Bernadotte trembled against the building. Sneering viciously, Tilton raised the weapon, staring down his arm until the gun's sight was in the middle of the cat's terrified face. Grinning with insane hatred, he squeezed the trigger. The firing pin clicked against an empty chamber.

At the sound of the click, Bernadotte bounded off into the thick woods. She did not emerge until the man was gone. Then, mewing softly, she approached Schmidhuber and, as she had every night since she was a kitten, curled up against the stiff white hair of his beard to sleep.

In his office on the Bahnhofstrasse in Zurich, Gunter Toombs opened a twenty-five-year-old file and extracted two letters—one written by Albert Einstein and one by Hans Schmidhuber. The addressee on both envelopes was Eric Ivorsen. A note attached instructed that Einstein's letter be sent on Eric's birthday in 1975, and Schmidhuber's letter sent in the event of the author's death. Toombs reread each letter as he had a hundred times before. Einstein's letter explained in detail that his work was to be revealed only under certain conditions. The letter by itself was of no use to Toombs, because it contained no detail of his contribution to the Viking Cipher. Its only value was to acknowledge the existence of a new theory and provide instructions for its use.

Schmidhuber's letter was no more than a series of complex equations that made repeated reference to Professor Ivorsen's letter—a letter Toombs had never seen.

Toombs, glaring at the file, recalled his desperate attempt to get the stubborn scientist to allow him to handle all the letters. But no matter how much he argued, Kyler Ivorsen had continued to insist that at no time prior to the revelation date, a date that he alone had decided on, would all three components of the Viking Cipher be united—and then, on that secret date, only under the plan that he had devised.

Toombs's festering hatred for Kyler Ivorsen rekindled whenever he thought of those arguments and was salved by one thought—the one concession that he'd been able to elicit from Ivorsen. Late one night in the New York law offices after a stormy session with Ivorsen, Einstein, and Schmidhuber present, Ivorsen had finally agreed, Toombs recalled with satisfaction, to have the law firm notified when his letter was finally sent to Eric. Gunter Toombs grinned, looking down at the confirmation notice that the Swiss banker had sent just weeks earlier.

And so twenty-five years of waiting ended. Action had to be taken quickly because of the damn Russians. Toombs had no idea how the Russians had become interested in the Ivorsens, but the Arpel Vienna office had been reporting KGB investigation of the central players ever since 1979. Fortunately, they seemed content just to ask questions.

But then upon Eric's notification and active involvement, there was one man who posed a threat to the plan, and that was Charles Ivorsen. Informed years earlier of the general nature of a project involving the world's most brilliant scientists, Charles Ivorsen was the only person besides Toombs with knowledge of its importance. And with his gambling and playboy life-style, Toombs concluded, he would be easy prey for an organization that thrived on human weakness, the KGB.

Toombs looked down at the neat notes that he had written twenty-five years earlier when he could still use his right hand—when he still had a right side—when women used to look *at* him, not away. A curl of bitter anger pulled his mouth down to the left as he thought to himself how the convoluted web of conspiracy had forced his hand. The double-edged sword cut just as deeply on the backswing—killing Charles Ivorsen to ensure silence had alerted the same Russians Toombs had hoped to keep in the dark.

He shook his head, trying to figure out how they had found out. Schmidhuber? Unlikely, he decided. Schmidhuber was an idealistic old fool who had to be kept alive. He was the only person other than Eric Ivorsen who could possibly piece together the three components of the Viking Cipher. If it became necessary to eliminate Eric, Toombs believed, he could always force the old man to explain the professor's code.

He folded the stiff papers back into the file and closed his eye, thinking. Eric would go now to Schmidhuber and then would know what prize he was after. The imperative now was to be there when the treasure was recovered. Complex but still manageable, Toombs decided. The girl, he was sure, was now the only way to keeping constant watch on Eric. He leaned forward and pressed for Katrine.

"Get the Vienna office," he growled.

The streets of Innere Stadt were rainwashed and glistening gray. The wavy images of reflected neon light from the fashionable shops along the Kärtnerstrasse shattered as Eric and Maggie splashed the thin puddles, hurrying through the drizzle from their hotel to the Wiener Rathauskeller restaurant.

Descending into the vaulted cellar fifteen minutes later, Eric pulled off his new raincoat and helped Maggie with hers. The contrast between the gloom outside and the colorful murals and ribbons of the restaurant was stunning.

"This is going to be an expensive meal, isn't it?" Maggie asked, looking around the medieval chamber.

"Not to worry," Eric replied.

"Oh, I'm not worried," she answered. "I'm just wondering why we just walked in the rain across the middle of Vienna when we could've taken a cab. Money being no object and all."

"Romance," Eric said and smiled, not wanting to reveal the real reason for the short wet hike.

Sitting in one of the comfortable booths, Eric relaxed, and after ordering a bottle of Sieveringer, held Maggie's hand beneath the table. He smiled into her eyes and whispered, "You are incredibly beautiful."

Maggie smiled back. "You're not so bad yourself."

Eric glanced to the entrance of the restaurant and watched a man enter, his hat dripping wet. When he saw Eric watching, he looked quickly away. Summoning a waitress, the grim-faced man eventually secured a table that gave him an uninterrupted view of Eric and Maggie as well as the door by which they would leave. For the next hour, he sipped coffee and ate nothing.

"Before we see Herr Schmidhuber tomorrow," Eric said, "I'll have to make arrangements to use a computer."

"Where?"

"I'm not sure yet. At any rate, I may have to leave you for a little while."

"No problem. I want to see Vienna. I'll do a little sight seeing."

The waitress brought Maggie a plate of *Wienerbackhendl* with *Gerostete,* and Eric, *Tafelspitz.* She served both with horseradish and chive sauce.

"This is fantastic," Maggie exclaimed, devouring her meal.

"The Austrians do know how to eat," Eric sighed.

Maggie tried unsuccessfully to stifle a yawn. Jet lag had begun to take its toll, coupled with the effect of strong slivovitz, Yugoslavian plum brandy. Maggie was more than ready for bed. Even though exhausted and full, Eric insisted that they walk rather than ride back to their anonymous little hotel behind the Stephansdom. He chose a route that was less than direct, twisting and turning down small side streets and alleyways. At the dead end of a small winding alley, they turned abruptly and Maggie was sure that they were headed in directly the wrong direction. Turning a corner, they came face-to-face with the grim-looking man from the restaurant.

As they passed, he looked away toward the ground. When they were once again on the Wallnerstrasse, Eric said, "You go on down to the end of this street and turn left on Kohlmarkt. Do a little window-shopping—I'll catch up."

Maggie blinked. "But where are you going?"

Mumbling about dropping something in the alley, Eric turned and sprinted back down the street, disappearing into the alley. Maggie shrugged and wandered toward Kohlmarkt.

Eric's prey was just emerging from the dead end when Eric smashed into him. Crashing to the pavement, the man rolled over in a stream of water rushing from a downspout and hit his head on a cobblestone curb. Dazed, he tried to reach for his pocket, but Eric was too fast. Standing on the man's wrist, Eric leaned down and extracted a KGB-issue revolver.

Dragging the man to the downspout, Eric asked, "Who are you?"

The man said nothing. Eric lifted his head under the rushing water and for a moment gushing rainwater poured onto his face, then bubbled back out through his mouth and nose as he coughed and gagged. *"Nyet! Nyet!"*

Eric's eyes widened, and he muttered, "Well, at least we know who you work for." He dropped the man on the pavement with a sickening thud. Eric tossed the gun into a storm sewer and ran to catch up with Maggie.

Maggie, staring through the window of Demel's pastry shop, looked up and asked, "Did you say you dropped something?"

Eric smiled. "Yep."

"What?"

"A Russian spy."

Maggie was too tired to press for a serious answer.

A secretary walked into the communications room in the CIA headquarters in McLean, Virginia, with an Eric Ivorsen update memo in her hands. Pete Burns and Bill Scriven, each holding a cup of coffee, stood with headsets on listening to a report from CIA Station Vienna. The radio was crackling with a transmission from the new chief of operations.

". . . arrived this morning with companion. Request surveillance instructions."

Scriven looked at Burns, who shrugged. Scriven had worked with Dan Traxler, the man who had just made the request, in Berlin during the late '70s and found him to be a reliable officer. Traxler's constant humorless enthusiasm sometimes bothered Scriven, but he overlooked it in light of the fact that Traxler had been instrumental in turning around a KGB station worker, and all within four weeks of being assigned duty in Vienna.

Scriven spoke into the headset's mike. "Nonpriority. Determine reason for visit, if possible."

"Subject can be networked immediately. Hard line feed available if so desired. Photographer also on line."

"Say," Scriven said into the mike, smiling at Burns, "I

have a novel idea . . . a new concept in intelligence procedure to determine reason for subject's presence."

Burns smiled back as Traxler responded, "Standing by to copy."

"Here it is," Burns said. "Why don't you just ask him?"

There was a moment of silence from Vienna, and then Traxler said, "Roger, will comply with directive to make hard contact."

Scriven shook his head, and Pete Burns grinned. As they walked back to Burns's office, the senior officer said, "Don't be too hard on him—you were like that for a few months too."

"Never that bad," Scriven protested.

"No, not that bad," Burns replied. "But close."

When they reached the hotel, Maggie started to undress but stopped when she saw Eric throwing their things back in the suitcase.

"I'm about to fall asleep on my feet, and you're packing?" Maggie asked weakly.

"I forgot to tell you," Eric said, hoisting one bag to the floor near the door. "We're moving."

"Why?" Maggie squeaked, her eyes closing.

"This place is just too far from good restaurants," Eric teased as he opened the door. Tossing a five-hundred-schilling note on the bed, he led Maggie down a back stairway and out the rear door of the hotel. Crossing the narrow Riemergasse, they reached the tram station on the Schubertring just as an A Tram rolled to a stop.

Falling onto the wooden seat, Maggie sighed. "What's going on now?"

"You want to sleep late in the morning, right?"

With eyes closed, Maggie nodded slowly.

"You want to just stretch out and wiggle your toes and have room service send up orange juice, coffee, and pastries, right?"

Maggie smiled.

"And you don't want to spend the morning being interrogated by KGB agents, do you?"

Maggie's smile disappeared and she opened her eyes. "What?" she asked, suddenly awake.

"If we move to another hotel before they pick up our trail, we can spend a luxurious morning in bed."

Maggie clamped her hand over her eyes. Four tram stops later, Eric picked up their bags and led Maggie to another small hotel.

"How do you know all these places?" Maggie asked, following him into the lobby of a modest little hotel on the Stadiongasse.

"I lived here for two summers."

"Don't tell me, let me guess," Maggie said as the hotel clerk selected a key. "Uncle Charles thought it best."

"As a matter of fact, no. Uncle Charles wanted me to accompany him to New Zealand, but Lady Barbara thought my education was lacking without exposure to classical music."

"Lady Barbara?"

"I told you . . . the woman on the deck," Eric said, pulling open the iron gate of the hotel's antique elevator.

"Oh, of course, when you were fourteen," Maggie replied, stepping into the etched-glass car. "What ever became of Lady Barbara?"

She still lives on the yacht, and now it's hers."

"Uncle Charles had class," Maggie smiled.

"Yes, he did," Eric replied.

After a hot bath and one of Eric's excruciatingly pleasurable backrubs, Maggie hit the pillow and was sound asleep. Eric rolled on his back and with his hands behind his head, thought about Lady Barbara, the only person beside him at the funeral of Charles Ivorsen.

Standing at the closed casket in a small church near Salzburg, Eric had been in tears and could not understand how Lady Barbara would retain her composure. At forty, she had spent the last twenty years with no man other than Charles, and yet at his funeral shed no tears.

A classically beautiful woman, Lady Barbara Falcounbridge had been the object of Eric's first crush. And he had been mildly in love with her ever since. Although her devotion to Charles never wavered, she was well aware of Eric's infatuation and kept it alive with a constant hint of sinful playfulness beneath her cool exterior—just as she did with every attractive man who had the pleasure of knowing her.

When she saw just how badly Eric was taking the death of Charles, she made him take her arm and walk to a pew. Sensing his incomprehension of her attitude, Lady Barbara explained to Eric that she simply chose to remember happily—and cherish—every moment of her life spent with Charles. And that if she were to let herself grieve, she would grieve for the rest of her life. And that that would be a terrible insult to the memory of the man they both loved. She leaned up, kissed Eric gently on the cheek, and whispered in French, "Live for today, my love."

Then she stood and walked to a beautiful floral arrangement that Eric had had delivered and extracted a single long-stemmed red rose from the center. Turning to the closed coffin, Lady Barbara placed the flower on top and then walked from the church with her head held high and a sad smile on her lips.

Turning to hold Maggie, Eric understood.

CHAPTER 16

Frieda Mueller's morning routine was no different from that of any other day. And as always, she enjoyed herself. Even though the rainy skies of the evening had cleared, the road through the woods would still be muddy. But Frieda would not have minded the daily journey even if it had still been raining. She found the task of delivering fresh eggs, milk, and bread to the home of Hans Schmidhuber to be always amusing, primarily because he never failed to pay a flirtatious compliment. Even though Frieda was fifty-five, she giggled like a schoolgirl whenever Hans compared her to one of Rubens's cherubic nymphs. Straightening up after the gentlemen was no bother, and although his cat, which she did not like at all, left long strands of hair everywhere, she merely considered cleaning up after her to be part of the job.

When she walked up the path, she did not sense anything wrong, although she was surprised to see the windows closed on such a nice morning. As always, the front door was unlocked, and Frieda let herself in. The first vague tingle of disorder came when she heard the repetitious hiss crackling from the speakers of the stereo as its needle slowly dragged across a skip in the record's final groove. Then she found Schmidhuber's work light burning in the bright morning sun. Calling his name and receiving no answer, Frieda frowned. When Bernadotte failed to appear for her morning saucer of cream, Frieda became truly frightened. She peeked into Schmidhuber's empty bedroom, crossed the room to the open window, and leaned out.

Lying in the shadow of the house with Bernadotte desperately trying to lick him awake, Schmidhuber was a rigid pale corpse. When Frieda saw his hands, she felt the room start to spin and sagged to the floor, gasping. It took almost five minutes for her to regain enough strength to stand. She did not look out the window again. Instead, she did what she had been told to do in the event of any unusual occurrence at the Schmidhuber cottage—she picked up the phone and placed a call to her other employer in Vienna, an employer whose existence had never been revealed to Hans Schmidhuber.

"*Ya?*" the gruff voice answered.

"Herr Schmidhuber has been murdered," she croaked in her thick German.

"How do you know it's murder?" the man asked calmly.

"Blood is everywhere on his shirt," she whispered desperately and then swallowed before adding in a stammer, "And his fingers have been cut off!"

There was a moment's silence before the man said, "Call the police and then wait there to learn as much as you can about the crime. Watch to see if any strangers come to the house. We are looking for an unusually tall man traveling with a woman. Call again when you know more. There will be a handsome bonus for you."

Frieda pushed down on the phone's cradle and then dialed the police.

The man who had issued the cold instructions placed a call of his own to his superior in Zurich. Gunter Toombs was on the line within seconds.

The man in Vienna said simply, "Schmidhuber has been eliminiated."

With his only insurance policy now lapsed, Toombs spat a vicious curse and growled, "It's the Russians. I'll be there within two hours. I want to know who did this. Pay whatever it takes to find out."

Money flowed quickly whenever Gunter Toombs was anxious for information. As with any business, unlimited cash made it easy for his people to function efficiently. With authorization to spend any amount to learn the identity of Hans Schmidhuber's executioner, the man in Vienna had arranged to meet his Russian "mole," a paid KGB informant, within twenty minutes of the conversation with Toombs.

One hour later, a small nervous Russian walked past the Opernring metro station and then turned abruptly to see if he was being followed. When he saw no one, he descended the escalator to the brightly lit concourse. Entering the men's room, he walked directly to the washbasin, next to one of the men to whom he betrayed his country's secrets. He reached down and ran the water but did not get his hands wet. Nevertheless, he took a towel and dried his sweaty palms. Without speaking, he turned and walked out of the lavatory. Toombs's man followed.

Waiting on the platform, neither man spoke, neither man acknowledged the other. But when a train pulled into the station, they entered the same car.

Convinced that they were safe, the small nervous man turned and spoke in Russian. "You said there would be a lot of money for this."

Toombs's man nodded and extracted a thick stack of five-hundred-schilling notes.

The Russian licked his lips lightly, staring at all the money.

"There was a killing in the Wienerwald last night."

The Russian nodded. "Hans Schmidhuber. Physicist. Colonel Nikolayev came personally to oversee the operation. There are to be two more—a man named Eric Ivorsen and a woman named McCabe."

"Who is the contractor?"

"An independent from America . . . Lawrence Tilton," the Russian said. "He works for our man called Delahunt."

"Do you know if it was this Tilton who was responsible for a hit in Princeton?"

"Yes. I am quite certain. He has been the primary contractor on this project from the beginning."

"What else can you tell me?"

"We are assembling a team to search for a document. There is some sort of map . . ."

"I want a copy of this map."

"Impossible. I have not even seen it. And besides, the team leaves tonight."

"Where can I find Tilton?"

The Russian traitor mentally estimated the value of the stack of money, considered asking for more, but then thought better of it. "He stays at the Inter-Continental," he whispered as if this secret were more powerful than the others.

"You have done well. Contact me if there is more I should know."

"How much will you pay?"

"It will depend on what you have to offer."

Toombs's man rose and departed the train at the very next stop. The Russian, a true mercenary, stayed on until the train returned to Vienna. When he emerged from the station, instead of returning immediately to his job in the *rezidentura*, he walked past the CIA station observer on duty at the American Travel Bureay offices in the Innere Stadt. Within minutes he was approached on the Kärtnerstrasse by a long-haired young man trying to sell cheap jewelry.

The young man, wearing tattered bellbottom blue jeans and sporting a scraggy beard, looked more like an outdated hippie than the Stanford Law School graduate that he was. Recruited in 1978 by the CIA, he had since perfected an almost flawless command of the Russian language.

"You want to buy a ring?" he asked in the Russian's native tongue.

"I have something to sell Traxler," the Russian replied. "If the price is right."

"What?" the agent asked as he pretended to offer more jewelry.

"Details of an important operation."

"I would have to know more in order to requisition funds."

"Tell Traxler that it involves Nikolayev and a man from America named Ivorsen. Eric Ivorsen."

"Come by after six and I will have an answer for you."

Morning sunlight filtered past a small opening in the drapes of Eric and Maggie's room, casting a golden glow across the big featherbed on which they were lying like spoons. Eric, propped up on his elbow, stared down at the silky-smooth alabaster skin of Maggie's neck and, pulling aside the tress of her shiny chestnut hair, leaned down and kissed her lightly. Stretching, Maggie woke, turned, and saw the look in Eric's eyes.

With a sleepy sexy smile on her lips, she whispered, "Uh-oh."

Yuri Nikolayev wanted badly to finish up his conversation with Pyatigorsk in Moscow. The communication had been set up on a "clean" line. Even so, their dialogue was cryptic, and they made no specific reference to Ivorsen or the location of the Viking Cipher.

"We have selected a team," Nikolayev boasted. "They will leave tonight after a briefing. And we have taken care of the Wienerwald liability."

"What about the other two?" Pyatigorsk demanded.

"This too should be taken care of this evening."

"Should?" Pyatigorsk asked with intentional surprise.

"We expect no difficulty in that area," Nikolayev replied quickly.

"There is no more time for careless mistakes," Pyatigorsk warned.

"I said it will be taken care of," Nikoleyev snapped and then wished he hadn't.

There was a chilly silence from the other end for several moments. "Inform me as to your progress," Pyatigorsk said finally and then signed off.

Nikolayev walked down the hall to a grim little conference room furnished with an old table and folding chairs, entered, and sat at the head of the table. On his right was the man Eric had waylaid in the alleyway. Next to him was Delahunt. On the right side of the table were two strong-looking men who had been recruited from the KGB's tactical assault school. Terror-trained in all aspects of guerrilla warfare, espionage, and survival, they were two of the best in their bloody field.

Nikolayev turned to the man who had been hit by Eric in the alleyway and ordered, "I've altered the entire network to assist in correcting your incompetent mistake. In the meantime, you get back out to Durnstein. Ivorsen will probably return there. Follow him, and as soon as you are sure of his location, contact me. We will handle it from there."

The man nodded without comment, stood, and departed. Nikolayev then turned to the two commandos who had been selected to retrieve the Viking Cipher. He looked back and forth into their eyes as he spoke. "You will join me tonight for dinner. At that time you will learn your destination. You will speak of this to no one. If anyone except me should inquire as to the nature of this program, you will report it to me immediately. Anyone."

At Nikolayev's nod, both men stood and left the room. Delahunt looked nervously at Nikolayev and then at the table. He remained silent, waiting for his instructions.

Nikolayev looked up and said, "You and Mr. Tilton are to join me for dinner as well. Seven o'clock. Do not be late. I am certain that by then we will be able to tell your man Tilton where to find Eric Ivorsen and Maggie McCabe and we can be done with this problem once and for all."

Wrapped naked around Eric, Maggie teased, "Let's just stay like this."

With his breathing returned to normal, he smiled contentedly and replied, "I'd love to, but there's this business of saving mankind that I have to take care of this morning."

Maggie giggled, kissed his neck, and then asked, "Is all of this for real? I mean, do you believe what Mr. Schmidhuber said about your father and Einstein?"

"I just don't know." Eric sighed, staring at the ceiling. "For all we know, he's just an eccentric old physicist with delusions of grandeur."

"I think he's cute."

"If we're to believe him, he's spent the last fifteen years waiting for me to get these letters, listening to Mozart, copying French masters, and petting that crazy-looking cat—and all the while keeping the Durnsteiner vineyards in business."

"I think his cat is adorable."

"She looks as if she's been drinking as much as he has."

"I still think she's adorable."

Eric smiled into Maggie's eyes, kissed her, and untangled

himself from her warm embrace. "I'm going to take a shower. Care to join me?"

"Sure," Maggie replied eagerly, knowing that the invitation would probably lead to yet another uninhibited encounter in the steaming spray of the shower.

When they walked from the hotel an hour later, Maggie headed for the Kärtnerstrasse to explore the shops and boutiques. Eric hailed a cab and instructed the driver to drive around the Innere Stadt, past the Mercedes that they'd left at the first hotel. As he expected, parked nearby was a surveillance car, a battered-looking Citroën, with two men watching the Mercedes. Eric told the driver to return to the Stadiongasse near his hotel and drop him off two blocks away at the Universität.

Upon entering the university's huge main building, Eric asked a receptionist for directions to the computer science laboratories. He had to walk up two flights of stairs and down a series of long hallways before he found the room he was looking for. Eric knocked on the door and a young girl opened it. Explaining that he was interested in learning about computers for a report he was preparing, Eric convinced the young student to activate and access the system. While the hardware was not state-of-the-art like the Dec 10 system that he was used to at the Princeton Plasma Physics Lab, it would serve his needs. He took note of each step, and then, certain that he would have no difficulty repeating the procedure, thanked the girl and left. Unfortunately, the mag tape that he'd brought from Princeton was not compatible, and that meant he would have to recreate his father's program before applying Schmidhuber's. Eric mentally calculated the time it would take to be at least an hour.

He spent the rest of the morning walking around the sprawling buildings of the university to determine the best way to reenter after everyone else had left. He found a service door with a damaged lock on the basement level at the back of the main building. Apparently broken for some time, the locking mechanism was rusted open. Returning to the computer labs, Eric memorized the route, knowing that the hallways would look vastly different in the dark.

Eric spent the rest of the morning in the university library poring over astronomy books. He then reread several volumes that concerned Viking exploits, myths, and legends. Still, nothing clicked.

Maggie had been spotted as she crossed the Opernring. That fact was relayed to the Arpel offices with instructions to pass it along to Toombs the moment he got off Arpel's ebony Bell JetRanger helicopter.

Maggie spent the morning strolling along the Kärtnerstrasse, stopping to browse in many of the small shops. Then, deciding that it was more fun to shop for clothes with an admiring Eric Ivorsen along, she made up her mind to do a little less shopping and a little more sight-seeing. At the Stephensplatz end of the crowded pedestrian mall, she came to St. Stephen's Cathedral and walked inside. Awestruck by the majestic beauty of the soaring gothic nave and baroque altars, Maggie gazed up at the high stone archways and stained glass.

Wandering across to the pulpit of the Master Pilgrim, she became intrigued by the intricacy of its sculpted carved stone. She listened in as an English-speaking tour guide described the work and then moved on.

As the tour group followed, Maggie tagged along. She walked with them to the iron gate at the entrance to the cathedral's catacombs, but feeling a little guilty for eavesdropping, did not follow as they descended the dark stone stairway. When the group returned ten minutes later, she casually peeked to see if the guide had locked the gate. He had not, and so Maggie ambled down into the deep vaults beneath the altars. After several turns she found herself in the catacomb of Emperor Frederick III, who had been entombed in 1493.

The silent stone sepulcher, octagonal in shape, had a high arched ceiling and a polished stone floor. In the dead center of the ancient room a massive red marble tomb rose five feet behind a carved marble railing. Maggie walked over cautiously and gently touched the edge of the tomb and then heard the iron gate above clang shut. The lights in the catacomb went out, plunging her into total darkness along with a five-hundred-year-old corpse.

Momentarily panic-stricken, Maggie turned and started

toward the oak doors of the vault. Then, realizing that she was not alone, Maggie froze. An eerie squeak from the entrance that sounded like a rubber-soled sneaker twisting on stone was the only sound in the burial chamber. Maggie began backing away, feeling her way along the cold marble coffin that held the emperor's remains. Suddenly a match was struck, and for an instant the granite cell flickered in yellow light. When Maggie saw the bizarre gathering at the vault's entrance, she gasped.

Standing in the aura of fading light were two men—one holding out a votive candle stolen from the apse of the sanctuary above and one setting it aflame with the match. To their right was a stunning young woman with long blond hair and a blank glazed stare. And below her, propped up in a wheelchair, was a deformed little creature with one eye wide and the other narrowed. Maggie felt the presence of something evil and shuddered.

"My name is Gunter Toombs," he whispered slowly. "And yours is Margaret McCabe."

Maggie, still trembling, stared down at the man's face. Only his left eye moved.

"You have been . . . shall we say, keeping company with Eric Ivorsen."

Maggie did not respond.

"I am going to tell you something now, and then you are free to go," Toombs said, rolling forward. "This Ivorsen is a very sick young man. He is responsible for the death of his uncle—murdered him to accelerate delivery of the vast inheritance on which young Ivorsen depends for his extravagant life-style. In addition, he has stolen a series of letters that belong to the United States government and now has apparently enlisted your help in carrying out a scheme to sell highly classified data to the Russians."

"I don't believe you," Maggie whispered.

Toombs closed his eye and slowly shook his head as if disappointed by Maggie's reply. He remained silent for a moment and then said, "His only uncle, federal agents in Princeton, and now a retired old scientist here in Vienna—he has killed them, or arranged for them to be killed, all for one purpose: He needs money. But for some reason we don't yet understand, he needs you too. All I ask is that you keep the United States government informed as to his activities. You can reach me day or night at our consulate. Or face the consequences as an accomplice."

Toombs rolled forward, his rubber tires squeaking, and pushed a small white card under Maggie's hand gripping the red marble railing. Then he spun around and rolled out of the candlelit room with the young woman ahead and the two men behind. They left the stolen candle burning on the emperor's carved coffin.

Once they were back in the vast church, Toombs leaned back to one of the men who had lifted his wheelchair up the stairs and growled under his breath, "Follow that bitch."

Maggie gazed around the gloomy chamber, shivered, and then ran up and out of the church into the warm Austrian sun. Breathing fast, she stared down at the small white card clutched in her hand. It bore a phone number and nothing else.

CHAPTER 17

Sitting alone in the hotel room, Maggie heard the horrible little man's accusations over and over in her mind. With her emotions tearing at her, she tried to tell herself that what Gunter Toombs had said couldn't be true. And yet she couldn't get it out of her mind that it just just might be. Eric's seemingly endless money supply had to come from somewhere. And she knew that Princeton didn't pay for summers in Tahiti with side trips to Africa whenever a scientist got bored. Wondering to herself how she had gotten so deeply involved, Maggie clenched her fist and banged it slowly against the bedpost.

Biting her lip, she wished that Eric would come home to tell her that everything was okay. Then she stared again at the little white card. Licking her lips nervously, she picked up the phone on the nightstand next to the bed and dialed. The phone rang three times before a man answered. "United States Consulate, Supervisor Toombs's office."

Maggie swallowed and dropped the phone on the cradle. With suspicion gnawing at her gut, she started to cry.

In the elegant private office of Arpel Limited, Gunter Toombs sneered an evil grin and watched his man hang up the phone.

Eric squinted at the Citroën from an alley across the crowded street. The two men inside were obviously bored and apparently sweltering—they had both windows open and would occasionally wipe sweat from their faces. The

Mercedes sat waiting on the street about fifty meters ahead of their car.

Eric considered several devices to disable the Citroën, including stuffing the tailpipe with a rag. But he knew from experience as a kid that that was an uncertain technique. As often as not, the rag would just fire out the pipe with a black puff. Finally, he decided on the direct method.

Walking quickly up from behind, he slammed his hand down on the roof of the car, adding yet another dent. The two men inside jumped. Eric leaned in the driver's window, snatched the keys from the ignition, and sprinted up the street. Jumping into the Mercedes, he was screeching away from the curb by the time the first KGB agent had figured out what had happened.

Chuckling to himself, he watched the frustrated spies in the rearview mirror as they scurried around in the street not knowing what to do next. He drove out toward the canal, and then, after making several backtracking turns to assure himself that he was not being followed, he returned to the hotel.

"Hey, Irish, are you home?" he called as he walked through the door.

Maggie, red-eyed from crying, was still sitting on the bed.

"Hey, what's the matter?" he asked, sitting next to her.

Pulling away, she sniffed. "Nothing. I'm just . . . it's just all the excitement. I want to go home."

"Well, maybe you'll feel better after we drive back out to the country. I need that formula sequence that we discussed with old Hans last night. C'mon, I've got the car downstairs."

Maggie nodded and followed him out the door, but she was obviously still terribly distressed. She tried to think of a way to broach the subject—to come right out and confront Eric with Toombs's accusations—but Eric was in such a good mood that she found it impossible. And if what Toombs claimed was true, how would Eric react to being unmasked as a killer? she asked herself. Looking over at him, she told herself that it couldn't be.

She was so confused she couldn't carry on a conversation. As a result, the drive out to the Wienerwald was silent except for several unsuccessful attempts at lighthearted banter by Eric. When Maggie failed to respond, Eric simply assumed that jet lag, fatigue, or both had exhausted her.

When they reached Hans Schmidhuber's home, they saw the rotund little Frieda walking from the cottage door with a somber-looking policeman gently holding her arm. Eric jumped from the car and ran up the path.

Speaking in fluent German, he asked, "Where is Hans Schmidhuber?"

"Please," the policeman replied, "who are you?"

"My name is Eric Ivorsen. I am a friend of Herr Schmidhuber's."

"Herr Schmidhuber has been murdered."

Maggie, who had come up silently behind Eric, asked, "What did he say about Mr. Schmidhuber?"

Eric whispered in English, "Schmidhuber's dead."

Maggie gasped, "Oh my God." Toombs's accusation came flooding back to her—he'd said that Eric was responsible for the murder of a retired old scientist here in Vienna. Maggie backed away with her hand to her lips.

Feeling faint, she turned toward the backyard, breathing fast. Trying to clear her head, she heard the policeman speaking in German to Eric, but she could not understand a word.

The policeman explained, "The body has been taken into the city for examination." Then he asked suspiciously, "Why do you come to visit Herr Schmidhuber this morning?"

"We had an appointment."

"To discuss what?"

"Personal business," Eric replied defensively.

After fifteen minutes of questions and answers, the policeman reluctantly agreed to let Eric into the apartment. Claiming that he'd left some personal papers in the home the night before, Eric began rifling through the documents on the cluttered desk, under the watchful eye of the policeman and the unblinking scrutiny of Frieda. Eric saw what he was looking for at the top right-hand corner of the desk but did not pick it up. Fearing that one or both of his observers were involved in this madness, Eric chose to wait and see if he couldn't snag the paper without their knowledge.

Maggie rubbed her forehead and sat down on a wooden bench in the yard. Suddenly remembering Bernadotte, she called the cat's name. When Bernadotte did not appear, Maggie returned to the house and confronted the policeman and Frieda. "Have you seen the cat?"

Frieda, who understood no English, turned along with the policeman toward the open doorway. Frieda blinked at Maggie and shrugged. The policeman shook his head and answered with a thick accent, "No, *Fräulein*, we have seen no cat."

Eric took immediate advantage of the diversion, quickly slipping Schmidhuber's formula into his jacket. Turning again to Eric, Frieda Mueller looked on disapprovingly. Eric continued searching through various stacks of papers and documents, but after several more minutes he looked up and said innocently, "I cannot find what I'm looking for."

Maggie had returned to the yard to search for the cat. When she still could not find her, she went around behind the building and walked down the path that led into the woods, calling Bernadotte's name. Finally, Maggie heard a faint mew. Following the distant sound, she found the frightened cat hiding under a fallen log. When Bernadotte saw Maggie, she leaped from her hiding place up into Maggie's arms and clung to Maggie's neck like a child holding its mother.

Back in the cottage, Frieda raised her eyebrows at the policeman, who nodded and then, tapping Eric on the shoulder, asked, "Are you finished, then?"

"Yes."

"Then we can all leave."

Frieda had made careful note of each question and answer. Although she had no idea what it all meant, she knew she would be paid on the basis of how much information she related to her employer in Vienna.

This arrangement had not bothered Frieda until now, and she wondered to herself if she would somehow be implicated in the nasty business. As the policeman turned and locked the cottage door, she remembered her first meeting with Schmidhuber and how only weeks after accepting the job, the man from Vienna had called. He had contacted her at home one day after she had delivered a chocolate cake to Herr Schmidhuber. Explaining that there would be considerable sums of money available if she would simply keep the people in Vienna aware of the goings-on at the Schmidhuber cottage, the man peeled off one thousand schillings as a down payment. The only stipulation was that Schmidhuber was never to be told of the arrangement.

At first reluctant, Frieda soon came to see the money as just an extra bonus for doing work she would have done anyway. She agreed to the stipulation and made daily reports on the phone. The man then always paid, and when occasionally something unusual happened, paid more. This unsettling event would be good for thousands, she told herself, and besides, the golden goose had died along with Hans Schmidhuber.

Eric walked down the brick pathway with the policeman, who then climbed into his van and departed. Frieda said goodbye but followed Eric around behind the cottage to look for Maggie. She was walking from the woods holding Bernadotte.

"We'd better go," he said.

"Okay," Maggie agreed, heading for the car.

Keeping pace, Eric reached over and stroked Bernadotte's cheek. He patted her head and said, "Goodbye, Bernadotte."

Maggie blinked and said, "I'm taking her."

"What?"

"I'm not leaving Bernadette."

"Bernadotte," Eric corrected her.

"I'm calling her Bernadette," Maggie stated.

"Whatever—we can't have a cat," Eric said flatly.

"I'm not leaving her here," Maggie said in a tone that left no room for argument.

"Maggie," Eric argued anyway, "We cannot—"

"I said I'm not leaving this cat out here with no one to take care of her." Maggie's chin was out and her green eyes wide, determined.

"Mrs. Mueller will take care of her," Eric said, turning to Frieda.

"Nein!" Frieda shot back, throwing her hand in the air to emphasize her refusal. *"Nein."*

Maggie raised her chin higher, glaring up at Eric.

Eric, wisely sensing the futility of further debate, took a

deep breath and announced brightly, "Say, I have an idea—let's bring Bernadette along with us!"

With a final defiant nod of victory, Maggie carried the fluffy gray cat to the car. As they drove slowly back to Vienna, Bernadette was nestled in Maggie's arms and purring so hard she began to drool.

"I have to get back to the university," Eric said.

"Fine," Maggie replied. "I have some shopping to do for Bernadette."

"You'll be all right alone for a few hours?"

"I can take care of myself," Maggie snapped defensively.

Eric, unable to fathom Maggie's sudden coolness, shook his head, turned sideways squinting at her for a moment, and then kept driving.

Gunter Toombs rolled across his office. When the man who had hired Frieda returned from his meeting with the Russian informant, Toombs gazed up from behind his desk and demanded, "Who was it?"

"KGB, as you thought."

"I know it's KGB," Toombs hissed. "Who in the KGB?"

"An independent named Tilton. From Philadelphia, U.S.A. Our informant advises me that it was Tilton who shot Gregor, too."

"What else did he tell you?"

"He told me that they have instructions to put together an exploration team. They have some sort of map."

Toombs was silent. This was the worst possible news.

The man finally broke the silence, "The information was costly. Apparently a section chief from Moscow is here to oversee the operation personally."

"Name?" Toombs snapped.

"Nikolayev."

Toombs did not reply. Instead, his eye began moving back and forth across the desk. Plotting, he looked up slowly and said, "I want to see this Tilton. We'll take as many men as you deem necessary, spend whatever it takes, but I want to meet this Tilton."

The man wiped his mouth nervously.

"Well?" Toombs demanded impatiently.

"Tilton is a very dangerous man."

Toombs's steely eye widened in anger as he hissed slowly, "You do not know the meaning of the word 'dangerous.' "

The man reared slightly at the threatening reprimand. He blinked at Toombs and said weakly, "He stays at the Inter-Continental—"

"It should be simple, then," Toombs snapped, interrupting. "Have a car brought around."

Lawrence Tilton, naked in the bathroom of his suite at the Vienna Inter-Continental Hotel, stretched his neck to look at his wounds. He sneered at the bald image in the mirror and opened his shaving bag. After injecting a new blade into his razor, he stepped into the shower and began delicately scraping tiny stubble from his body. He began with the hair on his ankles and drew the cold steel up his leg.

At the same time, three men accompanied Toombs and Katrine as they entered the lobby of the hotel and rode the elevator to Tilton's floor. A quick deal was struck with one of the chambermaids and a passkey purchased that would open Tilton's suite.

Standing in the warm spray of the shower, Tilton carefully and delicately pulled the razor across his testicles. He shaved himself completely, scraping the razor in long continuous strips across his belly, over his chest, along his jaw, and then up and over his head. An almost daily routine, the process took only minutes.

After drying himself, he made certain that he washed the concentration of stubble and soap scum into the drain. Planning to pour his little tin of lye to dissolve telltale evidence and residue, Tilton reached into his shaving bag and removed the container.

Bending over the ceramic tub with the lye in his hand, Tilton heard movement outside the bathroom door and sank into an animal crouch. His Ruger .22 was under the pillow on the bed, and he found himself unarmed—except for the half-empty can of lye. Holding the tin with a washcloth, he ran a thin stream of water into the vessel and it began to boil. Squatting naked, Tilton crouched ready to spring through the door and cast the bubbling caustic muck into the face of whoever was on the other side.

The door opened and Tilton sprang. Three guns stared at him as he shot through the door, and he froze, glaring angrily at the group. With acid dripping onto the room's expensive carpets, he realized the hopelessness of escape.

Toombs looked up and smiled. "That will not be necessary. If you put down your little can, my men will put away their guns."

Tilton set the lye on the desk, and it began immediately eating through the finish. He turned to look at Toombs.

"You are responsible for the death of two of my men," Toombs said. "And now you planning to kill people that I do not want dead . . . yet. I assume that you are not involved in this procedure for some personal reason—rather, that you work for the KGB because they compensate you well. I too pay well."

"What's this?" Maggie asked as Eric pulled up in front of the Hotel Helmhof.

"We're moving again," he answered. "I believe we were followed from the last place."

"Who?" Maggie demanded. "Who is it that you think is following us? Why don't you call the police or the FBI or somebody?"

"We've been through all that. There's no one I can trust. Now I'll register us here and you can shop for Bernadette if you wish. I'll be back in about an hour."

Inside, Eric pulled out a stack of cash and paid the clerk for the room. Handing Maggie the key, he said, "I'll see you in an hour," and disappeared.

Alone in the room with Bernadette, Maggie drummed her fingers on the table next to phone and then reached for the white card in her pocket.

In the Arpel offices, Toombs's man looked down at the flashing private line and smiled. He answered the phone on the second ring. "United States Consulate, Supervisor Toombs's office."

"May I speak with Mr. Toombs?" Maggie McCabe asked.

"I'm sorry," the man replied, "Mr. Toombs is out of the office temporarily. May I help?"

"I want to leave a message. Tell him that Maggie McCabe called and that we've moved to a new hotel."

Toombs's man sneered, grinning as he wrote down the information. He thanked her and promised to relay the message. Another line started to ring and he picked it up as soon as Maggie was off. This time he answered in German.

"*Ya?*" he grunted.

Frieda Mueller was making her report.

In the Soviet *rezidentura*, Nikolayev reviewed the program that he would present at dinner. He decided that the meeting would best be held at his hotel room rather than in the *rezidentura*. He had suspected that one of his people had been turned, but wasn't certain which. He could trust Delahunt and Tilton. And he was sure of the two commandos. But everyone else was suspect.

"Colonel Nikolayev?"

Nikolayev looked up to see one of *rezidentura* clerks nervously fidgeting in the office doorway.

"We have located Ivorsen and the girl," the thin man said in Russian.

"Where?" Nikolayev answered.

"Hotel Helmhof. The clerk there is sympathetic to our cause."

"Sympathetic," Nikolayev snorted. "How much does this sympathy cost?"

The nervous man licked his lips and answered, "Five thousand schillings."

Nikolayev nodded, and the mole left with the money. He went directly to the hotel, gave the clerk four thousand, and pocketed the rest. Then he went to the Kärtnerstrasse looking for the hippie.

It took only one pass for the CIA to move on the Russian. Traxler himself made the contact and with the assistance of two other agents whisked the traitor off to a safe house where they could talk in relative security.

The Stanford hippie was waiting to translate.

"How much?" the Russian asked first.

"It depends on what you tell us," Traxler replied.

After an hour of questioning, Traxler had learned almost

everything about the case that the Russian clerk knew. The information included almost every detail that the Russians had on the Viking Cipher except its purported content and importance.

The cast of characters was impressive, and Traxler left the meeting with a windfall of intelligence data. Most importantly, he knew where to find Eric Ivorsen and Maggie McCabe. He paid two thousand schillings and promised two thousand more if the man would return with more specific information about the nature of the Viking Cipher. The Russian said he would try and then disappeared into the Viennese night.

Dan Traxler immediately contacted Bill Scriven in Washington, relayed a synopsis of the new data, and promised a full transcript of the interrogation within hours. A new cryptonym was assigned the case, and in the databanks of the Central Intelligence Agency, Eric Ivorsen became simply the Viking.

As soon as he finished the transmission, Dan Traxler left for the Hotel Helmhof.

Yuri Nikolayev took opportunities like this to treat himself well. His suite in the Wien Hotel had a complete bar and several trays of *zakuski*, Russian hors d'oeuvres. Tonight would be something of a celebration—the launch of an operation that was now well under control.

Delahunt arrived and explained that Tilton would be a little late. The two commandos arrived together and attacked the cold meats and caviar. Half a bottle of vodka was gone before Tilton knocked on the door twenty minutes later.

Sitting at a table that Nikolayev had had set up in the middle of the room, the five men devoured a goulash that was supposed to be the best in Vienna. Then Nikolayev cleared the table and brought out a sealed map. Somewhat drunk but at no time out of control, he began describing the role of each of the other four was to play. His tone was officious and at times even melodramatic. Finally, after a brief unnecessary speech about Soviet patriotism, he broke the official plastic seal that secured the Viking Cipher map. As he unrolled the document prepared in Moscow it became apparent that all graphic references were in Russian, but the final location was clear even to Tilton.

Mostly silent during the small feast, Lawrence Tilton looked down at the map and then spoke to the others for the first time. Walking across the room to his thick briefcase, he explained that he too had something of interest to demonstrate. Nikolayev, annoyed at being interrupted, looked up impatiently. Delahunt and the two commandos were leaning over the table staring at the map. They too looked up.

Tilton extracted an Autoburglar shotgun, customized in Philadelphia to his exact specifications. The weapon, which looked to Delahunt like a hand-held mini-cannon, had a massive steel pistol grip, the barrel of a sawed-off shotgun, and a two-inch-thick silencer welded to the end. Hanging from the middle was a ten-cartridge clip. Tilton pointed it at one of the young commandos, who grinned good-naturedly. Bracing himself with one leg back and his left hand fisted around the weapon's barrel, Tilton pulled the trigger.

A dull thudding boom filled the room and the young Russian was headless. The jolt of the kickback savagely jerked Tilton's arms. He leveled the gun again, a curl of blue smoke leaking from its maw.

"Jesus!" Delahunt began gasping as blood dripped from the table. "Jesus! Jesus . . ."

The other commando dove toward Tilton, but it was a futile attempt. The second blast knocked him right back under the table of *zakuski*. Delahunt screamed for mercy from God, and Yuri Nikolayev backed against the suite's wall. Tilton squeezed off a round that chopped Delahunt's vocal cords in mid-scream.

Nikolayev stammered in Russian, "I will pay you anything—I will pay you whatever you ask—just tell me how mu—"

Tilton did not understand Russian. He leveled the gun and fired once more.

As he walked through the lobby of the Helmhof Hotel with the map in his briefcase, Lawrence Tilton began organizing in his mind the equipment that would be required to reach the Viking Cipher.

CHAPTER 18

Eric tried to think of a way to lift Maggie's spirits. After taking a quick walk past the university building to make sure that there was no nighttime activity that would prevent an unofficial after-hours visit, he noticed a flower vendor just closing up shop across the street in Rathaus Park. With a bouquet of fresh flowers, Eric returned to the hotel.

He knocked on the door of the room and smiled warmly at Maggie when she opened the door. "Hi. Let's have a romantic dinner under the stars and then—"

"I'm not hungry," Maggie said coldly.

Eric was silent for a moment and then exploded, "What the hell is the matter with you?"

"I just want to know what's going on. No, I don't even want that—I just want to go home."

Eric took a deep breath and sighed. "Okay. Listen—"

A sharp rap on the door interrupted the thought. Motioning Maggie to get out of the way, he walked cautiously to the door. As Eric looked through the fisheye peephole, the man outside, standing purposely to the side of the doorway, reached over and knocked again. Eric hesitated for a second and then ripped open the door, grabbed Dan Traxler by the coat, and pulled him inside. Holding him against the wall, Eric frisked him thoroughly but found no weapons.

"Suppose I was just delivering room service?" Traxler quipped as he straightened his clothing.

"Unlikely," Eric replied. "You haven't pushed a food cart since working your way through spy school."

"How very perceptive for a simple mathematician from Princeton."

"My uncle taught me how to tell the difference between a well-dressed businessman and a government agent. There's no doubt which you are . . . just a question of whether you work for theirs or ours."

Traxler smiled. "Traxler is my name. Dan Traxler. And this must be Miss McCabe."

Maggie frowned and nodded. Traxler smiled and sat down in one of the room's two armchairs.

"My guess," Eric said to Maggie for Traxler's benefit, "is that Mr. Traxler works for the CIA but will tell us he's with the embassy here or the consulate or some bogus import-export company or—"

"Embassy staff," Traxler stated simply.

"Yeah, sure." Eric laughed. "Any identification?"

"Would you accept it?"

"I'd know a bad forgery."

Traxler tossed his ID to Eric, who looked carefully at the clarity of the United States Government imprint. It looked authentic because it was.

"A friend of mine asked me to stop by and have a chat," Traxler said, "because your name keeps coming up in various police reports. As an American citizen, you should know that the government can be useful if you should . . . let's say, find yourself in trouble."

"Very comforting," Eric replied.

"Would you care to tell me what it is you're doing here in Vienna?"

"Visiting an old friend of the family," Eric replied innocently.

"May he rest in peace."

Eric nodded once in deference.

"KGB hit, you know," Traxler said matter-of-factly.

"I thought it might be. I caught one of their people following us around the other night. Did they kill my uncle as well?"

"No, that was another party. The KGB engineered Miss McCabe's abduction in Florida, though."

"How did you know about that?" Maggie whispered.

Traxler remained silent, so Eric answered the question.

"Contrary to popular fiction, the FBI works closely with the CIA."

"Oh," Maggie said.

Traxler turned to Eric. "This Viking Cipher thing seems to carry with it a lot of interest and a lot of death. Care to tell me about it?"

"No, Eric answered politely.

"Well." Traxler sighed. "We'd like to know if the security of the United States is involved."

"I don't know that it is," Eric answered. "And until I do, we really don't have much to discuss."

"I'm willing to help you," Traxler said with a touch of annoyance creeping into his tone, "but it's a two-way street, understand?"

"Okay. Who killed my uncle?"

"Gunter Toombs."

A soft "Uh-oh" squeaked out of Maggie. Traxler glanced at her.

Eric threw his head back and laughed. "Toombs has been dead for fifteen years. You guys should update your files more often."

"No he's not," Traxler said.

"No he's not," Maggie confirmed.

Both men looked at Maggie.

"If he's an eerie little man confined to a wheelchair, I met him yesterday."

"Why didn't you tell me about this?" Eric asked.

"He told me things. Things about you."

"Ah ha. So that's why you've been acting the way you have."

Maggie, like a child chastised, looked down at the floor and said nothing. Eric smiled and took her hand. He turned to Traxler and said, "Gunter Toombs died in a fiery building collapse in Paris in 1968. My father's legal affairs were then taken over by a law firm in New York."

"That's what everyone thought until last week. However, a little more thorough review of the Paris police files has revealed that Toombs's body was never properly identified, and in fact the possibility is strong that the fire was intentional. Apparently he did not get out without injury, but he did get out with the freedom to operate incognito."

"He was my father's lawyer . . ."

Traxler nodded.

". . . and so he knew all about the Viking Cipher because he helped set up the fifteen-year notification program . . ."

Traxler nodded again.

". . . and therefore would be in the perfect position to steal it," Eric said, the light dawning. "But why now? Why not fifteen years ago?"

"I thought you might be able to tell me," Traxler said.

"The only possibility would be that my involvement is a key."

"Or was," Traxler suggested.

Eric shook his head and then asked, "How did the KGB get involved in all of this?"

"Don't know that either. Do you?"

"No," Eric said. "And I don't know why they'd hit Schmidhuber."

"Apparently for the same reason they are going to kill you. They have everything they want—you're simply not needed anymore." Traxler stood and moved toward the door. "Give me a call if you need my help. We're always there to serve the citizens of our country." He winked and flipped his card on the bed.

Traxler closed the door softly, then reopened it and leaned back into the room to add, "By the way . . . I was given your address by one of theirs. The owner here sells to both sides."

Eric was unimpressed by the theatrical departure, but Maggie was wide-eyed and ready to pack.

"Gunter Toombs knows we're staying here too," Maggie admitted.

"How?" Eric asked.

"He told me he was with the consulate, and I . . ."

Eric, silent for a moment, started to laugh.

"You're not mad?" Maggie asked, hopefully.

"No, I'm impressed. What a masterstroke on his part. If he could make you think he was with the government, you'd keep him up to date on our location. Very creative." Eric smiled, picked up the phone, and asked Maggie, "Do you still have the number?"

Maggie pulled the white card from her pocket and held it out.

Eric read it and dialed. Handing the phone to Maggie, he said, "Tell them that I'm not here but that I called and said we're going to leave tonight by train."

Maggie did as he instructed, and while the man who answered was busy dispatching people to the Westbahnof, Eric and Maggie finished packing. As they crossed the street from the hotel to the car, Maggie carrying Bernadette, Eric scanned the street but saw nothing unusual.

"I'll bet we're not alone out here," he mumbled as he climbed in the driver's seat.

Pulling slowly out into the traffic, Eric saw headlights suddenly appear in the darkness behind. As he braked for a traffic light that was turning red, he turned to Maggie and smiled. "You were beginning to think I was a bad guy, weren't you?"

Maggie looked up but did not answer. Eric smiled. Bernadette, curled up in the back seat, yawned. The car behind them, with two of Toombs's people, pulled up and waited.

"Hold on," Eric said as the light turned red. He stamped on the accelerator and slid his foot off the clutch. A screech of burning rubber split the night air. With its tires smoking, the 450 SL shot out in front of the oncoming traffic just starting to roll.

A Volkswagen swerved to avoid collision, and the driver shook his fist at Eric. The car that had been following, a BMW 320i, shot out right behind them and fishtailed into the Volkswagen's left front fender.

The smash-up halted the BMW's slide, and then the superficially damaged car took off in pursuit, leaving the Volkswagen standing in the middle of the Schubertring. The angry driver jumped out and stood with his hands on his hips, staring down at his badly mangled car. Eric accelerated and began weaving in and out of traffic on the Schubertring—busy at all times, being part of the main thoroughfare circling the Innere Stadt. Toombs's man was no mean driver himself and managed to keep pace even on the Opernring straightaway running past the city's famous Opera House.

Side by side, both cars were traveling at seventy miles an hour when Eric suddenly slammed on his brakes. The BMW flew past. Jerking the steering wheel left, Eric pushed the gas pedal to the floor, and the Mercedes spun around, heading directly into oncoming traffic. Maggie sank down in her seat as Eric accelerated through the parting cars. With her eyes closed, she heard the angry blare of horns and the sound of screeching tires as drivers swerved to get out of the Mercedes's path. She peeked once and saw a pair of headlights cut right in front of them. Ripping the wheel left, Eric drove the Mercedes onto the sidewalk plaza in front of the Opera House, scattering a gathering of beautifully dressed patrons. Bouncing over the curb, the Mercedes was back in the street. The BMW was right behind.

"Damn," Eric spat. "They're too fast. I can't outdistance them."

Then a chance presented itself—an A Tram pulled out of the trolley stop and began rolling along the tracks in the Opernring. Eric sped ahead and then slowed, trapping the BMW between a group of angry motorists and the two-car trolley. The trolley driver clanged his warning bell furiously as Eric paced him, jamming up cars to the rear. Then at the very last minute, Eric stomped on the gas and the Mercedes shot in front of the trolley, swerving across its path.

In a four-wheel drift, the Mercedes just barely managed to clear the front car of the trolley, sliding out of control onto the Goethegasse and leaving the BMW with Gunter Toombs's men carried away in a tangle of traffic.

As he fought the slide and brought the car back to the middle of the narrow side street, Eric asked calmly, "Did you mention the university to them?"

Maggie, rising in her seat, shook her head.

"Good—because that's where we're headed, and I'd hate to find them waiting after that beautiful job of driving I just did," Eric said proudly.

"Dan? I've been calling for an hour!" Traxler's secretary sounded terribly upset on the phone. "You'd better get on the horn to D.C."

"I just walked in the door, Liz. What's up?" he said.

"Somebody took out Nikolayev, Delahunt, and two others."

"Holy shit! Are you sure!?"

"No question. Double confirmation."

"I'm on my way over. Pull everyone off the streets. Everyone. Immediately!"

By the time Dan Traxler reached the CIA station headquarters located above and below a travel agency in Graben Square, all operatives and agents had gone to ground—disappeared from the streets, coffeehouses, and bars of Vienna. A hotline had been opened up to Washington with Bill Scriven, Pete Burns, and the director of the CIA all standing by.

"What the hell is going on there?" Scriven demanded.

"Unknown at this time," Traxler responded.

"Find out. We're getting heat from upstairs on this," Scriven said.

"It wasn't company-sanctioned."

"Jesus Christ! I hope to hell not!" Scriven shot back.

"I mean, we're dry here."

"Nothing?" Pete Burns piped in.

"Nothing."

"Possibilities?"

"Two," Traxler said.

"Who?"

"The Viking and/or the Lawyer."

Bill Scriven looked at Pete Burns and the director looked at both of them. Burns explained in a whisper, "New cryptonyms for Ivorsen and Gunter Toombs. It was in the brief that came through just over an hour ago."

"Next time, give me a little more lead time," the director commented. "I don't like surprises."

"Neither do I," Burns replied. "We have complete dossiers on all parties. They'll be on your desk in five minutes." He pointed at one of the junior officers, who rushed out of the communications room to assemble the documents.

Scriven asked Traxler, "Did you pull our people?"

"Everyone we could reach. We have one man incommunicado on the Copenhagen Program. And one team in the red zone. They're still out."

"Get 'em in. And for Chrissake, let the Russians know it

wasn't us as soon as possible. We don't need another tit-for-tat crisis."

"Working on it right now. But they've clammed up over there too. The streets are empty except maybe for the Lawyer's people chasing the Viking."

"Did you make contact?"

"Affirmative. Just left him."

"And . . ."

"He's cautious."

"Cooperative?"

"Not one hundred percent."

"Could he have set up the hit?"

"Uh . . . I think not. I don't think he had any idea."

"The Lawyer?"

"Prime suspect."

"But to knock off Nikolayev?" Scriven was incredulous.

"Full book will burst in twenty minutes. Your favorite author."

Scriven nodded at Burns. A complete transcript of the meeting with the Russian informant, taped at the safe house, was about to be coded and transmitted at super-high speed. Burns leaned to the director and said, "We'll patch it through to your VDT. I'll have transcripts run off immediately."

"We'll keep a line open. Don't be a stranger," Scriven said, which meant that Traxler was to report every hour until further notice.

As the communications officer flipped the line to a holding frequency, Scriven looked at Pete Burns and whispered, "Jesus, talk about powder kegs . . ."

"Gentlemen," the director said, "my office . . ."

The Universität seemed deserted. Eric pulled the Mercedes down around behind the main building and parked in a courtyard just outside the broken door that he'd discovered earlier.

"We'd better leave Bernadette in the car," he said.

But Bernadette did not care for that idea at all. Meowing loudly as they left the car, she could easily be heard throughout the cobblestone courtyard and even as far away as the corner near the Liebigasse sidewalk. Eric stopped and looked at Maggie, who shrugged.

"I didn't think a cat could be so loud," Eric whispered.

"I didn't think Bernadette knew how to meow at all," Maggie replied. "She's not the smartest cat I've ever seen."

"Mild understatement," Eric mumbled as he opened the car door.

Bernadette bounded across the cobblestones and welded herself to Maggie's leg.

Entering the empty dark halls, the click of the door closing made Eric wince. He slipped off his shoes and asked Maggie to do the same. They padded quietly down the halls with Bernadette running alongside. Eric remembered the route, hesitating only once at the last turn. They reached the computer laboratory without incident, but when Eric went to open the door, he found it locked shut.

The oak door had a frosted-glass panel, which he smashed with one quick jerk of his elbow. As the crash and tinkle of breaking glass echoed through the halls, Eric and Maggie held their breaths. But there was no reaction. When the last shard dropped to the floor and shattered, the halls fell deathly still. Maggie breathed out, and Eric reached inside the door and unlocked it.

Within five minutes, he had the system up and running. Within twenty he had entered his father's program. Within thirty he was back to where he had been all along: four sets of crude concentric circles and one jumble of circles by itself. Applying Schmidhuber's formula had no effect on the four concentric groups, but it did affect the jumble. Each time Eric entered the formula, the jumble would advance and several outer circles would disappear. New circles would appear in the center of the screen. Maggie watched over his shoulder.

Staring at the unusual graphic, Eric was once again frustrated.

Finally Maggie said, "What is it supposed to be?"

"If I knew that, we wouldn't be here."

"Well, I'll tell you what it looks like."

"Maggie," Eric began with exasperation evident in his tone, "I know what they look like—they look like constellations. But I'll be damned if I can tell which—"

"They look like topo lines," Maggie interrupted.

Eric glanced back at the screen, blinked, and mumbled, "Huh?"

"Topos," Maggie repeated, "I used to process photographs taken by an aerial surveyor. He took stereo pictures of an area, and then the photo lab I worked for would print them. The result was a topographical map of the area photographed. Hills, valleys, and streams. The lines of hills looked just like that."

Eric stared at the graphic again and then entered a command that began the circles twisting on the screen. With each twist the circles began to lie flat and then build one on top of the other until the screen showed three small mountains surrounding a towering peak.

"Zermatt," Eric whispered in amazement.

"The what?" Maggie asked, misunderstanding the comment.

"Zermatt, Switzerland. That's a graphic of the Matterhorn as seen from Zermatt. My father took my mother and me there often. Always telling us about some ice caves he had explored as a young scientist. In fact, Zermatt was one of the places he took my mother shortly before they were killed."

"What about that other squiggle?" Maggie asked, pointing at Schmidhuber's graphic.

Eric began quickly typing commands, and the image started to spin and tumble. Finally it stablized, and Eric realized that he was looking at the computer's attempt to display a three-dimensional map. With each command, the image moved forward as if the screen were walking into a tunnel. Or cave, mused Eric.

As it slowly progressed through the circles, it became obvious why Schmidhuber had developed a nonconverging sequence—the formula led the computer explorer through unending tunnels. The sequence never converged because the caves had no end, only more tunnels. Whenever there was a split on the screen and Eric had a choice of tunnels, he simply reentered Schmidhuber's formula and the screen shifted to the correct tunnel and continued down.

Eric initialized the system's printer and activated the paper feed. A hard copy of the video screen began printing out. As Eric commanded the computer program to advance through the deep caves, the location of the Viking Cipher suddenly became obvious. And so did the reason that his father had taken his mother along. Eric looked up at Maggie but said nothing. Maggie, smiling proudly because her suggestion had helped, did not suspect a thing.

Eric parked the car at the side of Vienna's Westbahnhof train station, in a no-parking area near the side entrance. Small groups of travelers milled throughout the modern facility, preparing to depart or welcome arriving friends. Eric walked quickly across the concourse with Maggie running to keep up.

"Won't Gunter Toombs's men be here? After all, we told them—"

"We don't have time to worry about it now," Eric said, turning toward the tracks. "Our train is going to pull out of this station within the next three minutes."

As they approached track 12, Maggie looked up and read "Orient Express" in neatly painted white letters on a green background.

"You've got to be kidding," she said, staring at the famous train's sign.

"The Orient Express left here at three this afternoon," Eric reassured her. He nodded toward a train three tracks away. "We're headed for that." The destination billboard in front of the track read: "Arlberg Express—Salzburg, München, Paris." The train itself, like many modern European trains, with its dark-burgundy cars, looked grim and somehow sinister in the grayish-green light from lamps that glowed in the high arched ceiling above. Eric carried their bags onto a first-class sleeper car, and Maggie followed with Bernadette.

As soon as they were aboard, Lawrence Tilton, watching from the dark doorway of a storage room across the station, emerged from the shadows and walked toward the train. Climbing up the same steps that Eric and Maggie had just taken, he walked through their car and found it empty except for three compartments with unpacking passengers and two with the window curtains drawn.

Turning back, he selected an empty compartment between the two with drawn curtains. Once inside, he too drew the curtains closed, assuring himself privacy. Then he reached into his heavy briefcase and extracted a pair of white surgical gloves. Stretching the smooth latex over his hands, he decided to kill Maggie first as a lesson, brief though it might be, to the man who had handed him his first defeat. The train began to move.

A few minutes later, the conductor knocked, entered the compartment, and sold him a ticket to the first stop, Linz. After that point, Tilton reasoned, he would have no reason to be on the train. The car swayed as the train picked up speed.

Then, following the trainman to the first of the curtained compartments, he excused himself to pass and glanced inside. He saw an elderly couple with two children presenting their tickets. And he knew that his prey lay two compartments away.

Returning to his own compartment, he sat down and waited. He waited almost an hour and then methodically unpacked the deadly Autoburglar and let it dangle in his right hand. Draping his coat over his arm, concealing the weapon completely, Tilton stepped out into the hall. Rocking gently in the night, the train sped closer to the town of Linz. With a blast of the whistle, its engineer acknowledged the approach of the Holland Express headed for Vienna.

Tilton stopped outside Eric and Maggie's compartment. There was no light on inside—he could see that from the hall. The conductor had moved on to the front of the train, and all the other passengers had settled in their own compartments. When the train suddenly shook from the blast of the express rocketing by in the other direction, Tilton glanced once more up and down the empty hall, then ripped open the door and leveled the shotgun into the darkness, looking for Maggie's long hair silhouetted against the lights of the passing train.

But the compartment was empty. And Lawrence Tilton's mini-cannon remained silent. Trying to control himself, he stiffened, the veins in his neck pulsating in a grotesque purplish bulge. Blind hatred filled him. Once again, Eric Ivorsen had laid to waste a meticulous plan. Standing in the flashing light of the other train, his weapon hanging limp at his side, Tilton grimaced, frozen with rage.

As the last car of the Holland Express rocketed by and the light outside the compartment disappeared, Lawrence Tilton brought himself under control by desperately whispering a self-bestowed mantra: "Zermatt." The word, he knew, represented the place of final redemption.

CHAPTER 19

As the Arlberg Express thundered through the Austrian countryside, it did so without Eric, Maggie, or Bernadette on board. As soon as they had entered the train, Eric had led Maggie back through two cars. He stopped twice—once in the first car to draw closed an empty compartment's curtains, and then in the second car to see if anyone followed them onto the train. Bending to peer through the car's dark-green glass, they watched Lawrence Tilton emerge from the shadows, and Maggie gasped, "I've seen that man before."

Eric, with an expression of exasperation, turned slowly to her and said, "Gunter Toombs and now this guy! What else have you been doing?"

"No . . . I didn't meet him. I saw him briefly in Princeton the night we went to your apartment. He was in a car on the main street."

"Nassau Street? Are you sure?"

"I'm almost positive. Look—he has no hair. You don't forget a face like that."

Eric, staring down as Tilton walked quickly by toward the car they'd just entered, mumbled, "Well, at least we know one of the players. Let's hope he waits until the train is underway before attacking."

Then Eric led Maggie to the platform between the cars and illegally disembarked on the wrong side of the train, climbing awkwardly down the little ladderstep that was supposed to be used only by train personnel. Walking along behind a train on the next track, they made their way quietly out of the train station without being noticed by any of Toombs's people. One hour later they were at the Vienna airport with three first-class tickets to Geneva. Maggie insisted that Bernadette ride with them in the cabin, and Swissair insisted that she pay a full fare.

"I sure hope there's life after death," Eric said to Maggie at the Swissair ticket counter.

"Why?"

Eric, smiling as he peeled off the cash, replied, "I'd like to think that the guy from my apartment is watching us spend six hundred Swiss francs of his money to buy Bernadette a first-class ticket to Geneva."

Once they were airborne, Bernadette, confined to a small travel cage graciously supplied by the airline as part of the expensive fare, was content to lick one of Maggie's fingers occasionally and then go back to devouring the tiny plates of caviar that Maggie kept pushing through the slot at the bottom of the cage.

After several minutes of silent flying, Eric leaned over and said, "So tell me . . . have you ever been spelunking?"

Maggie thought for a moment, turned, and answered, "My father took the family to Luray Caverns, if that's what you mean." Then, realizing that the question carried with it all manner of untold danger, her smile suddenly disintegrated and she whispered, "Why do you ask?"

"Just a random thought." Eric grinned, trying to sound casual.

The next morning, the Kärtnerstrasse saw the presence of no Soviet or American agents. Until ten o'clock. Then the agent on duty at the American Travel Bureau glanced up and could not believe her eyes. The Russian mole was trolling—wandering back and forth across the Kärtnerstrasse hoping to be seen. The agent buzzed Dan Traxler upstairs.

"Jesus," he whispered. "I guess we've gotta go for it."

Within minutes the Russian was picked up and driven to the safe house.

"I took a big chance coming here," the small nervous Russian said in his native tongue. "That should be worth ten thousand schillings."

The Stanford agent, still disguised as a hippie, looked up at Traxler and began to translate.

Traxler, waving the agent off, said, "I know what he said. Tell him I'll pay five thousand schillings if he can tell us more about the Viking Cipher."

The agent translated. The Russian listened intently and then began to speak. Explaining that the Soviet *rezidentura* was in complete upheaval over the assassination of Nikolayev and the others, he claimed to have access to information that would normally never have been available to subordinates. While he did not understand the exact nature of the project, he believed that it concerned work done by Professor Ivorsen and a secret formula. Most important, he said he knew that the formula could be found in Zermatt, Switzerland, on some sort of mountaintop. Thirty minutes later, Dan Traxler had a rough sketch of the entire Viking Cipher project and was making plans to visit the Swiss mountain resort.

An hour later, all information was transmitted to CIA headquarters outside Washington. The reply transmission carried all FBI data on Lawrence Tilton. Tilton was originally from Chicago, but his current whereabouts were listed as unknown. The last official record available was a psychological report that in 1965 had prevented Lawrence Tilton from enlisting in the United States Marine Corps.

Described as psychopathic to the point of being capable of the most heinous insane crimes, Tilton had been advised to seek immediate professional help. He did not.

Maggie ran her hand lightly over Eric's chest, across his hard flat belly, and along his muscled thigh. Sleeping in the morning sun, Eric shifted in their bed, and Maggie gently cupped him in her hand. Tracing her thumb and forefinger lightly across his length, she felt him start to swell. He sighed in his sleep, and Maggie felt him grow hard. Then, slowly wrapping her fingers around him, she began hard strokes that brought him absolutely rigid.

Feeling his warm smooth skin excited her, and she continued the gentle pumping until he woke. Sucking a deep breath, Eric stretched.

"Feel good?" she whispered.

"Mmmmmmmm," he sighed.

Naked, she climbed up and kissed him wetly. Then she began exploring him with kisses, all the time continuing her gentle demanding caresses. Trying to remain passive, Eric gritted his teeth and closed his eyes. But the pleasure was overwhelming and his instinctive need to reciprocate undeniable.

Tumbling Maggie on her back, he hesitated for a moment, gazing into her smiling hungry green eyes. Then, whispering love in her ear, he drove himself deep, and Maggie closed her eyes in bliss.

"Damn you, you stupid bitch," Toombs spat at Katrine.

Katrine quickly mopped up a squirt of saliva that had dribbled from his mouth.

"Get away," he snapped, his eye searching his jacket to see if it had been stained.

Katrine sat down to await further instruction.

If Ivorsen was not in Vienna, then he knew where to go, Toombs decided. He realized the little diversion at the train station had been planned and the girl was in on it. He began to fume and calmed down only after telling himself that Tilton would take care of her. He did not blame Tilton for the failure on the train because it was Toombs's own people who had promised that Eric and Maggie would be on board.

Tilton, like Katrine, did what he was told. Toombs smiled at the thought. Once the price had been agreed to, Tilton carried out his assignment quickly and efficiently. There was no last-minute bartering for delivery of the sacred map—he had simply walked into the Arpel offices and handed it over. Toombs, delighted with the performance, paid him cash on the spot and reminded him that the contract had been only partially satisfied. Recovery of the Viking Cipher was still expected, and the reward would be doubled upon the successful elimination of Eric Ivorsen and Maggie McCabe.

After a hearty breakfast of eggs, fresh fruit, and pastries, Eric and Maggie took the first train to Brig and three hours later transferred onto the cogwheel train that would carry them up to the alpine resort at the base of the Matterhorn.

As the train wound up through the spectacular green valleys, across rugged gorges, and along precipitous cliffs, the events of the preceding days seemed far away and unreal. While Maggie sat stroking Bernadette, gazing at the breathtaking scenery passing by, Eric busied himself by jotting down a list of equipment that he felt they would need to find their way through the ice caves.

The cogwheel train pulled into the Zermatt station shortly before noon. One of the town's taxis, a horse-drawn coach, took Eric, Maggie, and Bernadette to the Mont Cervin, a luxurious hotel that, like most of the buildings in Zermatt, had an unobstructed view of the Matterhorn.

"There are no cars," Maggie exclaimed, looking around at the narrow streets. Several small flat carts, operated manually by workers, wheeled silently up to the train.

"Only horse-drawn wagons during the summer and sleds during the winter," Eric explained. "And those little electric delivery carts."

At the hotel, the manager reluctantly agreed to allow Bernadette in the suite, but only after Eric suggested a five-hundred-franc deposit. The woman behind the desk spoke with Eric in German, and he translated for Maggie.

As they walked to their rooms, Eric explained, "The lady said we can have Bernadette in the room while we are there to watch, but she must be outside when we're not."

"That's okay," Maggie promised. "She'll tag along."

"I noticed."

Once inside the suite, Eric walked to the balcony's french doors and pulled them open. The Matterhorn, soaring skyward, disappeared into a cloud. Gray and shiny even in overcast, the lower east face of the towering granite mountain was slick with melting snow. Even from the hotel, Eric could see white water falling from cliffs near the mountain's base.

After settling into the elegant rooms and freshening up, they walked into the village climbing shop and Eric explained that he needed advice and equipment.

The owner, Pyotr Lenz, a broad sturdy Swiss with white hair and ruddy features, was a picture of health and except for a bad limp looked as if he had just come off the mountain. He spoke flawless English and laughed easily whenever he made one of his frequent jokes.

"We want to visit the ice caves near the base of Hornli Ridge," Eric explained.

"Then you are going to be disappointed." Lenz grinned, exposing his strong white teeth. "The caves are closed. Have been for many years."

"My father and mother explored them once."

"Not alone," Lenz insisted with a twinkle in his eye.

"I don't remember. It was when I was a child," Eric replied.

"There is a man who used to lead expeditions. He lives in town now. But he has retired."

"He might remember my parents."

"He might. But he is getting old and stubborn and he does not remember things the way he used to. He doesn't climb anymore, and now he just sits around getting fat." Lenz laughed.

"It sounds as though you know this man well." Maggie smiled.

"All my life." Lenz grinned proudly. "It is me!"

Eric and Maggie laughed. Bernadette pawed at a string of stainless-steel pitons dangling next to the shop's workbench counter.

"Well then, do you remember an American professor and his wife? Ivorsen is the name."

Lenz touched his finger to the side of his face and squinted. "Yes," he said suddenly. "A big man like you. Just about the time that the caves were closed. He insisted that he explore, on his own, one of the uncharted ice caverns. He came several times. The last, he brought a woman. Your mother?"

Eric nodded and said, "I want to see this place."

Lenz smiled but said, "I am afraid, my young friend, that what you want is impossible. The caves used to be open for exploration only during the winter when there was no flow from melting snow. Even then it was dangerous, and so they were closed to the public. No one ever goes in during the summer. So you see, even if you could go in, you would have to wait six months."

"I see," Eric replied. "What equipment did my father use to reach the uncharted caverns?"

Lenz thought for several minutes before answering. "It was in December, I think. We used ice gear to reach the entrances. Once inside, we needed only the minimum, because the caves are easy for the novice to explore. Crampons were essential, because we had to ascend a forty-meter iceflow. Then it was just a matter of avoiding the frozen sinkholes. Very little water ran during the winter months. Now, though, it would be like a thousand rivers and a hundred waterfalls."

"What kind of lights did he take?"

Lenz looked suddenly concerned. "Why do you want to know this? I have explained that it would be suicidal to enter the glacier this time of year."

"I'm interested because my parents died shortly after their climb here. I want to know more about them."

"Yes, yes, I see," Lenz said, diverting his eyes. "Death in Zermatt is too often. Our village graveyard has many headstones commemorating the last day of an exploration. You would not add to this, would you?"

"I don't plan to," Eric said convincingly.

Lenz stared up at Eric for a minute and then continued, "We used Justrite carbide lamps and Wheat Light electric torches."

"Well, if I'm ever here during the winter, maybe you could arrange it so that I could make the same exploration as my parents. Is anyone allowed entrance?"

"Just scientists from the university in Zurich. But maybe I could get you a pass. They will be exploring again in January. They have made a date, and they always still come to me for advice."

"That would be great. In the meantime, Maggie and I would like to hike to the Hornli base. Can you outfit us?"

"I can . . . but I will sell you no caving equipment," Lenz warned, waving his finger.

"I won't need any." Eric smiled. "I just want to see the entrances."

"They are barricaded shut."

Eric nodded. Tangled hopelessly in a coil of climbing rope, Bernadette meowed for help. Maggie unwrapped her as Lenz began selecting hiking boots and equipment for their use. Eric specifically selected two pairs of narrow-welt lug-soled boots that were equally useful in hiking and cave exploration. Lenz did not notice.

"If you are hiking to the Hornli base, you will not need very much climbing equipment," Lenz explained.

"Is there any small climb nearby to try just for fun?"

"Yes, you could make a small ascent on the Furgg iceflow."

"We'll take whatever you think we'll need. And a route map, if you have it."

Lenz put together a collection of crampons, the steel spikes that attach to boots for climbing ice, pitons, ice bolts, carabiners, Mammut ropes, and two ice axes—one large one for Eric and a smaller one for Maggie. Then, marking out a map, he called Eric over and traced the route to the Furgg iceflow.

"That is all you need to make a small safe hike," Lenz said, piling the equipment on the counter. "Except for one thing."

"What's that?" Maggie asked.

Lenz looked directly at Eric and answered, "The common sense to stay away from the caves."

"I wouldn't think of entering a cave without lights and a cave map. And we've already established that you won't sell them to me."

Lenz nodded but remained unconvinced. Eric paid cash for the equipment and thanked him. As soon as they were out of the store, Eric was asking for directions to another shop. Within an hour he had purchased a cavepack for himself and a backpack for Maggie. He had to settle for used caving equipment owned by the parents of a young man killed on a climb several years earlier. The shopkeeper had stocked the out-of-date equipment on consignment and was happy to be rid of it. They left the store with dented hard hats, questionable battery packs, and antiquated lamps.

Leaving the caving and climbing equipment at the hotel, Eric, Maggie, and Bernadette rode the cablecar lifts up to the Hornli Ridge trail. Explaining that he wanted to get a preview of what they would face the next morning, Eric led

Maggie almost halfway up the route. It was more of a simple hiking climb than an ascent, and Maggie was relieved to find that she could handle it with ease.

They were back in town just after dusk and decided to eat at the hotel. Eric ordered two thick steaks for himself at dinner and was fairly conservative in his consumption of wine. Insisting that Maggie eat more than she really wanted to, he explained that the caves would be cold, that they would probably get very wet, and the danger of hypothermia could be reduced by proper food intake.

"Gee, you make it sound as if it's going to be terrible. How bad can it be?" Maggie said after the little lecture.

Eric debated telling her exactly what it would be like inside the ablating prehistoric glacial caverns, but deciding that there was no sense in upsetting her at this point, he just smiled.

Standing on the balcony of their suite while Maggie was bathing, Eric glanced up at the two mountain ridges surrounding Zermatt. He noticed a tiny dot of flashing red light rise over the Riffelalp ridge and then descend into the village about two miles away. Turning to go to bed, he didn't give it a second thought.

Sweeping over the Riffelalp ridge above the village, the Bell JetRanger helicopter banked for its descent into Zermatt. The Arpel pilot pushed the stick left and the JetRanger turned into a landing pattern above Zermatt's heliport.

Settling down gently on the floodlit helipad, the shiny ebony craft glinted, reflecting the high-intensity lamps that had been turned on at the pilot's request. Two men climbed quickly out of the helicopter to assist in the unloading of Gunter Toombs. Katrine, her long hair whipping in the chopper's buffeting wind, stepped down behind them, lifted a lightweight collapsible wheelchair from the cargo hold, and opened it. Wrapped in a blanket and blinking his eye against the wind of the blades, Toombs was lowered into his chair.

After rolling across the tarmac, he made Katrine stop before entering the small modern terminal building. She pushed him around so that he could see the helicopter being unloaded. After pulling several pieces of expensive luggage from the cargo door, the men carried out two crates of special equipment purchased earlier in Simplon. When all the cargo was on the ground, Toombs watched his new employee emerge from the flying machine's belly. The glare of the helipad's floodlights gleamed on the man's bald scalp.

Lawrence Tilton was about to complete his contract with Gunter Toombs.

CHAPTER 20

Maggie woke first when the tiny Rolex travel alarm began to beep softly on the nightstand next to the bed. Stretching, she sat up in the dark bedroom and gently shook Eric's shoulder. Then she made her way immediately to the balcony doors of the hotel suite. Pulling aside the drapes, she got her first full view of the Matterhorn, unveiled in the purple predawn sky.

Cast in violet light, the majestic monolith soared to the heavens above Zermatt. Perpetually capped in snow, the jagged peak was just starting to glow in the morning's first rays of golden sunlight. Maggie stood transfixed, awed by the sheer size and solitude of the mountain.

"Something, isn't it?" Eric said softly, coming up behind her.

"I've never seen anything like that," Maggie whispered, still staring.

Stepping onto the balcony, they could smell the sweet scent of wildflowers, carried by a soft summer breeze.

"It's going to be a beautiful day." Maggie sighed.

"Too bad we're going inside the Matterhorn instead of on it." Eric smiled.

"We're not really going to be inside, are we?"

"No, not really. We're going to be inside what's left of the glacier that carved it. Just below the Hornli Ridge," Eric said, pointing at the jagged northeast edge that ran from the peak to the base of the mountain.

"Are we really going to need the heavy clothing and sweaters we bought?" she asked.

"Yes, we are," he replied. "It may be seventy out here on the surface, but we'll be in caves that have been frozen for millions of years."

Maggie, rubbing the sleep from her eyes, thought about what a million-year-old cave would be like, decided that it was beyond comprehension, and called Bernadette. Bouncing out from underneath the bed, Bernadette caught her front paw on the bed quilt and tripped, tumbling into a ball at Maggie's feet. Eric watched the clumsy display, shook his head, and looked up at Maggie.

"Graceful, isn't she?" Maggie asked.

"What are you going to do with her today?"

"We can't leave her here, so I'm taking her along."

"We can't take her."

"You said it would be a simple hike, a quick run into the cave to pick up this Viking thing and then home. So there's no reason why she can't come along."

"It might be a little more involved than that," Eric admitted for the first time.

"She'll be fine," Maggie insisted.

Eric could see that the debate could lead to an argument, and they had no time for arguments.

"Besides, if she's a problem, I'll carry her in my backpack," Maggie concluded.

Eric nodded reluctantly, wondering to himself just how difficult the descent would be. If the computer map was accurate and what Lenz said true, then the last cavern could be a roaring underground nightmare even for an experienced climber like himself. For a brief uncomfortable moment, he pictured Maggie trying to negotiate an ice chimney with Bernadette, but quickly put the thought out of his mind. There were no options now, he reminded himself. And there was no way to retrieve the Viking Cipher papers without Maggie McCabe.

As the morning sun broke free of the horizon, Eric and Maggie were well out of town and hiking up the foothill of the Matterhorn below the Hornli cablecar, which wouldn't begin operating for another three hours. Walking along the lift-line trail that ran to the ridge base, Eric carried all the caving equipment in the cavepack and Maggie carried their heavy sweaters in her backpack.

* * *

Two of Toombs's men, the man from Vienna and the Arpel pilot, began loading the Bell JetRanger with the caving and climbing equipment that Tilton had selected the night before. When they finished, they went back into the hotel for breakfast. Katrine, suffering from a small overdose, was too ill to attend the predawn meeting. She stayed in her bed, staring at the ceiling through half-closed eyes. Her untimely incapacity annoyed Toombs, but he had more important things to worry about than the inconvenience that she had caused. Her drug use was becoming more nuisance than she was worth, he decided, and as soon as he was in possession of the Viking Cipher, he would make arrangements for her retirement.

Toombs had insisted the previous night that the hotel people have a breakfast ready for his crew at 5:30. There was a protest from the hotel management that lasted until Toombs had Katrine write a check for the extra service.

Lawrence Tilton was waiting when Gunter Toombs's men rolled him into the otherwise empty dining room. Tilton, wearing a black turtleneck sweater and heavy gray wool climbing slacks, looked uncomfortable sitting by himself at the table. He had shaved carefully the night before not only as normal precaution but also because he had grown to like the ritual.

The petite waitress, the fifteen-year-old daughter of the hotel owner, brought out four steaming plates of poached eggs served on top of sizzling strip steaks. Although business was at hand, Toombs was taken by the girl's fresh beauty. He made a mental note of her name, thinking that she would make a splendid replacement for Katrine. He hoped she was a virgin. Following her movement as she set down the plates, he thought of a particularly interesting way to find out. Sneering to himself, he turned to Tilton and returned to business.

"I've decided that I want one of my men with you in the caves," Toombs began in his usual commanding tone.

"No," Tilton responded.

Toombs scanned over at the hairless man and said ominously, "You are in my employ."

"No," Tilton repeated slowly.

Toombs's men looked nervously at each other. Neither had ever seen anyone talk back to their employer. Not and live. But there was something about Tilton that held Toombs in check. It was almost as if he recognized—possibly even feared—the ungodly malevolence in the man's tone.

"You're sure that you can do it alone?" Toombs challenged.

Tilton lifted another piece of meat to his mouth and did not answer.

Toombs glanced at his two men, but they did not look up from their plates. He continued, "We will drop you off as soon as Ivorsen takes the girl inside the cave. Follow them. Wait until they have the document. Then apply your skills. We will stand by just outside the entrance."

Tilton raised a cup of black coffee to his mouth and sucked it down in two gulps. He did not acknowledge Toombs's instructions.

Toombs leaned forward, extending his bony left forefinger at Tilton. He issued one final instruction. "Do not bother to come out empty-handed. Understand?"

Tilton looked up, wiped a bit of egg from his mouth, and nodded once.

Fifteen minutes later, the pilot engaged the JetRanger's starter and the helicopter's blades began to swing through the still morning air.

When the shiny black machine lifted off the pad to deliver Lawrence Tilton to the mountain, Eric and Maggie were less than five minutes from the ice cavern's entrance.

Dan Traxler had telexed Washington from the Geneva section chief's home, where he'd spent the night. Based on the analysis done on intelligence data transmitted the night before, Traxler was authorized to reestablish contact with the Viking and determine the authenticity and disposition of the project described by the Russian mole.

Traxler spent the ride to Brig reading a dossier that had been put together in Washington and flown to Geneva overnight. It contained fairly complete biographical sketches of Eric Ivorsen, his parents, Maggie McCabe, and Hans Schmidhuber, but the information on Gunter Toombs and

Lawrence Tilton was sparse, confusing, and in some instances unbelievable.

Traxler had reached one concrete conclusion even by the time the train reached Nyon: Whoever had taken it upon himself to open fire on the KGB was either dangerously insane or incredibly powerful. Lawrence Tilton fit the first category and Gunter Toombs the second.

Dan Traxler looked up from the file and to himself mumbled, "Talk about a marriage made in hell . . ."

CHAPTER 21

The twenty-foot entrance to the ice caverns was as Pyotr Lenz had warned—securely barricaded by huge wooden gates padlocked shut. Abandoned for some time, the doors showed signs of deterioration. A split had cracked open across one of the thick posts supporting the exterior bulkhead, and the timber looked weather-beaten gray.

Eric used his ice axe to chop away the wood that held the lock brackets. Within ten minutes, the lock was dangling uselessly from a splintered chunk of hanging wood. Grabbing the ten-foot door, Eric strained and pulled it open far enough to gain entry. As he did so, a burst of wind rushed out of the cave, blowing his hair back. The whistling howl startled Maggie.

"What's that?" she breathed.

"When barometric pressure changes, some caves breathe. This one seems to be having an asthma attack."

When they had stepped inside and pulled the solid gate closed behind them, the wind eased, and Eric lit one of the electric lamps. The chamber in which they stood looked like the entrance to any cave. In the rocky wall ahead, a huge yawning hollow disappeared down into pitch blackness. Bernadette, trailing along, seemed unconcerned by the strange surroundings and waited patiently at Maggie's feet as Eric began unpacking the antiquated caving equipment. He handed Maggie one of the hard hats and then strapped on the other. After snapping the power cables into the battery packs attached to heavy canvas belts, he wrapped a belt around Maggie and helped her buckle it. Flipping the rusty switch, he looked up and saw that her headlamp worked perfectly, casting a steady yellow beam across the tunnel. He repeated the procedure on himself and turned to begin the descent.

Advancing, he pointed the hand-held lamp into the hollow, and they began walking down. Strange rushing sounds rose from the darkness before them, and as they descended deeper and deeper, Maggie began to feel uneasy. The slope of the path was not steep, and for a while the descent was easy. Then the texture of the walls and temperature of the air started to change. What had been solid dark rock was occasionally replaced by flutes of blue-white ice.

About half a mile into the depths, the walls and ceilings seemed to sprout icicles every two hundred meters or so. Large sections of the floor had turned to ice, and it became more difficult to walk. Eric stopped and fastened walking crampons onto their boots to ensure a grip as Maggie pulled two sweaters from her backpack.

Lawrence Tilton climbed down out of the hovering JetRanger and, running low, carried his equipment to the cavern gates opened by Eric. He pulled the KGB map from his cavepack and reviewed the route that would bring him face-to-face with the man who had now twice defeated him.

Once inside, he shifted the shoulder strap of the Autoburglar, looked down at the black hollow, and then began his descent.

Expecting deathly silence, Maggie was unnerved by the constant distant howl of wind and echoes of unseen churning waters. Occasionally, an ominous groan would echo from the darkness—signaling the demise of an ablating speleotherm as it lost its icy grip on a cavern ceiling, broke free, and crashed into the freezing waters below.

"Why would your father put these papers in here if it's changing all the time?" Maggie breathed.

"Only parts of the cavern change. The location on the map is in a prehistoric area. It hasn't changed in fifty thousand years, except for the microscopic buildup of ice."

"What are those creaking sounds?" Maggie asked nervously.

"Flakes, ice formations that come in all sizes, begin to melt in summer and break. The stalagmites and stalactites of ice are called speleotherms. Sometimes they grow so big they can't support themselves and fall. That's what you hear."

"It sounded more like footsteps," Maggie argued.

"Nobody would be crazy enough to come in here except us," he replied, smiling to himself at Maggie's first underground hallucination.

Glancing first at the computer printout, Eric looked up at a gaping division in the path. Comparing the scene to the printout, he saw that he was to take the tunnel to the left. He continued on and for the first time had to duck to avoid a thick cone of ice dripping from the ceiling.

Maggie, with her headlamp burning brightly, turned to make sure that Bernadette was still with them. She was. However, when Maggie looked back at the path they had just taken, she saw not one tunnel but four and could not tell which they had emerged from. The thought made her shiver and then jog to close the gap between herself and Eric.

The tunnel they were in was almost all ice, and the wind coursing up from the depths of the earth whistled through with bone-chilling cold. As they progressed downward, the walls and low ceiling suddenly opened into unbounded darkness. Hollow echoes of splashing water bounced from the seemingly limitless void. Eric turned on a bright electric lamp that lit almost the entire scene. They were standing at the edge of an underground ice cavern, glistening and dripping wet, all at once spectacular, breathtakingly beautiful, and, to Maggie, unnervingly eerie. Huge sixty-foot icicles hung like teeth from the ceilings and walls and rose daggerlike from the floor. Eric thought it was stunning, but Maggie had a sudden vision that they were staring into the gaping jaws of hell.

Eric judged the ceiling to be at least fifty meters high and the width close to thirty. The sound of rushing water came from the far-right corner of the chamber. Walking carefully, they came to a vast pool that turned out to be just a fraction of a huge underground lake—not shown on the computer map because it did not exist during the winter, when Eric's father had made his descent.

Making their way around the edge of the black water, Eric came to what he assumed was the proper tunnel. But he was unsure, and the first uneasy tingle of disorientation flashed through him. He began to feel better when they came to a long descending curve that was clearly marked on the third page of the printout. Meltwater, rushing along the same path, had cut a deep ridge in the ice floor, and they had to be particularly careful not to lose footing. Each step required a chopping stomp to ensure a grip. Bernadette meowed loudly as she started to slide down the pathway and could not dig her claws into the glassy surface. Maggie picked her up and put her in the backpack.

Emerging from the circular frozen tube, they found themselves in a small chamber floored with black openings four feet wide. The running water disappeared into the first of the sinkholes, and the sounds of rushing water filled the room. Scanning his map, Eric selected the fourth and smallest hole. Showing Maggie how to belay, he dropped into the darkness and slid ten feet to the floor of a new ice cave. Maggie dropped in behind him and immediately noticed the change. In this new location, the chatter of running water had deepened ominously. Instead of the gurgling trickles and drippings, the sound was more powerful, almost thunderous.

"We didn't have to do anything like this in Luray Caverns," Maggie breathed, glancing around nervously.

Eric looked at her and decided that it was about time she knew the truth. Most of it, anyway.

"Maggie," he said, "it's going to get worse before it gets better."

"What do you mean?" she whispered.

"This is the easy part. We're headed into a section of the cave that is almost all runoff. It'll be something like climbing down Niagara Falls at midnight."

To Eric's surprise, Maggie just nodded and pushed on.

With his headlamp dark, Lawrence Tilton had watched their progress across the canyon floor. When their lights disappeared into the ice tunnel on the far side near the lake, he climbed down and followed. Shifting the strap of his Autoburglar to his right shoulder, he sucked in a deep breath and dropped to the path they had taken.

As Eric and Maggie walked along, the pitch of the floor became steeper and steeper, and suddenly they were sliding. Swinging down with his axe, Eric stopped his slide and grabbed Maggie as she started to glide by into the darkness.

"This must be the spot Lenz was referring to. We'll have to set a piton and rappel," Eric stated, pulling one of the stainless spikes from his cavepack.

"What're you talking about?" Maggie asked, her voice betraying her growing apprehension.

"We set an anchor and lower ourselves on a rope."

He hammered the sharp spike into the shattering ice but found he could not set it properly. Maggie began to shiver while Eric removed an ice bolt from his pack and tried it. Drilling proved to be the answer, and within ten minutes he had planted an anchor upon which he could safely fasten his line.

Wrapping the rope around both arms, he began a simple rappel, descending sideways, crablike, into the blackness. Leaving the line secured, Maggie did the same and reached Eric waiting about 150 feet lower. He was studying the map intently. Maggie looked up, the light of her headlamp sweeping across a wall of tunnel openings.

"Which one?" she asked.

"Not sure," he replied. "This chamber is not shown on the printout."

"Maybe we took a wrong turn," Maggie suggested.

"This might be it," he said, pointing at a jumble of circles. "But it should've been more clear."

Looking up, Eric walked toward an opening that was emitting a distant muffled roar. As they entered the glistening chamber, Maggie could feel a damp wind. As they progressed deeper and deeper, the din of rushing water got louder and louder. When they stepped out of the tunnel, the roar was deafening, and they found themselves in a canyon twice the size of the one farther back. Everywhere they looked, walls of tumbling water were cascading down from holes, tunnels, and cracks in the walls. Bernadette hunched down inside Maggie's backpack.

"This is it!" Eric yelled over the roar.

"Where?" Maggie yelled back.

Pointing at the printout, Eric yelled back, "Across this canyon!"

Maggie nodded, and Eric led her out onto a narrow ledge. Below, a series of underground rivers, streams, and sluices smashed together in a continuous dazzling explosion of white water that then raced into a gaping lower tunnel. Dozens of waterfalls plunged from above, leaking and pouring from holes and faults in the ceiling. A two-hundred-foot cataract crashed into the foaming underground black billow. Countless pools and pockets of water cascaded from the walls, spilling into the subglacial sea, its runoff boiling across the canyon, disappearing in a huge sinkhole that led to unseen caverns below.

Clinging to high ground along the canyon wall, they began edging their way across the foaming tumult to the area explored by Eric's father—the frozen prehistoric caves.

Tilton reached the melt canyon as Eric and Maggie crawled up an iceflow on the other side. Scanning his map, he reckoned that they were only about a quarter of a mile from their goal. With a small pair of Zeiss infrared field glasses, Tilton watched Eric lead Maggie up into a high cave.

Crawling up by planting their axes and digging in with their cramponed boots, Eric and Maggie pulled themselves over the lip of the cave. Once inside, they sat on a ledge of ice to rest. The noise was much less inside the cave, and Bernadette crawled out of Maggie's backpack.

"How far?" Maggie gasped, out of breath from the climb.

"In two thousand meters. Down thirty."

"Let me catch my breath," she panted.

"Okay. You may want to take off your packpack," Eric suggested.

"Won't I need it?"

"No. Cavers don't usually wear them. They get in the way."

"I'll just keep it on, thank you."

"Not if we have to belly-crawl," he said softly.

Maggie blinked at Eric. "What's that?" she asked suspiciously.

"That's when the ceiling is low and you crawl on your stomach. The backpack would hinder progress."

"I won't be doing any belly-crawling," Maggie stated. "You can count on that."

Eric didn't respond. As they walked into the silent white world, the only sound was the hiss of black water racing along a parallel tunnel just inches away. After ten minutes, they reached the beginning of the prehistoric caves.

Entry would have been tricky during winter, when there was no water. Now it was deadly. They had to share their final descent with an unexpected small river that slid unimpeded into the same chamber. The chamber itself was a vast frozen wonderland of crystal walls, long delicate icicles, and fragile flakes, plates of ice that could be paper-thin or weigh tons. At one end was a wide pit into which the river water flowed. As the water boiled over the pit's edge, it fell about fifteen feet and then swirled into a slurping sucking whirlpool that looked to Eric to be another thirty feet deep.

"We must be on a ledge," Eric said, gazing at the twenty-foot black funnel of water.

"Why?" Maggie asked, peeking around his shoulder.

"The water looks deep. There must be a sinkhole below that's relieving the pressure."

Turning, Eric saw the entrance to the last cave, just as it was shown on the last page of the computer printout. And also, just as was shown on the printout, the entry hole was less than twenty inches wide—too small for a man like his father . . . or himself. But big enough for a woman like his mother . . . or Maggie.

"This is it, Maggie. Down here," he said, walking to the glassy aperture in the floor.

"You're kidding me, right?"

"I'm afraid not."

"You're never going to fit in there," she said, laughing.

"No, I'm not. You are."

"Oh no I'm not. Forget it. No way, José! Not a chance. I mean, just put the thought right out of your mind."

Bernadette padded over to the slick glassy opening and peered down as if to see what all the fuss was about.

Trying to convince her that the descent wouldn't be that bad, Eric began, "It looks worse than it is. You'll only be squeezing through the aperture and then it slopes into a room below us that's—"

"I told you before that I'm claustrophobic. I'll die if you make get in that—"

The debate was interrupted by a loud meowing scream for help. Maggie and Eric looked up just in time to see Bernadette plunge over the edge and disappear into the hole.

"Bernadette!" Maggie yelled, diving on her knees to try to catch the clumsy cat. But she was not fast enough, and Bernadette slid down the ice walls to the room below. Meowing loudly, Bernadette could just barely be heard over the sound of rushing water. Maggie looked up at Eric with tears in her eyes. He didn't say anything—he didn't have to. Trembling with fear, Maggie pulled off her backpack. And Eric tied the rope around her so that he could lower her into the hole.

With her body wedged against the close walls, Maggie had to exhale in order to get her chest through the opening. Then Eric had to push on her head to move her lower. Her hard hat slid off her head and cascaded into the darkness. Its lamp went dark when it hit the floor below. Jammed against the frozen walls, Maggie began to panic. Hyperventilating, she began to get dizzy. Then she heard Bernadette meow, and she calmed. She felt the pressure of Eric's push, slid for a few inches, and then felt the walls widen. A second later, she was sliding in the blackness. The thunder of pounding water got louder and louder the lower she slid. But she could still hear Bernadette's cries for help over the roar of the waterfall. She dropped another two feet and found herself dangling, and then a moment later standing.

When Eric felt the rope go slack, he turned on the rusty Wheat Light lamp and lowered it on a drop line into the hole. Gazing down, he watched the light disappear into curved steep tunnel.

Maggie stared up the chimneylike tunnel as the lamp bounced along, getting closer. When it swung into the small room, Maggie grabbed it and turned to look for Bernadette. Sitting on top of an ice-encrusted metal box perched on an icy table of ice, Bernadette sat licking her paws. Behind her, ten feet away, a twenty-foot column of falling water thundered from the sinkhole above. The column shot straight down through the room into another much larger opening smoothed by the passage of untold billions of gallons of water over thousands of years.

"You may need the axe to free the box," Eric called down. He lowered her axe and waited, peering into the tunnel, while Maggie went to work chipping at the ice holding the metal box. With her third swing, the box cracked free, bounced on the rock-hard floor, and slid to a stop several feet away. Bending with her weight against the rope, she managed to scoop it up.

"I've got it!" she yelled.

"Tie the rope around Bernadette and then the box," Eric called. "We'll take them out first."

Maggie made a loop of line that fit snugly around Bernadette's middle, tied a knot through the box's handle, and yanked twice. "Ready!"

As Eric drew up the line attached to the frightened wet cat and the rusty metal box, the upper chamber got suddenly brighter.

He looked up to see Lawrence Tilton holding a bright carbide light in one hand and his Autoburglar mini-cannon in the other.

"Give me the papers," Tilton said with an evil grin, pointing the deadly mini-cannon at the hole.

Eric looked down and saw his only chance dangling in the air. He reached down and grabbed Bernadette under her chest.

"I'm going to toss it to you," Eric cautioned. "Don't get excited with your howitzer there."

Then, slowly launching Bernadette gently into the air, Eric dived to one side. Bernadette arched and hit Tilton in the head. Clawing instinctively, her razor-sharp claws sliced through the flesh of his face as she rebounded like a shot into the darkness. Tilton screamed, falling backward, squeezing the Autoburglar's trigger. The action emptied half of the weapon's clip in a staccato thunder that blasted ice and lead across the chamber's ceiling and walls. The final blast slammed into a thick ice plate, cracking it loose from the ceiling above. In a slow creaking groan, the huge ice formation began to sag. Then a boom echoed through the caverns as it broke free and smashed to the floor. A wave of water poured from the hole it left in the ceiling above. The foaming wall of water smashed across the chamber and over Tilton lying on the floor, and he began to slide toward the sinkhole, pushed by tons of freezing water. Smashing his clawed fists at the ice in a futile attempt to stop himself, Tilton broke three fingers and then washed over into the whirlpool at the chamber's edge.

Swirling in the torrential funnel, Tilton screamed, his eyes wide in terror. Eric, lying on the chamber's floor above the new course of white water, watched as Tilton tumbled around for a few seconds, thrashing wildly in a useless attempt to climb the sucking wall of water. Then he upended, and the last Eric Ivorsen saw of Lawrence Tilton was the killer's hairless legs spinning into the whirlpool's deadly black vortex.

Maggie, deafened by the thunder of falling water, yelled again for Eric to hoist her up. She thought that the roar of the waterfall was drowning her out, but then suddenly the thunder ceased—the room fell silent except for the sound of dripping water. Maggie blinked and looked up at the lower chamber's ceiling. Protruding upside down from the sinkhole's mouth, Lawrence Tilton's naked head and shoulders had plugged the flow.

Water sprayed from small leaks near his right shoulder and left arm. Twisting and screaming in agony, he stared directly into Maggie's terrified eyes. His horrible screams echoed from the bottomless hole below. Then he fell limp, moaning. His pink head smacked in and out of a jet of water that suddenly shot from a crack in the ice near his grotesquely twisted shoulder. Forced past his body, water began gushing from everywhere, its increasing hiss slowly covering his moans. Maggie felt faint.

In the chamber above, Eric watched the whirlpool fill and realized how rapidly the water level was beginning to rise. Figuring out that a new level of water would find its easiest course to be into the tunnel that Maggie had to ascend, Eric scrambled for her line and began to hoist.

"Hold on, Irish!" he called as he ripped the rope upward.

Dizzy, Maggie lolled to one side. Then a spray of ice water hit her face and she shook her head.

"What's that?" she mumbled, blinking up.

"Nothing to worry about," Eric said as calmly as he could.

The flow in the tunnel increased, and Maggie shivered when a trickle ran down her back. She was only five feet from the tiny aperture when the first real wash rolled over the edge. Maggie gasped, sucking in air, expanding her chest. Eric pulled harder, but Maggie jammed.

"Breathe out," he called. But Maggie was panicked. She held her breath and the water began to spill in around her.

"Dammit, Maggie, exhale!" Eric yelled as the water came faster and faster.

Bubbling under the flood, Maggie let the air out of her lungs and popped out of the hole into Eric's arms.

Rocking her back and forth, Eric held her tightly and kissed her. Maggie remained passive for a moment and then kissed him back. Pulling away, she suddenly reached around him and grabbed the metal box just as a rising stream of water caught its edge.

"Don't want to lose this," she gasped.

"You're fantastic," he whispered in her ear and then turned to the box. Jamming the point of his pick in its rusted latch, he tried to pry it open.

Maggie fell back against the chamber's wall, closed her eyes, and panted for breath. When she heard the rusted hinges squeak, she watched through half-closed eyes as Eric transferred the box's contents to his cavepack. Then, sitting bolt upright, she asked, "Where's Bernadette?"

They each turned but did not see the cat. What they saw instead was water rising faster and faster.

"We've gotta get out of here," Eric warned, grabbing Maggie's backpack and pulling her off toward the tunnel they had come down earlier. Soaking wet and exhausted, Maggie stumbled. Eric, already laden down with his own and Maggie's equipment, supported her as they hurried away from the rising deluge.

"What about Bernadette?" Maggie cried desperately.

Eric shook his head. "I don't know. If she hadn't been here, I wouldn't be. Maybe she'll find us in the tunnel."

"But—" Maggie began.

"We've gotta go," Eric said sternly. Maggie realized he was right—the water was starting to lap at their feet. Looking around one last time, she did not see Bernadette. The return climb to the melt canyon was not terribly difficult, but when they came to a split in the tunnel, Maggie's hopes of finding Bernadette darkened. She knew that the return route would be confusing for an animal of normal intelligence. In Bernadette's case it would be impossible. Trying to hide her tears from Eric, Maggie started to cry.

When they reached the boiling waters of the melt canyon, they saw that rising rivers had changed course drastically and a new escape route had to be chosen quickly. The new route took them higher on the canyon walls and necessitated a difficult initial climb past a new and even more torrential waterfall. It took almost an hour of strenuous climbing to make the crossing, and Maggie knew that the difficulty of the passage made it impossible for Bernadette to have preceded them or to follow.

When they reached the safety of the other side, Eric pulled Maggie up over the last outcropping of ice. She fell back against an ice ledge, exhausted. They did not speak, but Eric could hear Maggie's muffled sniffling. After several minutes, they continued on and came upon the line that they had set earlier. Climbing back up the icy incline was not nearly as difficult as climbing down. A hundred feet ahead they came to the vertical climb. Chimneying, wedging himself aginst each wall of the vertical blowhole, Eric pulled himself up and out of the pit. He hoisted Maggie up easily, and the return through the silent first canyon proved simple.

When they came to the four-tunnel choice, Eric looked one last time at the computer printout and then proceeded directly into the tunnel that brought them back to the rocky caves of the cavern's entrance. When Maggie saw the huge wooden gates, she collapsed, sitting on a rocky ledge. Crying softly, she looked sadly up at Eric.

Dropping his cavepack and Maggie's backpack to the floor, Eric sat down beside to console her.

"If it hadn't been for Bernadette, we'd both be . . ." he began.

But Maggie wasn't interested. She was staring at her backpack. Moving by itself on the floor, its sides seemed to breathe. Then Bernadette poked her face out to make sure she hadn't been left behind. When she saw Maggie and Eric, she mewed softly and scrunched back down into the safety of the pouch. Maggie grinned and reached for the bag. Eric looked suddenly concerned.

"Do you hear something?" he asked, frowning.

Maggie, busy scolding the cat, didn't hear anything and didn't answer.

Walking to the tall wooden doors, Eric took off his hard hat and tossed it on the ground. He pulled the door open and leaned out into the late-morning sun. Maggie heard the whirring chop of a helicopter and then a blast of machine-gun fire. A line of bullet holes ripped across the door just above Eric's head.

"Eric!" she screamed.

Diving back into the cave, Eric hit the floor.

"Helicopter," he gasped.

"Are you hurt?" Maggie cried, crawling toward him.

"No. It was a warning shot. They had me dead if they wanted."

Peering out one of the holes, Eric saw the black JetRanger hovering three feet over the ground amid a small cyclonic swirl of blowing dust. Toombs was in the cockpit next to the pilot, and a machine gunner was perched in the passenger section behind. In the background, the CIA man, Traxler, and another man were crouching away from the line of fire. It looked like a Mexican standoff, with the clear advantage going to the helicopter.

Toombs spoke over a loudspeaker. "These people can do you no good. Come out with the papers and hand them over."

Eric said to Maggie, "Stay in here. I'll be right back."

Reaching into his cavepack, he extracted a thick white

looseleaf notebook, popped open the rusted rings, and quickly removed almost the entire last half of the book. After stuffing the loose pages into Maggie's pack, he stepped out the door. He raised the white book high and pointed to it with his free hand. Toombs's eye widened. Eric then pointed at the machine gunner, waving him away. Toombs turned to the man, and a second later, the gun was withdrawn, disappearing into the window. Eric advanced. The helicopter swung around so that Toombs had clear reach out his window. Eric, ducking under the deadly blades, walked to the JetRanger and presented the prize. Toombs snatched the book out of his hand, and for one split second their eyes met.

Then Toombs jerked his one good thumb up and the chopper leaped skyward, rotating for a clear shot. The machine gunner reappeared, but Eric was already diving for the safety of the cavern. A line of exploding dirt followed him across the ground. Thudding onto the rocks inside the door, Eric grunted painfully.

"My God, are you all right?!" Maggie cried.

"Stay down!" Eric ordered. Then he heard the JetRanger's chop start to fade.

Limping into the sunlight with Maggie supporting him, Eric met Dan Traxler and Pyotr Lenz twenty feet from the cavern entrance. They watched the gleaming black helicopter climb directly up the Hornli Ridge, make a wide swing around the Matterhorn's north face, and finally disappear as a tiny black dot heading directly for Italy.

Turning to Eric, Traxler said in exasperation, "Jesus Christ! If you had just asked, we could have had some firepower here to help."

Lenz said nothing, Maggie sighed, and Eric stared at the ground.

"So you want to tell me what it was that you just gave them?" Traxler demanded.

Lifting his gaze slowly to the angry Traxler, Eric sighed, "Yeah, okay. As soon as we get back to town."

There was a moment of uncomfortable silence before Traxler, still annoyed, asked, "You gonna be able to make it with that leg?"

Eric nodded and limped back to the cave. Maggie followed but said nothing. She picked up her backpack and then waited by the cavern doors. Zipping the cavepack, Eric hoisted it over his shoulder and turned to take one final look down into the gaping black hole. He drew a deep breath and let out a long satisfied sigh. Eric Ivorsen felt good. In fact, he had never felt better.

CHAPTER 22

The midday summer sun blistered Tampa. Eric pulled the rented Firebird into the McCabes' driveway. Maggie, beaming and gently stroking Bernadette, climbed out and waited for Eric to do the same. When he didn't turn off the car, she frowned. Eric climbed out and opened the trunk for her luggage.

"What are you doing?" she asked.

"I'm not coming in, Maggie," he replied. He walked the two pieces of brand-new luggage to the front doorstep and set them down. Then he walked back to the sleek gray car.

Maggie blinked and with an expression of deep hurt stammered, "Why not? I thought once we came home, you and I could, you know, kinda have a normal relationship."

Eric smiled sadly and shook his head.

"But the Viking Cipher business is over," Maggie pleaded. "Mr. Traxler said so. It's over and done with."

"Not quite," Eric replied. He touched her cheek and with a look of love in his eyes, said, "But I'll be back the moment it is."

He leaned down, kissed her hard, and then with a wink got back in the car and pulled away from the curb. Stunned, Maggie watched the car's taillights blaze red when he reached the end of the street. Turning left, Eric looked back and waved. And then he was gone.

Delta flight 23 touched down at Washington's National Airport at 4:05. A short cab ride later, Eric Ivorsen walked, with a definite limp, into the Hay Adams Hotel across from the White House. He crossed the elegant lobby into the bar in Danielle's and took a seat at the bar.

He ordered an Old Grand-Dad on the rocks, and the bartender served it along with a glass of water. Eric took a sip of the rich auburn liquid, and it hit his stomach with a not-unpleasant burn. Two men crossed the room, and one sat next to him. The younger of the two remained standing.

"You look like a man who likes to travel," Pete Burns said after ordering a beer for himself and a gin and tonic for Bill Scriven.

Eric turned and looked into the older man's soft blue eyes. "As a matter of fact, I've just returned from an interesting trip to Switzerland."

"I have a friend in Switzerland," Burns replied with a smile.

"Yes," Eric said and took a healthy drink from the tumbler of bourbon. "He seemed distraught when last we met."

"You know, Mr. Ivorsen, certain government agencies are not permitted to operate within the boundaries of the United States."

"I've heard that, yes. Don't believe it, but I've heard it."

"Nevertheless, at certain awkward times, it is impossible for other government agencies to deal with a domestic situation because of sensitive relationships."

"Let's drop the cloak-and-dagger, shall we?" Eric said. "I want Gunter Toombs, and so do you and so do your playmates in the Kremlin."

"Some people think he's a very dangerous man. Some want revenge for the loss of valued personnel. It would be good for my friends in Switzerland and Austria if Toombs were immobilized. It would also benefit you."

"Don't you guys have people to handle that sort of thing?"

"In some cases," Burns admitted.

"And in this?"

"Most of Mr. Toombs's assets have been confiscated. There is however, the matter of a relatively small personal account in Switzerland, his real estate holdings here in the U.S., and of course, the document you so readily handed over in Zermatt."

"So what are you proposing?"

"You can have the Swiss account. Our government doesn't want to explain to the Swiss government why we are removing money from a private account. Even though it will probably never come to light, we'd like to be able to point to you since you seem to do quite a bit of banking in Switzerland yourself," Burns answered with a grin.

"And what do you get?" Eric asked looking directly into his blue eyes.

"The FBI is going to visit Toombs's New Jersey farm at midnight. We fully expect to find that document since Toombs has taken up residence. We are sure that you can be a great deal of help in deciphering same. In short, we want what the KGB wanted. We want what you gave Gunter Toombs."

"I'll think about it."

"Do that, Mr. Ivorsen," Burns replied, looking at his watch. "It's four forty-five. In exactly six hours, a window will open. In six hours and five minutes, that window will close. We'll know your answer then."

Draining the last of the beer, Pete Burns stood and walked from the elegant bar. Bill Scriven set down a half-finished gin and tonic on top of a ten-dollar bill and followed his superior out.

When they reached the street, Scriven said, "Do you think you should've been a little more specific?"

Burns shook his head. "Nah, he's a bright boy. He'll figure it out."

Eric was confused. He squinted for a minute and then looked down at bar chair that the older man had been sitting in. An envelope was lying on the red leather cushion. Pulling out a packet of papers, Eric found himself gazing at a Central Intelligence Agency interdepartmental brief, carefully censored to accommodate his particular interests. Certain sentences and words had been blocked and the official letterhead seal had been cut off in the copying process, but the information that remained was complete and self-explanatory. The last of the smooth bourbon disappeared in two healthy gulps.

An hour later, Eric was sitting in a Ransome Airlines

Dash 7 commuter on his way to the Mercer County airport near Princeton. He flipped open the packet and began to read. The first document, a synopsis from an FBI investigation, detailed the Snowfield Farm operation. Attached was a transcript dictated by Katrine Nyberg, detailing the layout of the Hunterdon County facility and its daily routine. The next page was an agency biosketch of the author and her tragic involvement with Gunter Toombs.

As he made his way through the twelve-page report, Eric was astounded to learn the unbelievable lengths to which Toombs had gone to keep constant watch on him. Then he read the Interpol report. Somewhere over Baltimore, Maryland, Eric Ivorsen learned that Gunter Toombs could be linked to not only the murder of his uncle but also the death of his parents. Eric stopped reading for a minute and stared out at the setting sun. He thought of a fall night in Princeton when Uncle Charles had come for one of his infrequent visits, to proudly introduce Lady Barbara to the family. Eric released a sad sigh and read on.

The report went on to postulate that Toombs's physical condition resulted from the botched immolation of a Parisian transient whose charred remains so closely resembled Toombs that no one suspected he could have survived the fiery consumption of his law offices.

Eric flipped to the last page of the report, a CIA alert to the State Department and FBI. When he read the final paragraph of the report, he wondered how they would react when they raided Snowfield Farm and discovered that they were not first in line.

At the same time that Eric Ivorsen painfully climbed into the backseat of a taxi that would take him to Princeton, Gunter Toombs rolled into the planning room at Snowfield Farm and gazed around at what was left of his staff—the two men who ran Snowfield operations and their two assistants. The only other people on the grounds were the two security guards, who had no knowledge of the farm's real purpose or even that the man in the wheelchair was its owner. Although they suspected it, they never asked. They did their jobs and were well paid.

Toombs scowled at the white book that sat on the table

before him. This behavior further confirmed what the Snowfield staff had suspected ever since Toombs had arrived three days earlier. Something had gone drastically wrong. He was in a foul mood that grew darker by the hour.

Tapping the volume with his bony left forefinger, Toombs hissed, "This proves it! It is exact to the very last page . . . and young Ivorsen thinks he has made a fool of me." Toombs's eye widened and he glanced around the table.

His people shifted uncomfortably in their seats and waited for him to explain. But he was deep in thought—plotting and planning. He knew the final act had not yet been played. He would show this overgrown cretin who was the fool and who the master.

"Katrine!" he yelled, leaning back, "Bring me the . . ."

Toombs fell suddenly silent and lowered his head; he remembered that Katrine was no longer at his beck and call.

Katrine, left behind in Zermatt, had been scooped up by Traxler's men shortly after a "wet team" of Russians had hit the Zurich office of Arpel Limited, leaving it, and Toombs's right-hand man, little more than a pile of smoldering rubble.

In addition to losing half his staff, Toombs had discovered too late that the book given to him by Ivorsen was an infuriating tease—volume one of the Viking Forecast, 1950 to 1975. Absolutely correct in its predictions, the document confirmed that the rest of the Viking Project was everything he had hoped it would be. But its possession still eluded him. Not for long, he told himself.

Sitting up in his wheelchair at the head of the conference table, Gunter Toombs began, "I've decided what must be done. . . ."

In his office at the Institute for Advanced Study, Eric locked his telephone receiver onto a modem pad, reached behind the Vector Graphic computer on his desk, and flipped on the power switch. The dark screen of the video display terminal started to glow and finally a small message read: SYSTEM READY—HELLO.

Eric typed: INITIALIZE MODEM LINK.

The screen responded: LOADING.

Eric waited patiently and glanced at the clock. The time was 10:40.

The screen flashed: FUNCTION COMPLETE.

Eric looked at the notes he had made from the CIA packet and typed: ESTABLISH COMMUNICATION; WORLD BANK LINE 474409.

It took almost a full minute for the computer to respond, but finally the screen flashed: COMMUNICATION ESTABLISHED.

Eric entered: ACCESS ZURICH SUISSEBANK ACCOUNT 678 753 215 972 777 REFERENCE ARPEL.

The screen remained unchanged for a moment and then asked: AUTHORIZATION NUMBER?

Eric read from the last page of the CIA document and entered: USA56561239VA.

The computer responded: CODENAME?

Eric did not have to read from the file; he entered: VIKING.

There was a pause and then the screen responded: ACCESS DENIED.

Eric frowned, glanced at the clock, and then nodded understandingly. The window wasn't due to open for another three minutes. He reviewed his notes one last time and at 10:45 typed again: ACCESS ZURICH SUISSEBANK 678 753 215 972 777 REFERENCE ARPEL.

The access process was repeated, and he entered the authorization number and code. There was another short delay but this time the screen responded: ACCESS COMPLETE. REQUEST?

Eric typed: BALANCE AMOUNT—AMERIDOLLARS.

4,875,550.78 AMERIDOLLARS, the computer answered.

He smiled and entered: TRANSFER FUNDS.

AMOUNT? the screen asked.

875,550.78 AMERIDOLLARS.

LOCATION?

ALGEMENE BANK NEDERLAND NV AMSTERDAM HOLLAND.

NOTATION?

ESTABLISHED NEW ACCOUNT—KATRINE NYBERG REHABILITATION TRUST FUND.

TRANSFER COMPLETE—BALANCE: 4,000,000.00 AMERIDOLLARS.

Eric smiled and entered: TRANSFER FUNDS.

AMOUNT?

3,000,000.00 AMERIDOLLARS.

LOCATION?

Eric leaned over to make sure that he entered the correct account number and then he typed: CHEMBANK NEW YORK USA. UNITED WAY FUND CONTRIBUTION ACCOUNT 766654302.

NOTATION?

CHARLES IVORSEN MEMORIAL DONATION.

TRANSFER COMPLETE—BALANCE: 1,000,000.00 AMERIDOLLARS.

Eric, enjoying himself enormously as he spent Gunter Toombs's money, chuckled as he again entered: TRANSFER FUNDS.

AMOUNT?

450,000.00 AMERIDOLLARS.

LOCATION?

CITYBANK NEW YORK USA. SPCA CONTRIBUTION ACCOUNT 1020539.

NOTATION?

DONATION MADE IN THE NAME OF HANS SCHMIDHUBER.

TRANSFER COMPLETE—BALANCE: 550,000.00 AMERIDOLLARS.

TRANSFER FUNDS.

AMOUNT?

450,000.00 AMERIDOLLARS.

LOCATION?

PRINCETON BANK AND TRUST—PRINCETON NJ USA—INTITUTE FOR ADVANCED STUDY FELLOWSHIP FUND ACCOUNT 886754003.

NOTATION?

EINSTEIN MEMORIAL CONTRIBUTION. ANONYMOUS DONOR.

TRANSFER COMPLETE—BALANCE: 100,000.00 AMERIDOLLARS.

TRANSFER FUNDS.

AMOUNT?

100,000.00 AMERIDOLLARS.

LOCATION?

TAMPA FIDELITY TRUST—TAMPA FL USA. CHECKING ACCOUNT 2307886 IN NAME OF MARGARET MCCABE.

NOTATION?

DAMAGE REIMBURSEMENT.

TRANSFER COMPLETE—BALANCE: 0.00.

Eric thought for a moment and then entered: CLOSE ACCOUNT.

But suddenly the screen went blank. A moment later, a new message appeared: REQUEST DENIED ACCESS TERMINATED.

Eric, grinning like the Cheshire cat, sat back in his chair

and glanced up at the clock. It read 10:50. The window had closed.

In McLean, Virginia, a systems operator reported to the world banking system's central computer that the "Viking" authorization was no longer valid and should be red-flagged to the FBI if attempted.

Shortly before midnight, the security guard at Snowfield Farm walked out onto the farmhouse front porch to begin his rounds. Pausing to light a cigarette, he noticed a strange yellowish-orange light flickering on the ground behind the horsebarn across the grounds. Racing across the lawn, he skidded on the gravel driveway and looked up to see the entire north side of the structure being consumed by fire. He ran back to the house and alerted his partner, who immediately broke into the meeting still going on in the planning room.

Toombs rolled from behind the conference table, out of the room, and onto the porch. The one guard remained at his side as the others ran out to the blazing structure. Quickly assessing the situation, Toombs realized the real danger and shouted, "Let it burn. Get back in the house!"

But it was too late. Eric was already up on the porch behind them. One crashing right knocked the guard unconscious. As he fell, Eric grabbed his shotgun.

The other guard spun when he heard Toombs's command, but Eric had already pumped a round into the shotgun's chamber and now its barrel was pointed directly at his face. He dropped his weapon.

"So much for employee loyalty," Eric whispered to Toombs, who glared back.

"Where is the rest of the Viking Cipher?" Toombs hissed.

"I've got it," Eric replied.

"It's mine," Toombs growled.

Eric ignored him.

"I've waited twenty years for—"

Eric cut him off. "Enough of this reminiscing. Tell your people they are fired."

Toombs scowled.

"Okay, I'll tell them," Eric said, then turned to the five men and announced, "You are now free to look for new employment. My suggestion, if you wish to do so without criminal records, is to leave here immediately, because state police and federal investigators will be arriving momentarily."

The group did not move. Toombs whispered, "You are somewhat outnumbered, Mr. Ivorsen."

"There is no more money to fund Snowfield Farm, Arpel Limited, or Gunter Toombs," Eric announced and then pointed to one of the men, motioning him inside. "Check it out before your antenna burns up."

The man ran up into the building and into the communications room. The fire had not yet reached the electronics in the barn, and he was able to set up a quick link to the bank in Zurich minutes before the horsebarn's blazing roof caved in on the dish antenna, cutting him off. But not before confirming the intruder's claim—all Arpel accounts were empty. When he returned to the porch, the others looked up, and he simply shook his head. In the distance, the first piercing scream of approaching sirens could be heard. One by one, the men turned and ran for their cars parked in the carriage barn.

In the light of raging twenty-foot flames, a line of cars sped down the tree-lined drive away from an infuriated Gunter Toombs and a smiling Eric Ivorsen.

With the flames of the fire sparkling in his good eye, Toombs spat out venomous promises of vengeance on all of them. Then Eric leaned over and gently lifted Toombs into his arms.

"What are you doing?" Toombs growled as Eric carried him down the steps. They crossed the lawn and walked through high stalks of corn until they came to a farm lane that led into the woods. Eric's truck, a four-wheel-drive Land Cruiser, was hidden off the narrow, deeply rutted path.

"We're going for a little ride, Mr. Toombs, and we're going to chat. You're going to tell me what it was you thought you could accomplish by destroying my family."

But Toombs refused to speak. The one-hour drive was a silent one.

It was 1:30 in the morning when Eric pulled the truck to

the curb one hundred feet from the corner of 42nd Street and Eighth Avenue in New York City. Two prostitutes walked over and leaned down to offer their services but backed away when they got a look at Toombs's half-dead face.

"Well, here we are, Toombs," Eric said. "Home sweet home."

Toombs, who had been staring forward, slowly scanned the area's filthy sidewalks bathed in the flashing red neon light of a dozen porno theaters, sex shops, and peep shows. A drunk was sprawled across the doorway of a burned-out store and looked dead. Several derelicts wandered aimlessly along the street, begging handouts of whoever passed.

"What do you mean?" Toombs hissed, speaking for the first time.

"This is the end of the line for you, Gunter. The FBI doesn't want to touch you, because the best they can do is try you, and you've been so careful you'd get off. If you walk—pardon the expression—the Russians are going to be convinced that it was all a setup to blow away their people in Vienna, and so they will probably reciprocate by taking out some CIA. Since you've been glued to me since you had my parents murdered, you know that I don't care much for killing and you've probably assumed that I won't kill you. You're right. But I've done worse—I've emptied your bank account. And now, Toombs, you're on your own."

Eric climbed out of the Land Cruiser and limped around to the passenger door. He lifted Gunter Toombs to the sidewalk, setting him down against a boarded storefront. Walking back to the truck, Eric reached inside, opened the glove compartment, and tossed over a shiny tin cup.

Just before pulling away from the curb, Eric stared one last time at the pathetic monster and saw that another derelict was already trying to pull the cup away. Toombs held it rigidly with his left hand.

On the ride back to Princeton, Eric's thoughts were not about Gunter Toombs, his own family, or even Maggie

McCabe. He smiled to himself as he turned off Princeton Pike and onto the serene grounds of the Institute for Advanced Study, quiet during the day and absolutely still at the crack of dawn.

Stepping into his office to pick up the new looseleaf he had put together, Eric was surprised when the phone started to ring. He picked it up and said hello.

"Ivorsen?"

"Yes."

"You don't seem to want to play by the rules." Burns sounded tired and annoyed.

"Not when the other players can change them at will."

"I thought we had a deal."

"We did. You have the white notebook?"

"Yes and it looks woefully incomplete!"

"That is exactly what Toombs got and what you asked for," Eric pointed out.

A short silence followed before Burns sighed, "You think you're a pretty clever boy."

Eric did not bother to answer.

"We'll be keeping a close watch on you," Burns said.

"You've got your job," Eric replied, "and I've got mine."

Hanging up the phone, Eric wandered out into the cool morning air and strolled across B parking lot to one of the benches overlooking the campus frog pond.

Sitting in the first light of the day as his father had thirty years before, he listened to the soothing sounds of chirping crickets and croaking frogs, calling for mates. He thought about the eternal drive to propagate and wondered again if man really was capable of destroying all life on earth. Then he looked down at the new notebook in his hands.

Flipping it open, he glanced at the first page of what he had removed from the white original. It was the beginning of the Ivorsen Forecast, years 1976 through 2000. Smiling to himself, Eric scanned through the pages and stopped when he reached the neatly lettered title page of the final section. THE VIKING CIPHER—PHASE III.

As the first rays of morning light streaked through the trees, Eric Ivorsen turned the page and began to read.

CHAPTER 23

"I want you to marry me, Maggie."

Maggie, wearing shorts and a short-sleeve blouse tied at her middle, stood up from the garden at her parents' home. She had a muddy trowel in one hand and dribbling garden hose in the other.

"Somehow," she replied, "I always pictured a more romantic setting in which to hear those words."

"I don't care about that. I love you and I want to marry you."

The phone started to ring, and Maggie dropped the hose. "Stay right there—I'm expecting a call, but I'll be right back." Running into her parents' kitchen, she grabbed the phone. She listened to what the caller had to say and responded, "There must be some mistake."

"No," the voice on the phone answered, "I just checked again. The deposit was credited to your account last week."

Maggie, staring at her bank statement on the counter, frowned and insisted, "I show a balance of thirty-seven dollars and twenty-three cents and you're telling me that I have one hundred thousand, thirty-seven dollars and twenty-three cents."

"Correct."

"I did not make a one-hundred-thousand-dollar deposit."

"Someone has."

"That's what I'm telling you—there's a mistake and someone is going to call wondering where his hundred thousand is."

"No, Miss McCabe," the man replied. "I've checked and the transfer was wired into your account specifically. I know because we're required to report such large deposits. The IRS will make an official inquiry, and you should be prepared to pay whatever taxes are applicable."

"Oh, that's great," Maggie groaned. "I'm going to have to pay taxes on money that isn't mine?"

"No, of course not," the man answered. "I'll check on it again if you wish."

"Please, I'd appreciate it. I'll stop by the bank later," she said. After hanging up the phone, Maggie walked back out into the garden and declared, "The strangest mix-up has happened at the bank. They think I have a hundred thousand dollars in my checking account."

"Never mind that. I want an answer. Will you marry me, Maggie McCabe?"

"Carl, I've had a trying month. Do you think we could just give this a little time?"

"No, dammit," Carl snapped. "You're just buying time hoping that guy from Princeton comes back."

Maggie didn't deny the charge. Carl became more agitated.

"When are you going to accept the fact that the guy used you? He took advantage of you when you were vulnerable, banged your brains out probably, then used you to cover his ass while he ran from the police and whoever else he's tangled up with, and finally had you jumping in and out of little holes like some damn dog. Jesus Christ, Maggie!"

Maggie looked down at the ground and said nothing.

Carl moved in for the kill. "This character not only hasn't called you, he won't return your calls, will he? Huh?"

Maggie looked up with tears filling her huge green eyes.

Carl snorted. "I've seen the type before. Big talker—lotta flash—slam bam and in this case not even the thank you ma'am—and you ate it right up, didn't you?"

The sadness in Maggie's eyes changed quickly to anger. "Carl, you conceited sonofabitch, leave!" She reached down, grabbed the hose, and squeezed her thumb over the dribble, sending a spray at Carl. "And don't come back!"

"Hey, hey, hey!" Carl shouted. "Watch it, dammit, these are one hundred percent wool slacks."

Maggie sprayed the slacks.

"Awright, that's it. I've had it with you, honey. You wait for your big Princeton man. It'll be a cold fucking day before he shows up for you."

Carl stormed down the driveway, got in his Pinto, and drove away. Maggie watched the water dribble from the hose and then went back into the house. Bernadette climbed up on her lap and licked a tear from her cheek. Then a noise at the door startled them both. Maggie wiped the streaks from her face and ran to the door. Upon opening it, she deftly caught a can of coffee that tumbled out of one of the bags of groceries her mother was trying to balance.

"Oh, I didn't know you were home," Mrs. McCabe said.

Maggie just nodded.

"You really should get out of the house . . . go to the beach."

"Yes, Mother," she mumbled.

"I'll be here if he calls."

"I'm afraid it looks as if he's not going to," Maggie said in a cracking voice.

"Well, then it wasn't meant to be," Mrs. McCabe philosophized.

Maggie drove down to Gulf Boulevard and rode along the beach trying to decide whether or not she wanted to sunbathe. Finally she parked her car at Indian Rocks Beach and went for a long walk along the Gulf.

She thought about the previous two months, her self-deluding attitude toward Carl, and the trap she had almost put herself in by marrying him. Then she realized that even if she never saw Eric Ivorsen again, she still had grown more in the five weeks that she'd known him than she had in the seven years of subordinating her desires to those of Dr. Carl Millbank.

Standing a little taller and walking a little straighter, she wandered slowly back to her car. Although there was an uncomfortable emptiness in her heart and she admitted to herself that she would still probably cry herself to sleep that night, Maggie McCabe was proud of herself.

EPILOGUE

An unstable front moved down across the Gulf, bringing with it violent thunderstorms, hail, and high winds. The night seas were treacherous for small craft, and the Coast Guard issued strong warnings that were in effect until dawn. When morning broke, winds were still high and the air unseasonably cool. Eric was glad he'd packed a sweater to wear under his windbreaker.

His two-man crew handled the *Lady Barbara* well even in a vicious squall that deposited a half inch of hail on the antique motor sailer's teak decks. Just after dawn, they powered into Clearwater Marina and tied up in a visitor's slip. Eric treated the two young Frenchmen to breakfast, paid them their final wages, and said goodbye. He took a cab to the McCabe home and arrived shortly before 8:00.

"Hiya, good-looking!" he said to Maggie when she opened the door.

Maggie, wrapped in an old bathrobe, with her hair in curlers, and red-eyed from a poor night's sleep, felt anything but good-looking. Her mouth fell open at the sight of a tan, grinning Eric.

"I don't know if I should even talk to you," she said, trying to look angry.

"Why?" he asked innocently.

"You couldn't call?"

"That's right, I couldn't. I wanted to, but we lost radios off Bermuda."

"Huh?"

"I told Lady Barbara that I'd bring the yacht to the

States for her, and we lost our radios in a storm halfway across—a storm that almost ruined the surprise."

"What surprise?" Maggie asked suspiciously.

"I thought we'd take the *Lady Barbara* up to Newport together. Just the two of us for a week of restful sailing during the day, romance under the stars at night, and calm relaxation all the rest of the time."

Maggie's stern mask disintegrated into a smile and then a wide happy grin. Twenty minutes later, she carried a hastily packed suitcase out to the waiting cab for the ride right back down to the marina.

Maggie froze in her tracks when she saw the luxurious yacht. A seventy-five-foot William Hand–designed motor sailor, the *Lady Barbara* sparkled in the blue-green water. Eric climbed aboard and disappeared down the companionway into the master stateroom. Maggie walked along the dock gazing into the yacht's polished teak wheelhouse. A cool breeze from the Gulf made her shiver, and she mumbled, "Carl was right."

"What was that?" Eric asked, looking up from the companionway.

"It's a cold fucking day." She smiled devilishly.

"That's what I love about you." Eric grinned back. "You're so refined."

He stepped up on deck and offered his hand to help her aboard.

Before she took it, she stopped and said, "Romance?"

"Guaranteed."

"Rest?"

"No question."

"Relaxation?"

"Hey," Eric replied with innocent eyes. "What could happen between Tampa, Florida, and Newport, Rhode Island?"

ABOUT THE AUTHOR

Rick Spencer's interests include the acquisition and restoration of historic buildings. He and his wife Betsy live in a restored Victorian house in the heart of the Cranbury National Historic District outside Princeton, New Jersey. ICEBOUND, The Viking Cipher 1, is his first novel.